Evergreen

Also by Brenda Pandos

☙

The Emerald Talisman (Talisman Series Book 1)
The Sapphire Talisman(Talisman Series Book 2)
The Onyx Talisman(Talisman Series Book 3)

Everblue, Book #1, Mer Tales
Evergreen, Book #2 Mer Tales
Everlost, Book #3, Mer Tales
(coming 2013)

Evergreen

Mer Tales ⬯ *Book Two*

By
Brenda Pandos

OBSIDIAN MOUNTAIN PUBLISHING

Cover design and layout by the author herself.
www.brendapandos.com
Cover Images Fotolia.com
© Oleksandr Medvedyev # 36312949,
© Yulia Podlesnova # 13387253

Published by Obsidian Mountain Publishing
www.obsidianmtpublishing.com
P.O. Box 601901
Sacramento, CA 95860

ISBN: 978-0-9849835-2-0

10 9 8 7 6 5 4 3 2 1
Printed in the United States of America

To Mom and Dad.
For telling me I can,
and for keeping your promise to each other for over
forty years when it might have been easier to quit.

"... once he drew
With one long kiss my whole soul thru
My lips, as sunlight drinketh dew."

Alfred, Lord Tennyson (1809-1892)

English Poet

1

∽

ASH

Monday night, April 11th

I clutched Fin's first letter against my chest and crumpled onto my bed. He'd written yesterday's date—Sunday, April 10th—across the top, the day he left me. Already, something inside my soul had died and this ritual became crystal clear. Daily there'd only be a few minutes of bliss as I ripped open the envelope that filled my soul with his words. A temporary reprieve lasting as long as it took to read the letter. Then I'd be left, longing for more.

Our bond, sealed the day Fin kissed me, rubbed like a piece of glass lodged within the tender folds of my heart, needling its way further inside with each labored beat. He'd vowed to write, text, and call whenever he could until I reunited with him in Florida in a few months, but would that work? I could already see we'd be attached to the phone until we were together again. Would that keep us sane?

I traced my finger over the ink, wishing his hands were touching me.

"I miss you, Fin," I whispered, hoping God would help me deal with this in some way.

And I'd thought the countdown to college was unbearable before.

My dear sweet Ashlyn,

We've only left one another, and I had to write you. Your salty tears are still on my lips, and I smell you on my clothes. How will I get through this? Thank you for the pictures and the note. I'm going to wear both, reading and staring at your beautiful face all day. You're like the sun... bright and warm. They'll keep me rational until you are in my arms once again.

I hope this letter finds you soon. Once I finish writing, I'm forcing my dad to stop so I can mail it. I want you to have this by tomorrow. Hitting Phoenix today is the plan. I'm not looking forward to thirteen hours of traveling with my parents, but with all our stuff and towing my Jeep, we really couldn't fly. I'm glad I could convince them to upgrade to an iPhone on the way out, though.

On the map, I found a reservoir off the freeway for us to stay at. Let's hope it's decent. Only traveling during the daytime will make the trip longer, but Dad can't exactly drive with his fins. I know we'll talk all about this later, but I can't wait to hear your voice. It already feels like years have passed when it's only been minutes.

The desire to run my fingers through your hair and bring your lips to mine is haunting me. I miss you more than words can say. My parents are going to be so sick of me begging to come home to you—to escape this hellhole RV. I can't believe how long we'll have to wait until we're together again. Every minute is grueling. You're not suffering alone. I keep replaying our last kiss in my mind. I hear you speaking to me, and I'm keeping your sweet words close.

I love you.

Forever, Finley

I folded up the letter and held it close to my heart as a tear escaped onto my cheek.

2

ASH

Tuesday morning, April 12th

Mom white-knuckled the steering wheel and rattled on with her pep talk as she drove to school. Reassurance that the world wasn't ending because Fin had moved away was her apparent goal. I could have driven myself, but I think she secretly worried I'd head down Highway 50 for Stateline and keep going to Florida. If she told me "she understood" one more time, I'd scream. This wasn't your typical separation. The constant impending doom that I'd never see Fin again stole my very breath.

I twisted my ruby engagement ring around my right ring finger (my left had a strategically placed Band-Aid to cover my tattoo) and watched the lake out the window. Only ten days had passed since the wave toppled my boat over and changed my life. To think about it, today could have been my funeral. Instead of drowning to death, I'd awoken in the hospital with a row of stitches lining my thigh and a life-long promise of the mer on my lips.

Only after Fin's family escaped the oppressive rule from their underwater city, Natatoria, and sealed the hidden gateway under the waters of Lake Tahoe so no other mer could return, was Fin free to find me and tell me the truth. We had three glorious days together before the evil fish-doers found another way to get to the lake. Fin and his family had to pack up and leave for the safe house in Florida before they were captured. But not before Fin proposed, unbeknownst to my parents.

Returning to school without any fanfare was my secret hope.

Though I'd apparently won, I didn't want to be queen, especially after I'd ditched the king for no reason. Maybe my absence helped the Senior Ball vote-tampering drama to die down.

Mom gave me a hug and wished me an overly exuberant "have a good day" as I exited the car. I held my breath, disappearing in the swarm of students, and walked to my locker. I'd almost snagged my English book for an easy getaway to class when Georgia's squeal flooded the halls.

"Ash!"

My cheeks heated as I turned to greet her. "Hey."

She enveloped me into a hug. "I've missed you so much." She squeezed tight, then gave me a quick once over. "You're all better. Wow. "

I smiled weakly and bent my leg a few exaggerated times. "My injury wasn't as bad as the doctors thought. I'm good as new." *Thanks to Fin's magical healing blood.*

Her eye caught the crimson gleam radiating off my finger. "Holy... what is that?"

I tucked the evidence behind my back, kicking myself for wearing it today. "It's nothing. Just an early birthday gift."

"From who?" Georgia's eyes grew as she fought me pulling away from her grasp. "From Callahan?"

"No." I finally let her look at it. "Of course not."

As Georgia admired the ring, I caught none other than Callahan himself glaring our way. I looked away as he slammed his locker door and pretended he didn't see me.

The last time we'd been together alone was after Senior Ball where he'd been crowned king. He'd just asked me to be his girlfriend at the dance, and I couldn't have been more elated. But after my accident the next day, my feelings flipped. Lost in a swirl of confusion, I'd ignored his phone calls. Until Fin explained everything about the mer and the power behind his kiss, I had no clue what happened to me or why my feelings changed. From Callahan's expression, I needed to tell him something, or at least explain myself. Judging from his glare he never wanted to talk to me again.

As Georgia oohed and ahhed over the ruby, I played with the Band-Aid wrapped around my opposite finger. During my morning shower, my promising tattoo had developed into a disco ball, exploding into a party of light, and I needed to keep anyone from seeing it.

"It's from Gran. An heirloom," I quickly added to get her off the scent of who really gave me the ring.

Her eyebrow shot upward. "It's gorgeous. I bet Lucy was pissed."

"Yeah, something like that."

Actually, Lucy had no clue. After Fin proposed and left Sunday, I stayed in my room in a depressed funk until today when I was forced to go back to school.

"I have exciting news." Georgia shoved a beat-up piece of paper from her pocket in my face.

The Florida Atlantic University insignia caught my eye. An acceptance letter. My head swayed as I met her sunny eyes.

"I'm going to FAU with you!"

My words wouldn't form as my brain stalled. *Accepted? To FAU?*

"Well, say something."

"Wow," I managed to squeak out.

I could see it now. She'd want to be my roommate, take every class with me, be on the swim team, stalk me. My everlasting shadow.

"I'd applied to FAU too 'cause I knew you were going there. I didn't think they'd accept me, but they did. And now that you're all better and everything's cool, we can go together."

I couldn't listen anymore. Her happy words painted a drastically different picture for me—one with a permanent shadow following me throughout the college campus. The words "sorority" popped me out of my panic.

"I hadn't thought about that yet, Georgia."

"Really? It's instant friends, parties, fun all the time. Rush week... that's all we need to worry about."

My tongue felt like sandpaper in my mouth. I had no ammo for this conversation. I slammed my locker shut and headed for first period. Georgia followed, her words spewing out of her mouth in inhumanly fast speed.

"Okay," I put up my hand, "I'm on meds, so... I can't focus right now."

"Don't worry. I've got it all figured out."

"That's what I'm afraid of." I pulled open the door to English.

"Just hear me out. We'll live in the dorm first year, then we'll pledge to a sorority and live in the house the next year. It'll be fun."

The thought of lots of girls sharing one bathroom, or cycling on their periods all at the same time didn't sound fun in the slightest. After I moved to Florida, the school could burn to the ground for all I cared. I didn't really plan on attending anyway.

"I might have other housing," I said as I moved to my seat.

"What?" Georgia yanked on my arm to stop me mid-stride.

"I have relatives there..." I cringed at my lie.

"You're going to live with relatives?" She released my arm as if I had a catching disease.

"It's cheaper... I don't know."

"Doesn't your scholarship pay for housing?"

Her voiced echoed. I ducked into my chair as curious eyes bored into me. Mrs. Keifer stood in the front of the room, tapping her foot, the delay hanging in the air like a stink bomb. Georgia finally took her seat with a dramatic humph.

"Nice to have you back, Ms. Lanski."

I smiled weakly and opened my textbook, hoping Georgia would quit for now. My pocket vibrated against my hip with a text.

- **Are you mental?**

I timed my return text once Mrs. Keifer turned to the whiteboard.

- **I haven't looked at the stuff they'd sent me.**

Georgia blew out a gust of air.

- **Then look at it. We've got a lot of planning and shopping to do!**

Shopping? Talk about the last priority on my list. Actually, since I'd received the okay from my doctor, I wasn't sure where I stood with school. Though FAU didn't know what had happened as far as the accident, I'm positive my grades suffered from my absence. And whether or not I could swim as fast as before was questionable. This afternoon's practice would soon tell if I still qualified for my scholarship.

I watched Mrs. Keifer scroll words across the whiteboard and next to me, Georgia scribbled dutifully in her notebook, oblivious that she'd disrupted my world. She for once was being the studious student, but I couldn't concentrate with the news she'd dropped. My name written across the top of on her paper caught my peripheral vision.

WHAT ASH NEEDS TO BUY OR BRING

I let out a gust of air.

Georgia mouthed, "what?"

"Nothing," I whispered.

She opened her eyes bigger as if to say, "tell me."

I shook my head and looked forward. There was no way I'd share my Fin time with her. Maybe it was time to finally tell her I had a boyfriend.

3

∽

FIN

Tuesday afternoon, April 12th

Exhaust lingered in the air as my parents and I (and all our human junk) rattled along the road in the RV somewhere in New Mexico—day three of the road trip from hell. I warred with myself as my finger hovered over the send button. I'd promised Ash I wouldn't bother her at school, but I couldn't stand it anymore. I had to hear from her.

- I love you xoxo

She'd be in English, and her eyebrows would push together in that cute way and highlight the scar across her forehead—the one I gave her accidentally when I threw a rock when we were kids.

- I love you too, rule breaker!

I chuckled, tempted to text back. It took all my control to just put the phone down. As I expected, she'd officially consumed my thoughts, my appetite, my concentration, my....

"Fin!" Mom yelled. "Didn't you hear me?"

I glanced up from the table as Dad harnessed the wheel after a sudden gust of wind blasted the side of the rattletrap. "What?"

"Have you GPS'd where we are going to stay?" she asked in her mom voice, the one that made me grit my teeth.

I clenched the iPhone tighter, purchased solely for assisting us with the trip, and sighed. Thank God Mom insisted on a phone instead of a GPS. I didn't know what I would have done without a way to contact Ash during and after the trip.

I mumbled under my breath and scrolled through the map for

Lake Altus in Oklahoma. Though pretty populated, we decided not to stay in any bodies of water off the beaten path. Anything was better than the muck hole where we'd stayed in Albuquerque.

"Yeah, you're fine. Stay on highway 40, then go south on 283. We've got about 200 miles or so to go."

She turned and settled in her seat, watching the horizon as if we were high-tailing it from the police. I shook my head and went back to the map on the phone. Instead of checking out the lay of the land, I zoomed in on Tahoe. The little pin I'd placed on top of her school ridiculed me. She was there, surrounded by the deep everblue of Tahoe, and I wasn't. The growing anxiety I'd made a mistake left me filled with dread. Should I have fought harder to stay?

I took out her picture and reread her letter once more. Just a few more hours, then I could call. The time ticked on slower, as if it were doing it on purpose.

Dad said to focus on the future. Mom suggested to take things one day at a time. I didn't think I could do it. Ash was my air for life. Without her, I'd surely shrivel up like a fish out of water and die.

I was never going to survive this.

Never.

4

ASH

Tuesday afternoon, April 12th

I slammed my bedroom door shut and sunk to the floor, out of breath. I'd run the entire way home from Gran's store, marking off every hour in my notebook until this moment. I willed the phone to ring.

"Ring, darn it!"

The phone finally came to life in my hands.

"Fin." My throat accidentally pushed out a painful sigh.

"There you are, my ginger girl," he said, relief lacing his voice.

I closed my eyes, wanting with all of my might to crawl into the phone and into his arms. His voice was sweet to the taste, like melty marshmallows in my mouth, crispy from a campfire. I tapered back another breath threatening to explode from my lungs and grinned. "I've missed you so much."

"Me, too."

Our souls entwined over the line as a heavy tear trickled down my cheek. Muscles in my throat constricted and I worried he'd hear how torturous today had been, day three of our separation.

"It's so good to hear your voice," he said.

I gulped as another tear followed the first. "Yours, too."

"It's going to be okay, Ash. We can do this."

"I know—"

"Please don't cry."

The pain in his voice wracked my chest. Why couldn't I control myself? I never cried.

I swallowed again and forced everything deep. "I'm okay. Where are you?"

"Oklahoma, the Sooner state, though I'm not sure what a Sooner is exactly. We're at Lake Altus—"

I jumped up and typed in the address on Google maps on my laptop. I zoomed in on the lake and imagined I could see him.

"—how was your first day back at school?"

I bit my lip as a guilt-drenched vision of Callahan's disappointment flipped through my mind like a fish out of water. I didn't get a chance to settle things before swim practice. "It was okay."

"Did people ask about your miraculous recovery at practice?" Fin repressed a snicker.

"Kind of." I eased into a rhythm with his humor, my emotions under better control. "My tattoo, though, glowed in the water during my shower this morning. I had to put on a Band-Aid to cover it up. I thought maybe someone might see it, especially at practice."

"How could you cover up the symbol of our love with a Band-Aid? Where's the ring I gave you?"

"It wouldn't fit now. I had to move it to the other hand, Sorry."

He chuckled. "Didn't I tell you your promising tattoo would glow underwater?"

"No." A grin pushed up my lips. "But... yeah. I'm going to need to keep a stash of Band-Aids close by—"

"Or you could wear a sparkly white glove." He broke out in a rendition of Michael Jackson's, *Billy Jean*.

I snorted and started to laugh. "You're ridiculous."

"I can moon walk. Want to see?"

"Oh, puh-lease."

The phone jostled as if he were actually dancing wherever he was. He made a high-pitched squeal.

"Any other requests? 'Cause you know I'm bad, I'm bad, you know it. Who's bad?"

"Goofball." I moved to my bed and snuggled up in the covers. This was the stuff I'd miss—I couldn't believe he wasn't next door anymore. I hesitated, afraid to tell him about our new FAU stalker. "There's something I need to talk to you about—another problem."

He snorted slightly. "Besides the fact that you hate my singing? Hit me."

"I don't hate your singing." I giggled, enamored at the fact he could always make me smile, and clutched the phone tighter to my ear, still worried about his reaction to what I'd say next. "I just found out Georgia is going to Florida Atlantic." I let the words hang in the air, hoping the admission would make them untrue. His silence unnerved me. "Apparently, she thinks going to the same college as me would be a good idea."

"Hmmm," he said plainly.

My gut pinched. "I'm sorry. I promise I didn't encourage her. I wanted to warn you now. She's going to follow me everywhere," *and never stop talking,* "I know it."

"Does she sing, too? 'Cause I'm looking for some back-up singers."

I frowned. "Seriously?"

"Well, I hadn't planned on sharing you that much, but if she insists, she can tag along with us, but only at school and band practice."

I blinked. Did he say he'd be at school with me? "Don't you think that'll be awkward?"

"How else are we going to rehearse if she's not there?"

"Stop joking. I meant the being at school part."

He snickered. "Well, what else did you expect me to do all day? Hang out at the boring beach house with my parents and text pester you?"

"Well—"

"If I can't stalk you in class, then I'll legally attend. I'm sure the Dean of Students would love for me to join their fine establishment, how's that?"

"It's not that simple. You need to apply, and I think the deadline has passed—"

"Deadline, shmedline. With my *amazing* mer mind-powers, I've got it under control."

I bit my lip and tried not to smile. "I thought you could only erase memories."

"Oh, my dear ginger, there's a vast array of things I can do." He laughed evilly.

My mouth hung open. "Really?"

"I'm able to plant thoughts. How about I persuade a boyfriend for Georgia? That'll keep her busy."

My gasp couldn't be withheld this time. "You can do that?"

He laughed again—problem solved. Elation pulsed throughout my body, making me shiver. Though I'd never be able to concentrate with him sitting with me in class, I couldn't imagine a better idea. "I kind of like the way you think."

"Believe me, that's all I've been doing in these muck holes across your beautiful country the past three days. I figured I should at least learn a trade if I planned to care for you for the rest of your life."

A trade? "Why would you need a trade?" I asked.

"Because I like to do things on my own merit whenever possible."

"But you said you were going to use fishy powers on the Dean."

"Sometimes I make rare exceptions, but as a human, I won't have my super fishy powers any longer."

"Human?" I swallowed hard and sat up. Though I wasn't sure who'd convert to whose race in the end, I didn't expect him to choose humanity over his mer life—at least not that easily. "When did you decide this?"

"Well, I haven't officially decided, but I figured I should be prepared just in case."

"But you said, if you were to change into a human, the promise bond would break. What if you forget—?" I couldn't make my lips say it—that he'd forget he loved me.

"Never. I adored you before the kiss, and I'll adore you even more after, especially at night." He laughed evilly again, making my belly quiver. "You're stuck with me, Ashlyn Frances soon to be Helton, whether you like it or not. I plan to be happy and in love forever, surrounded by our kids or merlings—however we do it is your choice."

I gulped again, giddy and sad at the same time, my throat way too dry for this conversation. Too much pressure. How could I choose? Either way, one of us would say good-bye to our family and friends, and shed the thing that made us who we were and what we knew. Neither seemed win/win. I wouldn't feel right if Fin sacrificed everything to join my human world, and I didn't want to become a fugitive of Natatoria.

A deserted island sounded more blissful. But eventually, we'd need to live somewhere practical and provide for ourselves and children apparently. Which world would be most supportive of our relationship? Which was worthy of our sacrifice? I wanted parts of both.

"Now you're freaking me out, Ash. Did I scare you?"

"Well, kind of."

Fin exhaled in defeat. "My ginger girl, there's no pressure. We'll work this out when you get to Florida. I'm sorry I mentioned it. We have lots of time to decide."

I pressed out a sigh. Easy for him to say. I gnawed on my nail, anxious to change the subject before my brain imploded. "Too bad you can't use persuasion on me."

Fin launched into an unexpected coughing fit, propelling me upright in bed once again. "Wait. Did you? Before?"

"Yeah… well, but I can explain."

"You'd better." I pursed my lips in an attempt to sound upset. "What did you do to me?"

"Nothing big." He laughed some more.

"What?"

He couldn't stop laughing.

"Fin. What?!"

"Okay, okay. When we were kids, we were swimming and Tatch thought it would be funny if I showed you my tail and—"

"And?"

"You freaked out. Like I was Jaws or something. Screamed bloody murder. We had to swim after you and calm you down."

"I screamed? Really?"

"Yeah… it's etched in my mind forever, believe me."

"And you erased my memory?" I gulped. "What else did you make me do? Tell the truth, Fin."

"Nothing else. That was the only time, I swear." He continued to laugh nervously, which made me believe there was more to the story than he let on.

"Humph." I tucked one arm under the other. He needed to be punished a while longer for keeping such a huge secret from me.

"Ash, please. I promise. If you were here, you could look in my eyes and know I didn't do anything else. At least not that day."

"What?"

"Kidding!"

I softened in response to his adorable voice. How could I not believe him? "Why didn't you tell me before?"

"Because you'd freaked, and I was afraid you'd do it again. And I can't persuade you now."

"Well, that's good to know, unless—" I squinted my eyes. A traitorous smile cracked on my lips. "Is there something you'd like to persuade me to do?"

His laugh, nervous and deep, tickled my tummy. "Now that you mention it… " He breathed in slow.

"All you have to do is ask." My heart galloped at my words, at my boldness.

"Oh, do I now."

"What do you want me to do?"

"If you were here, there's no telling what I'd want."

I giggled, my cheeks warming as I snuggled back into my covers. "Too bad I'm not, or else… " I paused, secretly hoping his mind would wander the same direction mine was.

"You're such a tease," he said before he groaned. Then a ripping noise flooded the speaker as something crashed in the background. Fin's voice sounded further away. "Oh, crap."

"What? What's wrong?" I threw off my covers and jumped up.

"I—crap—I did it again."

"Did what again?"

He groaned. "Missed the sunset and busted through another pair of jeans."

"You what? Oh." I repressed a chuckle, visualizing the sight.

"I need to get in the lake before anyone sees me."

The image of Fin dragging his tail behind him like a seal toward the water, danced through my mind. "I'm sorry. I shouldn't have kept you so long."

"It's my fault," he said. "I lose track of time when I'm talking to you. Until tomorrow?"

"Yes, please. Same time, same station."

"Remember I love you—now and forever, Ash." Goose bumps spread over my skin.

"I love you, too. Please be careful."

"Always. Goodnight."

As the phone went dead, a piece of my sanity shredded like his jeans, and I clutched my chest. This torture would be the slow death of me. I turned to the window and noted the sun beaming sickening happiness over the tops of snowy mountains. Different time zones. Different worlds.

"Ash," Mom called from downstairs. "There's someone here to see you."

I shoved my phone in my pocket and breezed down the stairs expecting to see Georgia, and stopped mid-stride. Colin, Fin's traitorous cousin, stood on the porch. Mom's lips were propped in a weird smile.

"Colin's here to see you."

I narrowed my eyes. *What the heck does he want?*

He grinned, his dimples pressing small divots into his cheeks, and tilted his head. "Hey, Ashlyn."

I walked over, my fists balled up at my sides. Why couldn't the sun have set here, too?

Unfortunately, it made sense why he'd shown up. Yesterday, after I thought all the mermen had vacated Fin's house, I'd spotted him spying on me from the deck. We met a few weeks ago, but now I knew what he was—a merman like his cousin. He'd been responsible for turning Fin over to the bad mer guys of Natatoria. Did Colin know I was promised to Fin? Was he here to quiz me? It didn't matter. No amount of his fishy mer mojo would get me to spill. I was looking forward to watching his attempts fail.

Mom cracked a sappy smile and nudged my shoulder, pushing me toward him. He must have used some on her to get her to be so cordial. I shooed Colin away and joined him on the porch, closing the front door behind me.

"What's up?" I planted my hand firmly on my hip.

"I'm wondering if you know where my cousin Fin went?"

A spark of anger ignited inside, and it took all my control not to slap his cocky smirk off his face. I pushed my lips into a fake smile. "He went somewhere?"

"You'd seemed friendly before. Thought he'd tell you where."

"He told you we were friendly?" I smiled. "That's news to me."

I knew exactly what he referred to—the night he'd betrayed Fin and Tatchi at the beach.

"Oh, I must have been mistaken." Colin flashed a confident smile. "You wanna go out sometime?"

"Really?" I squinted at him in disbelief.

His cockiness melted away. "Well, yeah. Why not?"

I fluttered my eyelashes innocently, enjoying my power over him. His cuteness might have worked on me before, but now I saw through his mer swagger. "I'm sorry. I can't."

His nostrils flared while he clenched his jaw. "Wow." He turned toward Fin's house and took a deep breath.

"You seem surprised."

"Well, yeah. I mean, the last time, you were all over me—" He furrowed his brow.

"You're delusional." I turned my head to the side and sneered. "I'm taken. So… sorry."

"Poseidon!" he barked and then before I could do anything, musical words came from his lips. "Dump whoever you're seeing and go out with me!"

I didn't expect him to mojo me so quickly. I tried not to react and kept a straight face while my brain screamed for me to tell him to shove it. But I couldn't. Not unless I wanted to reveal I knew his precious secret and that my promise blocked him.

"All right." My stomach clamped in disgust. If Fin knew I was entertaining a date with the enemy, he'd come back to Tahoe tomorrow and rip Colin's head off. But curiosity captured the reigns. Why, if I said I knew nothing, would he want to date me?

"Great." He let out a relieved exhale. "How about tomorrow?"

"No good. I won't be home. I'm free Saturday." There was no way I'd give him valuable Fin time. Morning was safe knowing Fin would be on the road within earshot of his parents, which would make for a boring phone conversation.

"Uh, yeah. At my place?" He gestured off to Fin's house.

I withheld a grimace. How dare he take ownership over the Helton's house. "Sure. Nine sound fine?"

His shoulders relaxed. "Perfect. It'll be *fun*." Visions of choking him overtook me as my blood rocketed through my system.

Yeah, I'll show you fun, buddy.

"Oh, I'm sure it will be." I spun in my spot and exited inside, leaving him alone on the porch.

Through the gossamer curtains, I watched him saunter across our driveway. On the deck in the shadows of Fin's house, someone stirred. I strained to see a face, but they disappeared just as Georgia pulled up.

Georgia remained in the car, mouth agape. Fin's future plans for her sent a smile to my face. Little did she know the surprise we'd have for her at FAU—boyfriend-wise. She waited until Colin disappeared before she jumped out of her car and ran to the porch.

"Who the heck was that?" she asked as I opened the door.

"My creepy neighbor, Colin."

"Creepy? He's like… amazing. Did you see his shoulders?"

I rolled my eyes and motioned we head upstairs.

"Hey, Mrs. Delatore. Gorgeous ring," Georgia called over my

shoulder.

My legs swiveled my quaking body around to meet Gran's curious eyes as she stood in the hall.

"Why hello, darlings," she tilted her head to the side, "what do you mean ring?"

Adrenaline sapped my strength, caught ruby-red handed. "Oh, nothing. Come on, Georgia." I tugged her arm a little harder than I should have toward the stairs.

"The ruby ring," she said as she sailed behind me. "Ash said you'd given it to her."

I pulled her into my room and slammed the door.

"What the heck." She rubbed her arm. "What's wrong with you?"

"I don't want you to talk to her about the ring."

"Why? Didn't you say she gave it to you?"

"It's nobody's business, okay?

Georgia dumped her bag on the floor. "What's wrong with you?"

I pulled my lips into a straight line. "Nothing. Just don't mention it to my family again. It's a sensitive subject."

"Why? Because a guy gave it to you instead?"

The back of my neck burned hot. "No. It's just… I don't want to talk about it."

She crinkled her brow. "You've been acting totally strange… ever since your accident. It's a guy, isn't it? The one who rescued you!"

"No, of course not." I rolled my eyes and pulled out my history book from my backpack, wishing I had fishy mojo to silence her once and for all. "Near-death experiences change people. Now let's get on with our homework. You're here to tutor me, and I've got a ton of catching up to do."

She shrugged as she pulled out her book too.

I didn't know why I'd felt like I needed to keep Fin a secret from her. He was, for the most part, a guy after all. Maybe I should tell her... of course I'd leave out the part where he was my knight in shining scales.

I turned to chapter twelve when the guilt sunk my heart like a stone. I'd already forgotten about the date. How could I have allowed Colin to sing to me? If Fin knew, not only would he be furious, he'd be crushed.

Curiosity aside, I couldn't keep the date. But how could I break it without revealing I was impervious to the merman song? I ran my finger over my lips and wished for a perfect solution to my problem—one that didn't involve me taking the next bus headed to Florida.

I'd figure out something.

5

FIN

Tuesday evening, April 12th

Barely able to reach the dashboard with my mertail in action, I strained to hide the phone inside the glove compartment of the RV. Luckily, no one was around to see me as I slithered the few feet toward the lake on the rocky ground.

I laughed at myself. College? Did I actually tell Ash I wanted to attend college? What a change. Two months ago, I'd sworn I'd never abandon the mer and chewed out Tatchi for wanting to leave. But now, for love, I'd do anything, including singing Michael Jackson songs. Crazy.

The water washed away the dirt as I plunged myself into the current, still singing *Bad* in my head. Sharp twigs jutted uncomfortably from in between my scales, and I yanked them out. This would be something I wouldn't miss, the unavoidable scale-filled time-bomb at sunset. But the reason I hesitated to convert came to mind—Tatch. I needed to be mer to save her.

But I would change if Ash asked me and once the time came, Mom and Dad, though they would be disappointed, would have to understand. The King would never allow Azor to have his fins stripped for what happened, and I wouldn't dare bring Ash into our communal drama. Maybe my sister and I would convert together.

But how far would Dad go when erasing our memories after the change? Couldn't he leave them there? It wasn't like we were law-abiding citizens anymore. But until then, one thing was for sure: I needed to look into getting a waterproof case for the phone, so I could talk while in the water and stop busting through anymore of my jeans by accident.

"Fin... what took you so long?"

Dad's abrupt voice startled me.

"Late... sorry." Shame whirled around in my gut as I dislodged the last rock embedded behind my pectoral fin.

Dad shook his head. "You can't keep staying out past sunset. Someone's bound to see you."

"Yeah," I laughed, "on this remote side of the lake, I'm sure lots of people saw me and they're running for the tabloids now. Merman removes rock from his pectoral fin in Oklahoma, news at eleven."

Dad remained stoic. "Were you talking to Ashlyn?"

The way he said her name made me cringe—like she was the enemy. "Don't worry, Dad. I won't let it happen again."

I swam away in the murky soup the locals called a lake and looked for cleaner water. In my distracted state, I'd apparently picked another dud. Google needed to add a water purity index on the lake listings ASAP.

"Wait, Son. I need to talk to you about something." He swam to catch up.

I turned around. "What?" Obviously, I wouldn't be lucky enough to escape his lectures tonight.

"When we get to Florida, we need to keep things under tight wraps about what's going on, got it?"

I leaned my head to the side. "But you've been telling Hans and Sissy everything?"

"Not from them, from Galadriel."

"Really? She's still around?"

"She's—become a bit of a problem."

I withheld my eye roll. Galadriel, the King's eldest daughter was the source of this whole mess to begin with. Because she'd run away, the King had sent Dad on a mission to find her, Mom, Tatchi, and I were forced to stay in Natatoria and wait for his return. And since Tatchi and I couldn't abide by the rules, we were forced to promise with people we didn't like in order to control us. Dad ambushed the ceremony just in time for me to get away, but Tatiana wasn't so lucky. Azor, the King's son, kissed her against her will. Galadriel was the last person I wanted to be friends with.

"Well, I hadn't planned on becoming BFF's, if that'll make you feel better."

"I'm being serious and don't get smart."

I balled my hands, trying to keep my cool. "What's the big deal?"

Dad sighed. "The big deal is we'll be living under the same roof until we get a place of our own, and it'll be tempting to befriend her. She mustn't know anything about us. Are we clear?"

"Under the same roof?" I hoped this roof was large enough for me to have my own room. "Who all lives in the safe house besides Sissy, Hans, and Galadriel?"

"Just them, for now. Galadriel's situation is complicated and to protect the other runaways, they've been redirected elsewhere."

To protect the others? Sheesh. Why even ask? Mers and their love of drama. I fought back a yawn. All I cared about was Ash. When she got to Florida, we'd be together during the day, and I'd stay in the Atlantic at night. No need to make friends with anyone else if I had my way. The safe house was only a temporary storage place for my things.

"I'll keep my distance in the ocean."

"Good. She was the reason for the 'mission' that lost me Tatiana to the King's son in the first place, and since her botched conversion, she's reluctant to become human. She'd also been disappearing for days at a time without word. We aren't sure who she's communicating with or who she's connected to. She's more than likely a spy."

"A spy? You think she planned her near death so she could snitch about the safe house and our location? That's a little far fetched, don't you think? I bet she ran away from an overbearing King."

"Unpromised mermaids are fickle, Son."

I shook my head in disgust. "Really? You blame her genes after all of this? I'm sure she's not unlike any other mermaid in Natatoria, just smarter to run away. Being cooped up drives them all crazy after awhile, especially if they aren't allowed to get promised to whom they wish."

"She's worse. She's royalty." Dad pitched a brow. "And it's not unfounded why females need to be chaperoned."

Yeah, blame the girl. "But what I really want to talk to you about is Ash. Your mother and I have been talking—"

"And?" I ground my jaw.

"Son, we know things have been difficult being apart, but once Ash gets to Florida, she's not invited to the safe house, nor to be given the address. And don't tell Galadriel anything about her—or even that you're promised."

I held up my ring finger and smirked as the tattoo glowed purple shards of black light. "A little difficult to hide."

"Yes, well... until Ash is mer, she needs to live her normal life."

"Why? Because she's human? I'm not hiding who I am from her. Don't forget Ash is going to be my wife and you sure seemed fired up about that on Saturday. How can she make the decision if she wants to be mer if I don't show her what it's like? Or do you want me to become human instead?"

"Now you know that's out of the question." Dad's nostrils flared. "My request isn't ridiculous. We need to keep the girls apart until Galadriel chooses humanity. Otherwise, she could return to Natatoria, beg for forgiveness, and tell the King. Please... for

Tatiana's sake."

My sister's name sent a wave of pity through my gut, stopping my next rude remark. I actually did have higher regard for Galadriel once I heard she'd run away from the King's unfair rule. But if she ever betrayed my family—there would be no telling what I'd do.

I saw the ever-praised Hans and Sissy in my mind, the mer nobility of dry land my parents raved about. They'd been lecturing Dad on the phone over their expectations once we arrived in Florida; their kingdom otherwise known as the safe house. But the delivery often seemed pushy. Were their rules no different than King Phaleon's? Whatever lurked in our genetic bloodline that made us crave royalty to lord over us, I'd ignore once I became free to do what I wanted. I didn't need them or their archaic ways influencing or approving my decisions.

"Fine, whatever," I finally said.

"I knew you'd understand. Things are complicated, especially since we've lost touch with Badger."

"What? When?"

"After he tipped us off, we haven't received word from him. Hans hasn't heard from our other contacts as well. But one thing is for sure; no one has been able to leave Natatoria since our escape, runaways or regulars. Has Ashlyn said anything about the house? If anyone's been there?"

"She hasn't mentioned anyone. Should she?" I asked, suddenly alarmed. "I should go back. Protect her."

"No. She knows to stay away if mermen show up. They can't influence her. Just ask she not speak with them. I wouldn't want her to tell them something innocently. If they knew the truth—" A somber look crossed his face.

"They'd what?" I flipped my tail, propelling myself forward in the water. "They'd take her, wouldn't they? I can't stay here, Dad. I can't!"

Dad lunged and grabbed my arm. "No, Son. We have to continue on to Florida and make plans to rescue Tatiana. They have no reason to bother Ash, and she'll be in Florida soon enough. She needs to keep her distance and things will be fine."

I gritted my teeth. Dad didn't know that the night Tatchi and I were abducted from Lake Tahoe, Ash had run to the beach and seen us all in the water. Luckily, the promise had blocked Blanchard's attempts to erase her mind, but if he or any of Azor's goons were at the house right now, they might get desperate and suspect Ash was more than just my neighbor. Uncle Alaster or Colin might go so far as to try to persuade her to tell them where we'd gone. She'd be able to deflect the questions, but her family wouldn't.

I had to warn her tonight.

6

❧

ASH

Wednesday afternoon, April 13th

"So, Colin, huh?" Georgia said between sips of her Sprite as we sat together in the cafeteria. "Maybe you could set up a double date… after you make up with Callahan of course."

My heart sputtered, jolting me from my daydream. Colin had become my worst nightmare. And last night, while Georgia and I were working on homework, Fin had left a frantic message for me to stay away from his house. It was as if he knew what had happened.

Georgia nudged my arm, dislodging my fist from my chin.

"What?" I said after scrunching my nose.

"Didn't you hear what I said? About Callahan?"

"Yes." I crumpled up my chip bag and threw it at her. "We were never together. Okay?"

I peered over Georgia's shoulder to the other side of the cafeteria. Callahan sat with his back to me, his arm wrapped around Jaime's waist. Ironically, she was an employee at Gran's shop on the pier. Though I thought it might bother me, relief covered my guilty conscience instead.

My eyes snapped back to Georgia. "I've been horrible to him and honestly, he deserves better." *And I prefer blond mermen anyway.*

I withheld my smile and gently squeezed my phone, my lifeline to Fin.

"Seriously?" she shook her head. "No way. I know you still care. Technically, you're still together. I mean, he never officially broke things off. And you're going to let Jaime move in on your turf?"

The last phone message he'd left played through my mind. "Ash. I don't know why you aren't returning my calls, but I can take a hint. Don't worry. I won't bother you anymore."

I cringed. I'd been such a coward.

"He's better off without me and besides, he's going to Stanford to play ball. Jaime's nice—" I lifted my chin toward their location, "all I want to do is get my grades up and leave this drama far behind."

"Fine. Whatever." Georgia's shoulders slumped down in defeat, then a smile pushed up her lips. "That reminds me, do you know where Colin is going to college?"

I chuckled and almost said, "Natatoria University." But when Fin said he'd fishy mojo Georgia a boyfriend, I'm sure Colin wasn't on the list of suitors. "Why? Are you going to switch schools if he's not going to FAU?"

"No. I thought if he was going also, that would be a crazy coincidence. Right?"

"He's going to UCLA," I lied, hoping she'd stop talking about him.

"Really? Bummer." Her eyebrows rose. "Well… you're so right. FAU is going to be totally awesome and there will be much better guys for both of us—"

So, true. You don't know the half of it.

"—so for the meet on Saturday, did you see what heat you're seeded in?"

The vision of Fin and me reuniting with a passionate kiss crashed and burned at the thought of the swim meet Saturday. "No."

"Seriously? It's championships. You're slated against Meredith again."

My back stiffened. Visions of the last race played through my mind: the tie, the broken record, Callahan sitting on the bleachers with my dad. I massaged the scar on my leg as it tingled.

"You swam pretty good at practice yesterday."

My teeth clamped onto my lip to hide my smile. I'd purposefully tried to swim slower, but the water exhilarated me for some reason. I ended up swimming my best split with little effort. Maybe the mer blood still pumped in my system from when Fin healed me. I hoped it would last until Saturday. Beating Meredith Hamusek would be worth all the trouble.

"Yeah... taking a break must have recharged me."

"I'll say. Completely opposite of what happens to me. I stop swimming for even a few days and get all slow and mushy."

The whole time, the perfect excuse stared me right in the face. How could I have forgotten the meet? Though no-showing Colin seemed like the best way to dump him on his dorsal fin, I wasn't sure if the persuaded had a choice once they were commanded to do something. But I could always leave him a note.

As I contemplated my next move, Callahan and Jaime walked by, their laughter filtering through the noise of the cafeteria. He hugged her tighter as his glance caught the corner of my eye. I looked away, suddenly engrossed in the fraying hole in my jeans. Honestly, I couldn't be happier he'd found someone else, but he appeared hurt. I needed to apologize, somehow.

❦

The note shook like flimsy butterfly wings in my cold hand. Fin's explicit warning last night not to come near the house rang in my ears, but my feet moved forward anyway, creaking along the wooden boards of the porch. His memory hugged every square inch, haunting me. A deep longing for him to pull up in his Jeep grabbed me, turning my legs to JELL-O. Energy to keep myself from falling apart moment by moment rendered me emotionally exhausted, but finally being here, facing the past, I had to shove the pain further under that barrier I'd locked him in.

As I looked for an actual place to leave my handwritten excuse for Colin, I contemplated the mailbox next to the door. Would mermen know about the postal service? I gave up the idea and squeezed the paper into the door jam when the door popped open with a creak.

"Colin!" I heard a man say.

My blood turned to ice.

"What?" Colin barked.

I didn't dare move or breathe. He sat right there, on the couch beyond the wooden door that separated us.

"Azor is coming here tomorrow, so get off your ass and pick up your crap. He wants to know what's taking us so long, and inspect the house. And don't you dare tell him about the girl."

"Of course I won't! I'm not an idiot," he yelled with a huff. "She's not coming over until Saturday anyway."

At the squeak of the couch cushions, I willed my reluctant feet to move, to get me the heck away from there.

The unknown voice interrupted my descent. "She better come, but before you do anything, I want you to check first and see if she has the mark. I don't want you making a fool of us with the wrong girl."

"I know," Colin tsked, "what do you think I am, a merling?" he said in a low tone.

Approaching footsteps pinched my lungs. I pressed myself up against the siding, trying to blend into the topiary next to the door. How did they know I was promised to Fin? If they caught me eavesdropping, what would they do? Turn me over to Azor?

"In time, it'll all work in our favor and we'll see who's barking orders at whom," the man said within practical touching distance. "Why is this door open?"

A white haired bearded man peered outside. I held my breath and pinched my eyes shut. I was caught.

"Remember, it'll be me on the court and not you," Colin said from inside.

"Hmmm," the man mumbled.

I kept my eyes shut, praying he didn't see me.

"Well not now!" he yelled and the door slammed shut.

Something inaudible boomed from inside. Amazed I'd adverted capture, I let loose of my breath and snuck down the porch to the driveway. Once my feet hit the gravel, I ran the rest of the way home.

"What's wrong, Ash?" Dad asked as I darted inside and slammed the door.

I turned in a panic. "Nothing."

"You look like you've seen a ghost."

"It's… nerves for Saturday." I managed a smile.

"That's this weekend." He nodded his head in sudden understanding. "Well, your mom is on her way home and dinner will be ready soon. I hope you're hungry for tacos."

"Yeah." I took the stairs two at a time.

"Wait!" Dad said from somewhere on the bottom floor. "What am I, chopped liver? Where's my hug?"

"Sorry, Dad. Gotta pee." I disappeared around the corner.

I flung my gym bag on the floor and took off my wet sweatshirt. The scent of chlorine infused the room—a scent normally comforting to me, but I couldn't stop my heart from racing. They knew. Should I tell Fin? Or maybe a better question was could I tell him? Either way, I needed to get to Florida as soon as possible before Colin and Mr. White Beard cornered me and verified my promising mark.

I reached into my pocket for the note. It was gone.

Crap.

Sweat dripped down my cheek as I pawed through my bag. Did

the man find the note? Did he guess I was there the entire time listening in? Maybe in the scuffle, the note blew away.

I looked out the window at Fin's house filled with dread. I couldn't be alone with Colin, not after he'd been charged to confirm the truth. Not now. Not ever. Especially with Azor coming to the house. The thought of meeting him face-to-face, the merman who stole my best friend's promise, terrified me. He was coming here this week, looking for clues to find Fin and his parents, and maybe me.

Fear for Fin and Tatchi twisted in my stomach. What if there was an accident? What if Azor never returned home? Fin had said that only through death or mer-to-human conversion would the promise break. What if I made one of the two happen somehow? Then Tatchi would be freed and Fin wouldn't have to risk his life to try to force her home. She'd be able to leave.

But how? Could I even get close to him? The fact he'd stolen Tatchi from me made me hate him more than anyone in the world. But I could never hurt anyone.

The ringer on my phone filled the silence of my plotting, and I shook my head at my insanity. I'd overheard Colin's conversation for a reason, and I couldn't let the opportunity pass me by. I took a deep breath and answered the phone on the last ring.

Whatever I decided, I couldn't tell Fin.

7

ॐ

FIN

Wednesday evening, April 13th

Discouraged, I hung up and headed for the lake with a few minutes to spare. Ash's persistent questions about the conversion from mer to human didn't sit right with me. I'd told her what I knew, that they drained the mer of their blood, typically in a bathtub. Then the magical properties healed and brought the body back to life, regenerating new blood void of mer essence. Once complete, the supervising merman was to erase the mer memories and fill in a back-story.

But she'd continued on, asking if it hurt, if the person had to have their mind erased totally, or only certain events. But most important, she asked if I knew anyone who'd successfully converted. To her disappointment, I didn't.

My lack of answers made me wonder why I hadn't asked before. Did she expect me to convert? Had her longing been so horrible that she had no other choice but to subtly beg me to put her out of her misery? Though I'd let on I contemplated losing my fin, watching Mom slip further and further into a depression missing Tatchi, and her incessant talks of rescuing her put a halt to that idea. I couldn't now. Not yet.

I stepped into the slime at the waterline and stopped, sickened by the smell, when my parent's heads popped up one after the other.

"Don't," Dad said from the muck. "You shouldn't go underwater."

"It's filthy," Mom said behind him.

They came to the water's edge and sat on the bank, morphing out of their tails, covered in strings of algae.

"We need to find something cleaner for the night." Dad motioned to the RV. "Go get the phone. Quick!"

I ran back and grabbed the phone. Scales had already formed on my legs. We didn't have time to find, let alone drive to someplace else tonight.

I grabbed a bunch of bottled waters and took them with me as I bolted the rest of the way to shore before the sunset. My parents sat together in the muck, finned up once again. I gave them both a few bottles each.

"Thanks." Mom took a few sips and then splashed the rest over her arms and body. Dad did the same.

I joined them reluctantly, sinking three inches into the mud. Fire burned across my scales as I finned out after the initial plunge.

"Sorry," I finally said after no one spoke for several long minutes. "I didn't know."

"It's alright." Mom smiled weakly. "The lake looked good from the road. Next time, we need to arrive earlier so we can investigate and have a backup plan if it's not suitable." She pointed to my phone. "Where are we headed tomorrow?"

Still tired from the craziness of the night before, I opened up the map and waited for it to load. This had been our backup plan. If the drunken fishermen at the last lake hadn't been throwing explosives in the water to fish, we wouldn't have needed to rest during the daylight and had plenty of time to find a better location.

Through hazy eyes, I watched the circling ball inform me we were too far off the network for cell service. I turned off the phone. The fact the bog was missing a name should have tipped me off that it was a dump. Aerial satellite shots were so deceiving.

"I'll stay awake. If someone comes, we'll have to go under the water," Dad said.

Mom shuddered in response, but I doubted anyone would visit this horrible place anytime soon. "No, Jack. I'll stay up. You need your rest to drive tomorrow."

"I'll drive tomorrow," I mumbled as I leaned against the dry ground, unable to keep my eyes open.

"I'm driving," Dad said, "and we'll take turns."

With no more strength to fight, I finally gave in. After an hour of tossing and turning, Dad slammed his fist in the water, splattering Mom and me with mud. "I can't stand this. I'm looking for the inlet."

Mom watched as he slithered away in the stagnant swill.

"We should have bought a kiddie pool for times like these," I joked.

"That's actually a good idea—well, we'd need more than one." Mom laughed as she put her arm around me and squeezed. "Here, take a small sip of essence. That'll help."

I hesitated, staring at the precious vial she'd promised to give Ash when the time was right. I shook my head.

She smiled. "I've got more packed away for emergencies."

The sparkling blue liquid came alive in the moonlight, singing a faint song of our people, when the guilt hit me. What if I drank the potion and when Ash needed it in the future we'd run out? Though uncomfortable, sitting in a dirty bog wasn't something I'd call an emergency.

"It's okay, Mom. I feel fine." I gave her the precious commodity back and took another swig of water instead.

"No, seriously… we don't know what's in this sludge. It'll strengthen your blood." She nudged me again, holding out the liquid.

"I'm good," I finally said.

She grimaced before corking the vial, not drinking any either, and put the necklace back on. Seeing the vial on her neck daily reminded me of what I was and what Ash was not. And for some reason something inside compelled me to take it from her as if I didn't trust her judgment.

Mom placed her hand on mine. "I know what you're thinking."

I looked up, caught in her curious gaze. "What?"

"You're afraid there won't be any when it's Ash's turn."

"Well," I looked away. *True*

"I promise you, when Ash is ready, I'll give her this one. You don't need to worry."

I hated the way Mom kept ownership of the essence, as if she didn't trust me. I'd never trick Ash into drinking the essence—ever. That would make me no better than Azor.

"It's fine."

"It's not that I don't trust you. I'm trying to keep you both from pressuring one another. It's a big decision." Mom's eyes bored into me as grief stretched across her face—a worry I couldn't understand.

"Is there something wrong?" I finally asked, but already knew the answer. She worried about Tatchi.

"No." She looked away.

I skipped a rock across the water. I missed her, too. "Are we going to Natatoria as soon as we get to Florida?"

"I'm not sure. There's a lot to plan first."

Though I wanted to know more details, I was too tired to ask. Obviously the mission wasn't as easy as we'd all hoped. We couldn't just bring Tatiana home with us. We had to break the bond she had with Azor, and that meant one of two things—his death, or either of their conversions. Too much to think about and something heavier weighed on my mind.

"What was it like when you changed from human to mer?"

Mom let out a long, pained sigh. "Excruciating, like breaking all the bones in your legs at once, but it doesn't last long—"

Painful?

"—all good things come with a little pain, like childbirth."

"I guess," I said with a grimace.

Silence filled the space as we watched the other end of the bog for signs of Dad. He'd better come back soon, otherwise I'd have to figure out where he went.

"Was it an easy choice to convert?"

Mom chuckled. "Up until I finally decided, no. I struggled with what to do everyday."

"Why?"

Mom turned toward me. "I didn't want to abandon my parents."

I wanted to ask why Dad didn't change for her, but obviously there was something else going on. Maybe he was afraid he wouldn't survive.

"So what finally changed your mind?"

Mom flipped her tail in the water a few times. "Your father's continued acts of unselfish love. Before the promise, he'd sacrificed so much to rescue me from a life of servitude to Phaleon, and then after, he had undying patience with me. How could I not do the same for him?"

"You've never told me this."

"You never asked." Mom smiled and looked wistfully off into the distance. "When it came time for Prince Phaleon to choose a mate, he wasn't happy with his selection in Natatoria. So he came to Florida to stay with Jack's parents to find a human girl instead. And since Jack knew the ways of humans and could guard Phaleon on land while he chose someone, the King agreed. So, Leon and I met soon after he arrived, and unbeknown to me, he wanted me to be his mate.

"I have to admit, at first I was flattered with his attention. He swept me off my feet with his accent and charm. I didn't know for sure what he was exactly, until I caught Jack calling him prince once, so I became giddy with the possibilities—a royal life as a princess. I hadn't a clue where though.

"But, after a while, I tired of Phaleon's ego. I found myself drawn to your father. Though he was very proper in the Prince's presence, he was so attractive to me." Mom giggled like a schoolgirl—something I'd never heard before.

I shrugged it off as she composed herself and continued.

"But, unlike Phaleon, it was your dad who asked me about my goals and dreams, and the things that mattered most to me. He shared similar desires and we connected on a deeper level. Once Phaleon planned the big date to kiss me, Jack broke protocol and warned me not to go. At first I was shocked at his boldness, and thought he was saying so because he'd fallen in love with me. But when I flat out asked him, your dad said it was best I didn't get involved with either of them. I didn't understand and his rejection hurt. So when I told Leon I only wanted to be friends, they both disappeared the next day, and took my heart with them."

Though I knew this talk would be coming sooner or later, the timing sucked. I needed to turn off my brain before my own depression set in, but I continued to listen.

"Of course, your father had fallen in love with me, and a few years later when he rescued me from drowning, we were promised. I finally learned of the mer and exactly what Leon had planned for me. And your sweet father never wanted me to feel obligated to choose the mer life just for him, so he told me I never had to choose. We'd make it work no matter what. And we believed we could."

Mom swayed and put her hands back to catch herself.

"Are you okay?" I asked.

"Yeah." She rubbed her forehead. "I'm just tired from last night."

"Why don't you sleep then?"

"No... I want to tell you—"

If only Dad would let us know he'd found fresher water and she could rest.

"The thought of Natatoria suffocated me," she continued, almost as if in a trance. "A lonely place where women harvested merlings and the men supervised their every move. Everything was planned and provided for, right down to the rays of sunlight. But instead of seeing a blessed utopia, I kept telling Jack I wanted a career, a picket fence, and selfishly a home with an oversized bathtub for Jack to sleep in at night. But still, he never put pressure on me.

"But when Jack would leave me to visit Natatoria, I was the one alone. I worried he'd never return, or that if something bad happened, I couldn't go to him. I hated how the water separated us, so after my parents passed, I decided your father's love was greater than anything this world had to offer, and I became a mermaid.

"Then our lives fell into place. I had you kids. We were happy in our own world in Tahoe. But once King Merric became ill and Phaleon was given the kingdom, things changed. Phaleon began to do things that suggested he never forgave Jack for stealing me from him. And your father, so filled with guilt, continually allowed Phaleon to treat him like a servant.

"And when your father was sent to find Galadriel and bring her home, I thought it was the end for us. Though Phaleon doesn't seem to truly love Deidre, he wouldn't jeopardize his kingdom to steal another's mate—not in the public's eyes. The entire scheme was put in motion only to please his son, the future king. I believe Phaleon allowed us to stay away from Natatoria so Tatiana wouldn't have opportunities to meet merboys her age. And then conveniently, Galadriel runs away right before the coming of age festival. Phaleon had his perfect excuse. And I was afraid for Jack's life if I didn't comply. I should have insisted we stay in Tahoe. We should have discussed the situation as a family first before letting your father go, but he worried about discovery of the safe-house if he didn't. It's all my fault."

"No, Mom," I said, interrupting her. "It was my fault. I kept getting in trouble."

"Son," she said with glassy eyes, "they used every little infraction to tighten their control so they could justify forcing both of you to be promised as a punishment."

"We should have run, then."

Mom patted my arm. "I feared for Jack's life if we did. Accidents happen all the time to mers who don't succumb to the rules. For your father's sake, we didn't have a choice."

I shook my head. Mom carried the weight of this when it wasn't her fault. Phaleon had manipulated everything to give his son something he had no right to give—my sister. And they both deserved to be punished for their crimes.

All I wanted to do was rip Azor's life from him and watch him wake up a finless man. I could care less about his position or line up in the royal heritage. He was a bassface for stealing Tatchi's promise in front of everyone.

"I'm ready to fight, Mom," I said with gritted teeth. "Azor deserves to be brought to justice and I plan to give it to him."

"I know, Son," she said with a sigh. "You and your father both. But no matter how we look at it, someone is going to get hurt. And that's what I'm afraid of."

"Not if I can help it," I said.

A whistle from the other side of the bog caught our attention. Dad waved for us to join him. I jumped in first, the water sending pinpricks of pain over my skin. I swam quickly, anxious to get out of the toxic goop as soon as possible, but the soft tail splashes of my mother abruptly stopped behind me. I turned in horror to find her belly up, floating in the water.

"Dad!" I yelled.

"Oh, no. Maggie!" Dad moved to her side and gently lifted her as he flash swam for fresher water. "Don't leave me now."

I rode the wave behind him and dove in under the current once we reached clearer water. We all inhaled sharply. Mom floated limply in the current by Dad's side.

"I'm so sorry. This is all my fault." Dad opened the vial hanging around her neck and dumped the contents into the water near her neck. The essence floated in the water, then seeped through her gills. "Please don't leave me."

I watched on in horror. If anything happened to Mom, I'd never forgive myself.

She coughed and her eyes fluttered open.

"Jack?" she whispered.

"Yes, sweetheart." He put his hand under her chin. "I'm here."

"Thank you," she said and nestled against his chest.

Dad cradled her in his arms and gave me a stern look.

I looked away and swam further down the stream, settling on the sandy stream bottom. Homesick, I tried to sleep. Ash's face decorated the backs of my lids and I worried with everything we'd never survive let alone end up together. Who was I kidding?

8

ASH

Thursday afternoon, April 14th

I cowered in the bushes and watched Fin's house armed with a kitchen knife, hoping for a miracle. After waiting sixty minutes or so, the fear had dissipated and my only reward was a numb bum from sitting on a lumpy rock. What was I doing here?

But even with the danger of capture and Fin's explicit warnings to stay away, I couldn't. Like a shark in chummy waters, I had to see him, this spineless mollusk that robbed my best friend of her life. Still, I didn't know what I hoped for. I didn't see myself stabbing him—or even confronting him. And yet I lay in waiting, with my sister's spy-listening device disguised as a cell phone to my ear and the knife in the other, just in case.

I'd wanted to watch all day and actually faked a stomachache earlier, but Mom didn't buy it. With the amount of days I'd already missed, I'd have to be bleeding out my eyeballs for her to allow me to stay home.

The only other mers I'd seen were the ones in the water the night Fin and Tatchi were captured. Was he one of them? Moonlight hid their faces that night, and the next day from my dock, I spied a group of shirtless bearded dudes wearing dark colored skirts, circling the house. Fin had explained the attire made for an easy switch from fin to legs without flashing people. He preferred wearing jeans or his board shorts where he'd sewn Velcro on the inside seam. I smiled, remembering how he accidentally busted out of his jeans after sunset because I'd distracted him.

I checked the time again—4 PM. Twenty more minutes until Fin called. Disappointment took over. I'd either missed Azor, or he wasn't visiting today.

"Well, look who's hiding in the bushes."

I looked up in horror at Colin's Cheshire grin.

"I'm not. I'm—"

I tried to keep the knife concealed as I stood. Both phones clattered onto the ground. I snatched the real one up. Colin picked the spy device off of his feet.

"What's this?"

I cringed as he read the spy kids label on the front.

"It's my sister's play cell phone." I nervously chuckled. "She's always leaving her toys around." I pocketed the real one and held out my hand, hoping he wouldn't see the knife in the other.

"I see." He studied me for a second, then returned the toy. Something playful danced behind his eyes.

"I'm actually on my way home, so… nice to see you, again." I backed away when his eyes widened in anxiety as he glanced over my shoulder toward Fin's house.

I followed his gaze. A man in a skirt with dark, heartless eyes watched us from the deck.

Colin took my elbow. "Why don't I walk you home?"

I froze, locked in the mysterious man's gaze. Dark hair and flawless features matched his stoic appearance. He smiled, then turned to Mr. White Beard, gesturing in our direction.

"Ash. Let's go," Colin whispered.

I couldn't obey; my knees bolted in place. Was this Azor, my best friend's husband? I couldn't tear my eyes away. Sweat slicked my fingertips. He was the key to everything and within my grasp.

Both men stepped off the porch and headed in our direction. My heart sped off like a race car. Suddenly, I didn't feel prepared for the confrontation, for anything.

"Great," Colin mumbled.

With all these mermen near, escape was futile. I tried to move away.

Colin boxed me in. A musical tone sounded in my ear. "Be cool." His lips grazed my skin, sending a chill slithering down my spine.

My stomach clutched and I willed away a stave of nausea as a vision of my capture flooded my mind.

"Well, who's this?" The dark-haired man gave me a creepy once over.

"Colin's new friend, Captain," Mr. White Beard said.

Colin slid his fingers around mine as I struggled to keep a good grip on the knife.

"Human?" He pitched up a brow.

"For now." Colin squeezed my hand a little too hard.

The man's eyes fell into slits. "She doesn't talk much, does she?"

"She's persuaded," Colin said quickly.

"Hmmm. She looks like my sister… only younger." He cocked his head to the side and studied me further, like a specimen in a Petri dish. My heart thundered. I needed to lunge at him, do something.

"Oh, don't be silly. She's a local and was at the beach the night we finally captured my niece and nephew. Right, Colin?" Mr. White Beard's voice clipped upwards.

"She was, wasn't she?" The man looked off to the left in the direction of the water. "That's right. I remember." He returned his gaze on me and smiled; evil oozed from his pours. "Do you know where Finley went?"

I swallowed hard, willing my lips to move without success. I shook my head.

"I don't think she knows anything," Colin said quickly.

"Really?" He kept his eyes on me a moment longer before he waved his fingers in front of my eyes and stepped closer. Music flowed from his lips. "Where's Finley. You can trust me."

My chest heaved up and down. I had to speak this time or else they'd really know I was promised.

"I don't know." My meek voice was softer than I'd willed it to be.

But more important, he was right there—his naked chest within stabbing distance. I just needed to plunge the knife forward and all of this would be over. But was this Azor? Was this the right man?

The man's shoulders went slack. "I wish all females were this cordial." He turned to Mr. White Beard with a laugh.

"Trouble in paradise?" Mr. White Beard asked.

Anger surged inside me. Was Tatiana giving him grief? Was she okay?

"Tatchi," I breathed.

The man's head spun to me and he glared. Within the depths of his irises a bitter cold consumed and paralyzed me. His jaw locked. I couldn't breath.

"Keep looking, Alaster. They had to have told someone. Another neighbor, a friend, a lover. Find them. Persuade them. Jack has to be stopped."

His eyes didn't move off of me. A tear slunk down my cheek.

Mr. White Beard shuffled his feet behind him. "Yes, of course. I'd love nothing more than to bring you my brother's head on a platter."

He sang again. "Forget."

I tried my best to compose myself and closed my eyes for a second. I opened them to find him cordial again.

The man bobbed his head. "Good, now I'm hungry. Does she cook?" He gestured with an evil smile like I wasn't even there, "because my mermaid doesn't do a damn thing."

The men laughed and turned away from me. I gripped the hilt in anger, ready to stab when my phone rang in my pocket.

He spun quickly in alarm "What's that?"

"It's called a cell phone," Colin said.

"What does it do?"

"Allows people to talk to one another."

"Well, then…" he wove his hand in a small circle and stared at me. "Talk on it."

A lump formed in my throat. What if it was Fin?

"Now!" he barked.

My chest heaved as I dropped Colin's hand and retrieved the phone from my pocket.

"Ashlyn, where are you?"

Relief flowed through my body until the heat behind Mom's voice alerted my "you're in big trouble, missy" alarm.

Uh oh. "I'm out front. Why?"

"Come home. I need to talk to you, young lady."

"Yes, of course."

The man watched me hang up and pocket the phone. "Looks like you're in trouble."

Sandpaper lined my tongue. "I have to go home."

Colin frowned. "Well, then I guess I'll see you later."

Mr. White Beard looked fiercely at Colin for a moment. Didn't they get the note? Should I break the date now?

"Yeah," I mumbled, too scared to mention anything. Colin would eventually figure it out after I'd no-showed.

"Yes, so…" the man said, turning toward the house. "Procedures have changed. No one can leave until we know who the traitor is. If Jack can't communicate with anyone, he can't tell them what to do. Most of the betas have been arrested. We're still missing a few."

"I'm sure your traitor lies with one of them," Mr. White Beard said.

I stretched forward, wishing I could put Lucy's phone to my ear. I needed to know if the man was Azor, and then their plans. I tried to stall, but Colin didn't go away. Instead, he stared at me, making spying impossible.

"Aren't you leaving?" I asked impatiently.

"I wanted to escort you home." He motioned to my house as if to lead the way.

"Really, it's no trouble. I can go alone." *Leave already!*

"No, I insist." His dimples sunk into his cheeks as he smiled.

Great.

We watched one another as the men walked away. Then my phone rang again. I looked down. My heart flipped. This time it was Fin.

"Oh, man. I'm busted." I took off in a jog toward the house as if Mom had called.

Colin stumbled forward.

"Can't stay. Bye," I said and pushed my legs faster.

I peered over my shoulder to see his torso stoop with the familiar sign of defeat. Luckily, he didn't follow. The phone continued to ring as I crossed over the ridge; I shoved the knife in my bag and answered.

"Fin," I said breathlessly. An overwhelming desire to tell him what happened burned on my lips.

"Hey, ginger girl." Happiness infused his voice. "You okay?"

"Yeah, fine now." I hit the front porch and stepped through the front door.

Mom stood in the foyer, her arms folded over her chest.

"Hang up," she said plainly.

"Um…" I gulped. "I—I gotta go. I'll call you right back."

"What's wrong?" Confusion replaced his joy.

"Say good-bye, Ashlyn." Mom tapped her foot.

"I'll have to tell you later." Dread pinched its pointy claws under my skin. What did I do wrong now? "Sorry."

My heart sank as I cut Fin off mid-sentence while he told me he loved me.

Nothing was going my way today.

9

⤜

FIN

Thursday evening, April 14th

I hung up the phone in defeat. After the way Ash's mom sounded, I doubted she'd be calling back tonight. With my palm pressed into my forehead, I willed away my headache. Every time I moved, my brain rattled against my skull as a reminder of poisons from the bog we'd stayed in last night. All I wanted to do was return to Lake Tahoe, not only to see Ash, but to breathe in fresh snowy water, a vintage like none other.

Judging by the setting sun, I guessed I had twenty minutes to spare. Instead of texting (in case her mom took her phone), I opened my email and composed a letter instead.

> **My Dearest Ash,**
>
> **I'm sorry we couldn't talk tonight. I hope it's nothing bad and you and your mom work things out. It's been crazy since we last talked. Last night, we stayed ~~in~~ at a bog we later found out was contaminated. We're lucky ~~to be alive~~ that we didn't get sick. My head is pounding. I should have known something was up from the stench we'd driven past, especially since I hadn't seen any farm animals nearby. All I saw were rows and rows of big buildings. Do farmers keep animals in those things without sun? How inhumane. ~~What would they do if they ever caught one of us?~~**

I stopped and deleted the last line. What if this email fell into the wrong hands?

The algae blooms should have been a sign the bog wasn't safe. Nothing could live in these waters. It's a shame. Don't the farmers know they are poisoning the fish? We didn't get as far as we wanted today because mom couldn't handle the motion of the RV. Anyway, the lake we're at tonight looks and smells 100x's better. Like always, I miss you. How was your day?

I reread my words and cringed. Like knowing any of that garbage would help. Actually, Ash would worry and beg me to come home—especially after hearing about Mom. And at this point, I wouldn't fight her. I should have never denied Mom the essence the night before. As it was, she needed two full vials to recover. If only Colin and Uncle Alaster were truly harassing Ash in Tahoe, then Dad would have to take us home. If it weren't for Mom drifting in and out of consciousness all day, I would have unhooked my Jeep from the RV and driven back myself.

No. I needed to encourage Ash—tell her that things were okay. Lie. Contaminated bogs, overindulged princes, a possible mer war, and revenge of a heartless king—all stacked to separate us—couldn't get me down. We'd be together soon.

I took her picture from my shoulder pouch and touched her face through the plastic. Her beautiful lips, red hair, fiery eyes, God, I loved her.

I moaned and sprawled out on the picnic table. This stupid piece of crap email wouldn't help if she'd had a fight with her mom.

I deleted everything and started over.

Dearest Ash,

I love you. I'm sorry about today. Please write me back if you can't call or text.

I miss you more than you know.

Love forever, Fin

I smiled and hit send—short and to the point. Hopefully she'd check her email tonight. Overcome with exhaustion from detoxing all day, I closed my eyes and sucked in the cool breeze that blew over the lake, washing out my lungs. I'd give her five more minutes. At least tonight I'd remembered to wear my board shorts.

I'd dozed for a moment when something warm and wet touched my leg. A black-and-white border collie stared up at me. One of his irises was blue as the sky. A Frisbee lay at his feet.

"Where'd you come from?" I shook the grogginess from my head.

He barked and nuzzled the Frisbee closer with his nose. I closed my eyes for a second to clear my head before I picked it up.

"You want me to throw this?"

He barked again and bowed down on his front paws. I looked around for the dog's owner, seeing no one.

"Okay."

The dog took off, caught the Frisbee midair, and returned for another round. I laughed, amazed at his skill. I looked for his owner again before another throw. Scales popped out on my legs.

"Sorry, buddy. This is the last time. I can't play anymore."

The dog cocked his head to the side but wagged anyway in excitement. Because of what we were, Dad never agreed to let me have a dog and playing fetch rekindled my desire. As the dog took off, farther than the first time, I remembered I needed to lock up the phone.

Crap.

I put the phone with Ash's letter and photo in my shoulder pouch instead and headed toward the water when the dog returned. He dropped the Frisbee; this time right on my Jack Purcells.

Double crap.

I launched the Frisbee one last time before tossing my shoes. Only one landed under the RV door.

"Bring that back!" I yelled as the dog darted back and forth with my other shoe between his slobbery teeth. I picked up a stick. "Here, buddy. Fetch." The dog ignored me and moved to a nearby tree while gnawing on the heel.

"Hey! Give it back!"

As I approached, the dog's ears shot up and he froze. Then he dropped the shoe and took off. Confused and relieved, I grabbed the soaked shoe, pushed both of them through the crack of the window of the RV, and swiveled around to run. I turned and smacked into a little girl.

She fell on the dirt with a thud and started to cry.

"Oh, geez. I'm so sorry." I lugged her up to her feet. "You okay?"

Mute, she dusted off her palms and wiped away tears that streaked the dirt on her face. She gave me a once over before her eyes grew.

I already knew why. Within seconds, my legs finished the process of zipping up and this time I fell over and bounced on the dirt at her feet. The girl screamed.

"Forget you saw me," I sung in Natatorian, "and go find your dog."

Her big brown eyes glazed over.

I grabbed onto the earth and pulled my body hand-over-hand across the hard gravel, wincing in pain. Though my skin had somewhat recovered today, my scales were still raw and tight from the chemicals in the bog.

 58

"Gemma, what you doing?" a boy's angered voice said from behind me. "What in tarnation?"

I rolled over and sung again when another grimy kid appeared. He pointed at me. "What's that thang?"

"How many are there of you?" I shook my head and sung a third time.

Three more scraggly kids appeared making six; a wicked curious gleam glinted in the newcomers' eyes. No wonder the dog ran away. I sang louder, the crowd growing by the second. Luckily the song worked on each one and I tumbled the rest of the way down the hill. When I was just about to hit the water, pain ripped into my side. The gunshot registered in my ears a moment later.

"Ahh!" I felt alongside of my dorsal fin. Blood coated my hand.

"I got 'em! I got 'em!" I heard someone scream and a sound of a gun being cocked drew my attention. "Wez gonna be rich!"

Another shot hit my side and landed me flat on my back. The edges of my vision fuzzed over and darkened as a multitude of dirty faces and mouths with missing teeth gathered above me. They squealed in jubilation. Unable to keep my eyelids open, darkness surrounded me, and my body yanked upward and floated off into nothingness.

10

❧

ASH

Thursday evening, April 14th

Anger infused Mom's eyes as she stood in the foyer. "Where were you today?"

I hesitated. Did she mean just now? Or earlier? "School."

"Don't play games with me, Ash. You weren't at school. Where were you?"

I stood speechless. "I was, too, all day!"

"You said you weren't feeling well earlier. Did you cut?"

"No, I didn't cut." Although I'd wanted to. My body shook in fury because she didn't believe me. I tried to backtrack and remember if I had some sort of proof I'd actually been there. "Who says I cut? A teacher?"

"The record clerk called and said you didn't come back after lunch and your hair isn't wet."

"During fourth I took a make-up quiz in the teacher's lounge, which made me late for fifth, and sixth was my meeting with the school counselor, but Mr. Branson knew. I even have a note you need to sign from Mrs. Harlow."

Mom's glare remained on her face. "What note?"

I bent down to rummage through my bag. "Practice was canceled today and here are the papers you need to sign."

Before I could give them to her, something pinched the side of my calf. I looked down as blood gushed from my leg onto my sock.

"Ash, you're bleeding." As Mom came closer to investigate and moved the bag away, a triangular hint of silver protruded through the canvas.

"What's this?" She rummaged through the bag and pulled out a knife.

My head swam as my heart jumped around in my chest. I couldn't answer.

"William! Come here!"

Terror flooded me as Dad rounded the corner and caught sight of the knife Mom held and then my leg.

"You're bleeding!" He used the dishrag he held to stop the blood flow. "How did this happen?"

Mom pinched the knife by the hilt like it was poison. "This was in her bag and the school reported she ditched class today."

"I didn't ditch," I said defensively. "And I can explain the knife." *Maybe.*

Dad applied pressure to the wound. I tried to pull away, wincing in pain. "Let me," he said, gripping my calf gently. Once the bleeding stopped, he helped me limp to the couch. "Why are you carrying a knife?"

I looked down, unsure what to say.

"Does this have anything to do with the boat? With—" Mom stopped and brought her hand to her mouth. Tears glinted in her eyes. She swayed a moment, then sat down, gripping the edge of the cushions.

The situation went from bad to worse. I knew what she'd guessed—that I'd tried to drown myself on the lake on purpose and since that didn't end my miserable existence, I was going to do something drastic. I wanted to stop the train I knew was racing through her head before it wrecked, but I couldn't explain the knife. Lucy's head peaked out from behind the wall by the stairs; she smirked.

"I don't want Lucy here." I pointed my finger revealing her hiding spot.

Mom looked up and wiped away a tear. "Why? She loves you. We all do." Mom's voice waffled. "If you're struggling with something, you can tell us, or talk to Dr. Whistle again."

You mean Dr. Weasel? I shook my head and pursed my lips as Lucy continued to gawk.

"Lucy, go to your room please," Dad called out.

She groaned and within a few seconds, her door slammed. Dad investigated to make sure she'd left for sure, then returned and gripped Mom's knee. "Ash, tell us what's going on. Are you missing Fin? We won't judge you, whatever it is. We love you."

I cringed, appalled I had to defend my sanity to my parents. "I'm not trying to kill myself. I only borrowed the knife for—"

My brain continued to freeze. I couldn't think of an excuse beyond wanting to wound Azor so he'd bleed to death and morph into a human permanently.

"Is someone threatening you?" Dad's voice sounded harder than usual.

Sort of. "No."

I looked down at the dried blood on my skin and at the Band-Aid ring wrapped around my finger—covering my secret. More than anything, I wanted to come clean. To tell them I loved Fin with all my heart. That I wanted to be with him now and forever. That we were engaged. That he made me happy and without him, and only without him, did I want to die. But that would definitely grant me time on Weasel's couch. How could they even begin to understand the pressures I faced, the actress I've been day in and day out? That at any moment I was on the verge of snapping, so much so I was contemplating stabbing someone.

Then the perfect excuse came to mind—one to set me free.

"I used it to carve our initials on a tree," I said plainly.

Mom and Dad's eyebrows creased before a collective sigh filled the room.

"Why didn't you just say so?" Dad asked as he laced Mom's fingers with his.

"I don't know." I gulped again. "It's silly."

Mom's face softened, then she smiled. "Did I tell you your dad and I have our initials on a tree in Napa."

They looked lovingly at one another, almost as if they'd forgotten that their wayward daughter, injured and bleeding, sat awaiting her punishment or release. Thank God I thought of an answer.

But even though their fears were alleviated, Fin's was not. He only had a few minutes of sunlight before I could explain why I'd hung up so quickly.

"Can I go?"

"Yes… Of course." Mom rose from the couch and wrapped the knife in the bloodied towel. "Dinner will be ready soon."

Dad stood up with her and stayed an extra second. He hugged me.

"Ash. We really do mean it when we say we love you. You know that?"

"Yeah, of course, Dad," I smiled weakly. "I wasn't trying to scare anyone."

"Okay." He pulled away and smiled, distrust still hanging out behind his eyes.

I darted around him and took the stairs by twos. But somewhere in the middle of the ascent, pain from nowhere wracked my chest and then disappeared, like an elephant had jumped on me. The overwhelming crushing dread that I'd never see Fin again, that I lived with daily, had evaporated. More normal feelings of our separation remained, like I could wait a few weeks to see him and survive.

I started to hyperventilate. Something was wrong. Fin was in trouble. I dialed my phone. Every call rolled over to voice mail.

"No." I crumpled onto a step and my wound broke open. Blood began to trickle down my leg once more.

The rest of the night all my calls to Fin rolled over to voicemail and besides a short sweet email I'd received from him earlier, I didn't hear anything further. I wanted to remain hopeful and believe nothing physically had happened to him, but my heart felt hollow and numb. Even my promise mark seemed extra dim in the shower the next morning.

I yawned again as Mr. Branson droned on about the Nazi's in France. I couldn't listen. I could barely function.

"Ms. Lanski," Mr. Branson said. "And when did the French police arrest the Jews in the Vel' d'Hiv Roundup?"

I froze. "Ummm." This was the first I'd heard of the Vel' d'Hiv Roundup.

"I assure you the answers are not laying in your lap." He gripped the edge of his podium. "Please, Mr. Davis, will you help Ms. Lanski with the answer?"

"July 1942."

"That's correct." He took a deep annoyed breath. "People, if you don't take the time to learn your history, you may end up being carted off to a concentration camp for your race or religion. Do you want that?"

My cheeks ignited as Jeremy reveled in giving the right answer. Mr. Branson gave me a look before continuing. I cared, especially where the Holocaust was concerned, but dates didn't make one a scholar on the subject. Details were the most important piece and that was why Mr. Branson was the teacher—to teach me.

My phone buzzed to life and Fin's name blazoned on the receiver. I squeaked, unable to control myself. My hand flew in the air.

"Mr. Branson, I have to use the restroom. Now."

He shot me a glare. "We've only a few more minutes of class."

As the phone silently rang and tugged at my heartstrings, I contemplated using the most embarrassing excuse in the world. "This can't wait!"

The entire class seemed to turn in unison and gawk as Mr. Branson's eyebrows furled. "Fine, but leave your phone on my desk."

I gulped and didn't move. If I stayed, I'd be a liar and later, a laughing stock. But my phone? He'd threatened if he caught texters in class he'd keep the phone 'til the end of the year. But he couldn't, could he? I didn't actually get a text.

"I thought you needed to go, Ms. Lanski."

"I—I do." I stood and silenced the last ring by pressing OFF. I mustered all of my courage and left the phone on his desk. Hot bolts of lightening zapped through me, ones that wanted me to steal the phone and run through the door, never to return. I could have when Mr. Branson continued with his lecture, but I didn't.

I exited the classroom for the bathroom, afraid I might actually get sick in the hall. Alone, I gripped the sink and stared at my reflection. Grey smudges lined my eyes. I plunged my ring finger under the running water while removing the bandage. Sparkles of light made rainbows on the wall of the bathroom. Fin must have been okay. I had to take hope in that.

Within minutes, the bell rang and I went back to Mr. Branson's classroom. The phone had disappeared.

"Ms. Lanski, nice of you to return."

"I need my phone."

"You know my rules about cellphone use in class."

I squinted. "I'm sorry. I was expecting an important call—about a friend who's in the hospital."

"Well, then. You have a serious decision to make."

"What do you mean?"

"If you want your phone now, you'll have to serve detention with me next week in which you'll write a five-page paper on someone in history who lied and the consequences of such."

I clenched my jaw. "But I didn't lie and I have swim practice."

"Then, I surmise you'll be missing it."

"Or?"

"Or you can come back after class and I'll have a note I want your parents to sign about what happened today."

I cringed. That's all I needed was another reason for my mother to ground me.

"This is so unfair."

"Unfair? You interrupt my class and complain my consequences are unfair? If this phone call is so dire, go to the office and ask to use the phone—or use the payphone."

I exhaled hard and stared at my phone trapped in his hands. I couldn't miss practice if I wanted to do well in the meet, but the note would mean I'd end up being grounded from my phone, no less.

"I guess I'll come after class." I looked down.

"In my day, Ms. Lanski, we didn't have such devices. Use the privilege wisely."

"Yeah," I said under my breath as I turned away and shut the door, "I'm trying."

11

๛

FIN

Friday afternoon, April 15ᵗʰ

I rolled over with a groan as the bed shifted underneath me. Pain ripped through my thigh, freezing me in place. Mom sat next to me, pressing a cold compress on my forehead.

"Fin," she brushed my hair back, "you're awake."

"What happened?" My throat felt raw.

She gave my shoulder a quick squeeze.

"We barely escaped with our lives," she said, breathlessly.

I blinked slowly as bits and pieces came to me. Dad had warned not to push the limits and I'd done just that. I pulled back the covers and took a good look at the big bandage on my thigh and the other one around my ribs. "Geez."

"When we heard the shot, we weren't far from shore. Dad persuaded them to drop you in the lake, but we couldn't stop them all."

"What? Why?"

"I think the one with the gun is mostly deaf, that's why the song didn't work. Luckily, he fell asleep this morning. Dad persuaded the rest to sleep so we could get away."

I felt for my sling pack on my chest. "My—"

"I've got it." She produced the pack.

I fumbled through and found the phone—my most important possession next to my life. The screen illuminated and so did over eight messages—all from Ash.

"How long have I been out? What day is it?"

"You've been touch and go for at least a day. It's Friday."

I gripped the phone. A whole day? I needed to call her now.

"And," Mom said slowly, "you needed a vial last night so there's only one left now." She frowned and dangled her necklace to show proof.

I sat up and winced. "What?"

"Fin." Mom put her hand on my chest to force me down. "I tried to hold off considering everything but you needed it to heal faster. You'd been shot in multiple places and lost a lot of blood. We didn't have anything to take out the bullet until we got into the RV. They were trolling the lake most of the night and we couldn't have you convert underwater accidentally and drown, could we?"

I turned my back to her, mad as hell, but mostly furious at myself. If I'd left the dog alone and headed to the water, none of this would have happened.

"It's fine. I need to call Ash now."

Mom touched my arm. "Don't be mad. We had no other choice. I didn't want to take her from you, Son."

Take her from me? How would the conversion take her from me? Maybe allowing me to convert in the RV later, after we'd escaped was what she should have done. But they viewed converting as a sin, like all the other mers of Natatoria. This was another convenient excuse so Mom wouldn't lose me. Why they still insisted my memories be wiped, I didn't understand.

"You had to do what you had to do. Thanks."

"I did." She gripped my shoulder and forced me to look in her eyes. "I know it's been rough, but—your memories, your love for Ash, everything would have been gone if I didn't give you the essence."

I laughed at the idiocy.

"Really?" I glared. "After what we've been through? Dad would still have to follow Natatorian law and erase my memories."

"No." Mom frowned, confusion settled over her face. "The conversion takes the memories, not Dad or any merman."

"What?" My blood ripped through my veins. "That's not what you said when we were kids."

"I—what?"

"You said the merman erases the memories."

Mom brought her hand to her lips in a gasp. "No, Fin, when a mer converts, they forget everything and everyone. The merman is only there to soften the amnesia."

My mouth dropped open. "You've got to be kidding me."

"I'm not. That's what happens. I'm sorry I misled you—I don't remember saying that."

I made fists around the sheet and squeezed to stop from punching the headboard. "And Ash?"

"She'd be broken out of the bond, but," Mom hung her head, "she'd still remember what you two shared and have feelings for you. But you wouldn't because she'd be a stranger to you."

"Why didn't you mention this the other night?" I bellowed.

"I thought you knew."

I gritted my teeth. "I told Ash the exact opposite."

"Oh, dear."

I laughed bitingly. "And I thought this entire time Dad put pressure on you to change when he could have changed himself."

"Oh, Fin," she rested her hand on mine. "I'm sure he would have, if it were that easy."

"This is insane. I can't believe I didn't know."

"I'm sorry. We should have made sure the details were clear."

In respect to my mother, I refrained from cussing like a sailor. I'd been making life decisions based on assumptions. I fisted the pillow, still anxious to punch something.

"Then—what about Tatch?"

Mom grew stern. "Azor must be stripped of his fins in order to free her from the bond, period. And we will fight to make sure that happens."

I looked up at the ceiling, breathing out my anger. With the pure desire to do the courageous thing, I'd almost erased the most important person in my life. This needed to be common knowledge. An accident could rip the world from someone. And Sissy and Hans did this on a regular basis? How? Why would a person want to forget everything they knew? Unless something horrible happened…

"I want to call Ash."

"Of course." Mom bowed her head and left the room.

I dialed and closed my eyes while it rang. She'd be in class, but I wanted to let her know I was okay. My stomach knotted when I heard her voice on the message. I'd taken a stupid risk because I was clueless.

I softened my voice not to alarm her. "Ash, it's Fin. Sorry about last night. Things got crazy. Call me when you can."

I hung up and dangled my legs over the edge of the bed. The door swung open from the movement of the RV. Mom folded clothes in the living area just beyond the tower of boxes. My bag wasn't in its typical place under the desk.

"Don't tell me." I tried to stand, but the motion of the RV landed me on my butt. "Ugh."

Mom looked up in surprise "No way, mister. You rest."

I didn't want to rest. I wanted to find my bag.

She glared after I didn't obey right away. "If your father sees you up—I don't want him yelling again."

I reclined back with a roll of my eyes and stared at the ceiling, afraid to ask what happened to my bag. I scrolled through the phone. Ash's messages haunted me. I couldn't listen to them. A slew of text messages also caught my attention.

- **Are you okay? Call me as soon as you can.**
- **I had this weird feeling just now. Please call when you can.**
- **I'm up early, call me.**
- **I hope you didn't forget and took your phone underwater.**
- **I feel ridiculous for all the times I've called and texted. Sorry.**

I typed back.

- **I'm okay. Phone died. Sorry.**

I hated lying, but I had to. If she knew otherwise, she'd freak out. I was fine. But how would I tell her the truth about conversions now? She'd never believe me. I'd look like a manipulative jerk saying I'd convert when she was the one who needed to all along. I'd have to tell her in person so she couldn't hang up on me, but only after this all blew over.

But she'd felt something. Would I know if she was in trouble? I hoped so.

12

ᓚᕐ

ASH

Friday afternoon, April 15th

I bolted from Mr. Branson's room and turned on my phone, slowing my steps as I approached the gym. Fin's return text hit my inbox and my legs momentarily trembled.

I dialed frantically.

"Fin!" I exhaled as I fought back my tears. "I'm sorry. I just—" I gulped down the lump in my throat and tried not to sniffle as my teammates walked by me and gave funny looks.

"I'm so sorry, Ash. I forgot to charge the phone." His scratchy voice skipped like he'd been yelling at a rock concert.

"So nothing happened?" I wiped away a tear with the back of my hand, embarrassed by my overcharged emotions.

"Nope." His voice was peculiarly happy. "Things have been great."

Great? He'd never said things were great before. They needed to be horrible, like they'd been for me, especially after I hung up on him and he didn't call back for twenty-four hours.

"Well... that's good. I'm doing great, too." A pang of dread stabbed me in the chest. What if he'd figured out how to stop missing me, so much that he forgot to turn on his phone this morning? Did the bond break earlier somehow and now he didn't have feelings for me anymore? Was he still a merman?

"How are you?" he asked. "My cousin hasn't returned, has he?"

My heart somersaulted. "No. Why?"

"Just checking." Fin laughed, but it sounded forced. "Are you and your mom cool?"

"Um, yeah. She was upset, like always."

I explained our misunderstanding with the knife, but his happy-go-lucky reaction didn't reassure me. He didn't act himself at all. Or maybe it was me—that the guilt for hiding secrets from him had worked its evil into my heart.

"You carved our initials in a tree? That's awesome. Where?" Fin asked.

"Oh, between our properties."

Something else I'd need to do later.

I put my ear against the gym door and listened. The coach's whistle chirped in the background, signaling people needed to finish with their warm-up. I cracked the door. The gym was empty. But I didn't care that I was late; I needed to figure out why Fin was acting so strange.

"You're quiet, Ash. Are you mad at me?"

"No," I whispered as I snuck into a stall at the back of the locker room. "I'm supposed to be in the pool working out, but I had to talk to you first."

"Oh, well then don't let me keep you."

What? Keep me? My stomach rolled over. Something had changed. He'd never voluntarily get off the phone. And now he wanted to hang up. He didn't feel the same for me anymore, that's why I'd felt the shift in the hallway yesterday.

"I guess," I looked at the floor, holding back a giant sob.

If he didn't love me anymore, I didn't know how I'd stop this horrific ache in my heart. I slid against the wall and crumpled to the ground.

"Lanski! Are you in here?" the coach called.

I swallowed hard, fighting back a near panic attack.

"Yeah, Coach? Sorry. I'll be there in a second."

"I'll—I'll let you go," Fin said quickly. "I love you, Ash. Always remember that."

His words smacked me across the face. Did he mean it? Or was he saying that to hold me over until he officially broke things off later? "Okay, yeah. Me, too."

"Call me after school?"

"Sure."

I hung up and clutched the phone to my lumbering chest. Luckily the water would hide my tears, but I was terrified at what he'd tell me later.

"I meant today, Lanski!"

I swung wide the bathroom stall door and darted for the pool, only to remember I hadn't changed into my suit.

❧

My damp hair fell around my shoulders, making my sweatshirt wet, as I held my phone with clammy hands in my darkened bedroom. The moment I'd dreaded was here, and a vulnerable sinking feeling Fin was about to leave me hit hard again. What was I thinking putting all my hope and trust in a... fish?

He'd called three times already, though I'd said I'd call him first, but I didn't pick up. If what I'd suspected was about to happen, I wanted to speak to him alone in the dark.

My pulse whooshed in my ears. Maybe he knew I was lying. Maybe this was a test. Should I come clean about Colin and Alaster? What if all mermen were crafty liars who liked to kiss girls and string them along? Did he ever intend to marry me?

The display read FISH and the ringtone poured out the sad song of *My Jolly Sailor Bold* I'd programmed special for him.

My heart is pierced by Cupid, I disdain all glittering gold,
There is nothing that can console me but my jolly sailor bold.
Come all you pretty fair maids, whoever you may be,
Who love a jolly sailor bold that ploughs the raging sea.

I sighed, identifying with the lyrics. I'd been pierced and only Fin could console me, and now he was about to leave me.

"Fin." I said, answering on the last ring. My voice shook.

"Ash, what's wrong? Did something happen?"

"No." I swallowed hard. "I'm okay." The silence lingered painfully. "You wanted to talk to me?"

"Of course I do. I always want to talk to you."

I sucked in a controlled breath. "Then why didn't you call last night?"

Fin paused for a moment. "I couldn't."

I wanted to tell him I didn't believe it was because his phone wasn't charged. Something else happened and he wasn't telling me the truth.

"Don't be late again, Fin," I heard his dad speak gruffly in the background.

"Yeah," Fin mumbled. "Don't worry."

"Late again?" I asked. The only phone call he'd been late on and tore his jeans was earlier in the week. "What does he mean?"

"I had an incident the other day—it was nothing."

"An incident? What happened?"

Fin took a deep breath. "I got shot."

I nearly dropped the phone. "You what? When?"

"I'm fine, Ash. My leg is healing fast," he said quickly. "It happened last night. I—I didn't want to tell you, but I think you felt something and you sound upset, so—yeah."

I flopped into my pillows on my bed and put my hand over my racing heart. "Oh, Fin. I can't believe this. Yes, I did feel something—like you were torn from me."

"I wanted to tell you. I didn't want to upset you. I'm sorry."

"How did it happen?"

He told me about the dog distracting him, then about the hillbilly kids seeing him finned up. I nearly passed out when he told me one had a gun and wanted to stuff and mount him on their wall. He'd been shot not once, but twice.

The sobs locked in my throat came crashing out. "I—I thought you'd broken the bond and you were about to break up with me."

"What? Oh, Ash…. No." He let out a sad sigh. "Sh-h-h. I'm sorry. Never. I don't ever want to be without you."

My lip trembled as tears trickled down the sides of my cheeks pooling into my ears. "Good, because that scared me—a lot."

"I feel horrible about not telling you." His voice was pained. "Please… don't cry. This is killing me."

"I'm trying."

"Just curl up in your pillows and pretend I'm next to you. That I'm holding you and stroking your hair and kissing your cheek."

"Okay," I whimpered.

I curled up next to his virtual presence and listened to him breathe. Beyond him, I could hear the wind and seagulls crying in the background.

"Sing to me in your language," I whispered.

His beautiful voice poured out a ribbon and wrapped my

heart up tight, my jolly merman bold. I imagined us in his underwater world, swimming together.

"What's it like, Fin. Natatoria?"

"It's beautiful," he said, breathless. "Not as beautiful as you, but it's pretty amazing. The mer songs are always being sung and people are very happy there. And the buildings are covered in gems and precious metals. The light bounces around and everything sparkles. You'd love it."

I hummed.

"I have to go, Ash. But close your eyes. I'll be thinking of you and wishing you luck on your race tomorrow. I love you."

"I love you, too."

Exhausted, I drifted off to sleep.

13

*

FIN

Saturday afternoon, April 16th

A shiver jolted my skin as I watched a fly wriggling in the web hanging over the RV kitchen window. Earlier it had been buzzing low circles over my head, driving me crazy. Though I felt sorry for it now, I'd never set it free. I wasn't afraid of much, but man, I hated spiders.

My last conversation with Ash kept playing over in my mind, stabbing me in the chest. I'd hurt her, and I felt horrible about it. The moment she arrived, after I kissed her passionately, I'd show her my brand of idiocy etched in my leg—ironically one matching hers. She'd be getting ready for her race and I wished I could watch her swim. I missed my girl.

We rounded the bend and the Atlantic came into view. I slid open the window over the table to feel the breeze. The salty air clung to my skin and the inside of my nose, healing me in places I didn't know I'd injured. After driving through ten states in six days, I couldn't believe we'd finally made it to Florida in one piece.

We rolled past rows of mansions and I salivated at the water sprawled out behind them, anxious to wiggle my toes in the sand before diving in the water. The shush of the waves played music to my merman ears and tonight I'd finally work out the kinks in my muscles, swimming in the warm current.

Dad must have known where to go. Once we'd pulled off the highway, he stopped asking me for directions. Beyond simple navigations, he still wasn't speaking to me, still angry apparently.

Dad wove down a winding street, stopped in front of a tiny beach house, and killed the engine.

"Is this it?" Mom's voice hid nervousness as she opened the RV door. "The safe-house?"

Dad came around to her side of the vehicle and took her hand. "Yes, Maggie."

They walked up the small path toward the front door. I limped behind, sizing up the landscape.

Mansions on either side pressed in with their lofty intimidation as if the meager structure or its inhabitants didn't belong. White chipping paint on the siding screamed for attention as weeds staked their claim in the flowerbeds.

How long would we stay here anyway? My parents had said they'd planned to get a house and start up their business again. My only hope was that would happen soon, hopefully before we rescued Tatch.

Dad knocked but didn't wait for a response before walking in. I peered over his shoulder, curious of what lay ahead. The interior housed typical blue beachy stuff, uncomfortable furniture made of wicker, and white cabinets stuck in the wall filled with books. But at the sight of a girl on the couch, my mouth fell open. A vision. A dream. Her green eyes shone under red hair. Ash. But she looked a few years older. How'd she get here?

"You look like you've just seen a ghost," the redhead girl said with a thick Natatorian accent.

My shoulders slunk. Am I going insane? I blinked again, wondering if anyone else saw or heard her. Was she actually a ghost?

"Well aren't you talkative," the redhead cocked her head to the side and laughed, bouncing off the couch. "It's Mr. and Mrs. Captain Jack, I presume?" She smiled at my parents.

Dad bowed his head. "Princess."

Mom followed. "You can call me Maggie."

The girl took Mom's hand. "A pleasure."

"Look at what the crab drug in," an older woman with long curly white hair said. She rose from the table where an older man sat. A huge smile accentuated the wrinkles of her face. She zeroed in on me. "Don't worry about Galadriel, Finley. She's having a rough go of it on land." "Rough go?" Galadriel's face turned from sweet to sour. "You think these plastic boys running amuck is my fault? The uncultured sea slugs! Gah!" Galadriel flipped her long red hair over her shoulder and exited down the hall. Within seconds a door slammed. Mom turned in confusion. "That was abrupt."

"I see things haven't changed." Dad gave the woman a hug and rested his arm on her shoulder. "Son, this is Sissy," he gestured to the table, "and Hans."

Mom and Dad had spoken highly of them the entire drive, but they'd forgotten to mention they were human. All the Natatorians I knew were youthful, even the old ones. For that fact alone, Hans and Sissy couldn't possibly be mer.

"Hello, Fin." Sissy took my hand. "My, you've grown. The last time I saw you, you were a newborn merling. So adorable." She pinched my cheek with a cold, wrinkled hand.

I shrugged and backed away once she let go. Her hand caught the light and sparkled with the promising mark, same as on Hans' hand. How could that be? Were they mer after all? This left me with more questions than answers, especially over the coincidence of Galadriel's resemblance to Ash.

"Has it been that long, Sissy?" Mom asked.

"Too long, my dear friend." The women embraced.

Dad stepped to the side with Hans. "Has there been a report?"

Hans lowered his eyes and tilted his head. "Yes and no. There's been an uprising—"

Dad clapped Hans on the shoulder, interrupting him. "Why don't we speak on the porch."

Sissy flicked her head in the direction of the hall where Galadriel had just escaped. "Good idea, Captain."

I followed behind the crowd toward the door. Dad turned with a glare. "We'll only be a moment, Fin."

What?

Sissy frowned momentarily until Mom took her arm and led her outside. Dad ignored me and closed the door. I stood alone, rejected and angered, with only my demons to comfort me.

I limped over to the island counter and pounded my fist. How long would Dad fume over what happened? I'd already apologized. Didn't he see it was an accident? I'd never intended to fin out on the beach, especially in front of a group of toothless freaks.

If he intended to replace me with the washed-up mer couple, and leave me to tend to the house, he had another thing coming. I'd rescue my sister with or without his blessing.

"They're always doing that, but I can hear them most of the time."

I turned around to meet Galadriel's piercing green eyes. My heartbeat sped up. A part of me desired to kiss her right then and there, but her voice and demeanor revealed she wasn't Ash—an evil older twin messing with my head.

"Old, aren't they?"

I narrowed my eyes in confusion.

She pursed her lips and rolled her eyes. "I'm talking about Sissy and Hans. It's what happens when you stop swimming in essence filled waters. You get all old and icky." She moved to a bar stool and crossed her long tan legs. "It's something you and I have to look forward to if we stay here. We'll sprout grey hair and wrinkles, living unhappily never after." She leaned her cheek into her hand and produced a sappy smirk. "Speaking of which, why the limp?"

She gestured to my leg. Part of her hand though, where her ring and pinky finger should be, was missing. I frowned.

"Don't look at me like I'm a freak. You're the silent one over there with a limp. Do you talk, boy? Hook got your tongue? Or have they warned you not to speak with me—that I'm the enemy?"

I stopped staring at her deformity and gained composure. "I was shot."

Her eyes lit up. "Like with a gun?" She froze momentarily, her mouth gaped half-open. "You have to tell me what happened. Every detail."

Galadriel's innocent reaction tore away the illusion she'd wanted me to see earlier. She wasn't some evil spy for her father. No. She was a curious mermaid kept under the sea from a vast world with so much to offer.

I limped around the other side of the island and retrieved a cup from the drainer. "May I?" I said, gesturing to the tap.

She pursed her lips. "Yes, by all means."

After her snippy comments, I wanted to toy with her for a bit. Slowly I filled the glass. "It was really nothing. Just some locals thinking they'd poach me for sport."

"How did you get away?"

"I almost didn't. The one with the gun was deaf."

Her eyes grew. "That's incredible. What did you do?"

I smirked. "They planned to stuff me and mount me on the wall. Somehow I made it to the water and we waited until he fell asleep, then snuck away."

"Did you save the bullet?"

"Um…." I scratched my head and Galadriel gasped.

I froze, trying to figure out what freaked her out. She pointed at me with huge eyes. If a hairy spider was crawling on me, I'd scream like a girl and run from the room.

"You're promised?" she whispered.

My lips clamped shut, surprised that that was what freaked her out. I didn't answer.

"Oh." She brought her deformed hand to her lips. "You're separated—must be killing you." She shot me a conflicting look, one mixed with glee and sorrow, like she understood.

"I'm managing." I drained the glass in one long pull; something to stop the questions. I could still feel her eyes on me. I couldn't stay here, not with Ash's twin.

"So what's your story?" she asked.

I washed and rinsed the glass before I turned around. "There's no story."

"Everyone has a story." Her conniving smile lit up her face in an eerie way. "Come on," she held out her perfect hand, "…spill."

Her eagerness sparked a warning from Dad. He'd said to be careful. She'd get *Cliff Notes* with a pointed edge.

"Because you ran away, my sister had her promise stolen by your spineless mollusk of a brother. So now we're stuck here and are planning to get her back." I flashed a patronizing smile. "Your turn."

She looked away in disgust. "Not fair."

"Well, it's the truth." I shot an arrogant smirk.

She pouted her lips. "I never intended for that to happen to your sister, but good luck with my… brother. He's a self-important sea sack and he won't relinquish your sister without a fight."

"I'm not afraid of Azor."

She lifted an eyebrow. "You should be."

I stared her down. My sister suffered because of her actions. She owed my family. "So?"

"So, what?"

"Why did you run then?"

She slumped onto the counter and blew out a gust of air, blowing her bangs off her forehead.

"Mr. Darcy."

"Is this someone I should know?"

"Don't you read, pretty boy? The books… they've ruined me. I thought those men existed but apparently they don't, and ironically my own pride and prejudice prevents me from stooping to their level—I should have known that mermen aren't anything different than the land dwellers. There's no one here that is chivalrous or romantic. They're all a bunch of frat boys. They look at me with dreamy eyes and promise me the world; anything to get me in the sack. It's so pathetic."

She laid her head on the counter, her red hair within touching distance of my hand. I splayed my hand flat to keep from yanking it.

She continued, "now I'm stuck here. Sissy won't let me leave and I refuse to be made human after what I've experienced. It's a living nightmare."

Living a nightmare? I couldn't believe my ears. What about Tatch? "I'm sure my sister's in paradise."

She looked up at me, water rimming her eyes. "Stop blaming me for something Azor and my father did. They have nothing to do with me."

I could barely control my rage to hear my sister suffered over a search for her quest of fictional book characters. I wanted to choke her neck. Galadriel turned her back to me and faced the large bay windows. Her hand rose to wipe her face.

I stood there, my fists shaking. She cried because the men in books didn't compare to the men in real life, how insane.

"Your little lass is lucky to acquire such a catch," Galadriel said before she turned and slid her arms forward on the counter, looking deep within my eyes. I caught a glimpse of her cleavage pressed into the countertop. I glanced away. "Maybe I wasn't looking in the right place, or for the right land dweller. Maybe I need to trade in big metropolises for small lakeside towns—for boys like you. Will you take me to your lakeside town, Fin?" She flitted her long eyelashes. "I'll tell you all my secrets."

My stomach lurched. I was ready to chew her out good when Mom and Dad returned with Sissy and Hans behind them. Dad watched us with a questioning frown. I looked away like I'd done something wrong. Galadriel snapped her body upright as if we'd only been discussing the weather.

Galadriel was worse than a spoiled princess. She was a manipulative witch and I had to find another place to stay. I knew if we kept having conversations like this one, I'd lose control and who knew how far I would go. For her safety, I needed to leave.

Everyone had mistaken Galadriel to be the fly, but in all reality she was the spider.

14

⤸

ASH

Saturday, late morning, April 16th

My heart thrummed as I looked at the stands. Dad, Mom, and my sister all watched with rapt attention. The day had finally come for the championship meet, the biggest day of my swimming career, and I'd missed almost all of my practices the past few weeks. I was going to make such a fool of myself.

As I stood on the block, water dripped down the backs of my legs from my suit. The glistening oasis below called silently, beckoning me to wash away my cares in its goodness.

"Swimmers take your mark," the announcer called.

Here goes.

I took one last look at Meredith before we both dove in at the starter. Heaven enveloped me into her watery weightlessness as I glided in my underwater home. My body flowed through the current, my skin tingling over exhilarated muscles. I pushed the water down my sides and naturally sucked in a breath of water. I choked. My head emerged and I coughed through the next few breaths between my strokes.

Whoa! What was that?

I peeked to the side and instead of everyone passing me by, I still held a lead against the pack. I put my head down and developed a rhythm with each stroke, zoning out into mindlessness. Before I knew it, my hands hit the wall. I pulled up my head to find I'd finished almost a full lap ahead of everyone else. The crowd leapt to their feet in applause.

I checked the board for my time as Meredith finished next to me.

"Ladies and gentlemen, for the first time ever, with a time of 53.44, Ashlyn Lanski has tied the NCAA record for the women's 100-yard butterfly."

My mouth fell open as my time lit up and flashed. I'd told Fin of my new abilities, but this was ridiculous. He'd promised his blood would have long escaped my system by now, but this? How did I swim so fast? Did the promise secure one foot, or should I say fin, into the mer world and give me the ability to swim like a fish?

Whatever it was, my elation was out of this world. I wanted to swim backflips.

"Lanski, you did it!" Coach Madsen hoisted me out of the pool like a fish on a hook. She clasped herself around me in a hug, unconcerned that I soaked her sweatshirt.

The sea of congratulations continued when I caught Meredith's beet-red face from the poolside. She faked a smile. I pushed through the throng of people and helped her out of the pool.

"Good race," I said.

She nodded back. "Yeah."

I wasn't sure what else to say. Guilt set in. Had I really won the race fair and square?

❧

The hubbub continued on the way home from the meet in the car.

"Ash," Mom turned around from the passenger seat, "I can't believe it. Even after your accident. Did you hear your coach? The Olympic trials are in June. Maybe you could qualify."

"I don't know, Mom." I felt guiltier by the second. I'd practically cheated because of the promise. I needed to disqualify myself, or people would start questioning. What if they demanded a drug test? What if there was something in my blood?

"Mom's right," Dad chimed in from the driver's seat. "There's so much opportunity for you now. You tied the NCAA record."

Mom and Dad continued on about the possibilities while Lucy looked out the window and yawned in boredom. I had to tune them out as my heart fluttered with anxiety. All I wanted to do was get home, check the mail, and call Fin. He had to know why I'd been able to swim so crazy-fast.

Once we pulled into the garage, I bolted from the car and scurried through the house to the mailbox on the front porch. I practically plowed right into Colin skulking by the front door.

I steadied myself and gasped in surprise. "What are you doing here?"

His eyes smoldered over a fluff of pink petals. "These are for you."

I blinked at him and then at the huge bouquet.

"When did you get these?"

"Today," he said with a smile. "I realized after you didn't show up, I hadn't asked you out properly."

On the ground by his feet lay a white note with the Tahoe Florist emblem.

"What's that?" I asked.

He kicked the offending slip of paper off the deck into the shrubs. "Trash. Here." He held the flowers more firmly out to me.

I glared, annoyed he'd littered, but even more so, confused how he purchased the flowers to begin with. Did he rob Fin's piggy bank? Or worse, steal his aunt or uncle's credit card?

"Oh, my stars," Mom said from behind me. "Colin. They're so

lovely." She nudged me. "Aren't they?"

"Yeah," I moved around him to the postbox while Mom took the flowers from his hands. I wanted nothing to do with him or his stolen flowers.

From inside the mailbox, Fin's penmanship on a letter addressed to me sang a love song. I folded the precious envelope and slid it in the pocket of my swim jacket before anyone could notice.

"Bills and junk mail," I chirped. "Can't wait 'til I'm on my own to get some with my own name on it."

"Oh, just wait," Mom said jokingly as she went inside, "that day is coming sooner than you think."

"You going somewhere?" Colin asked.

An evil smile played on my lips. "Wouldn't you like to know? Gotta run. See ya."

I tried to walk inside when he moved into my path. "When?"

"When what?"

"When are you moving?"

"Soon." I tried to push him aside with my hand. "Do you mind?"

"You stood me up today," he said.

"I left you a note that said I couldn't make our date. You didn't get it?"

"No." He frowned. "You shouldn't have been able to stand me up. I mean after I'd—"

"Yeah, well, another time." I tried squeezing between his hulking frame and the door.

He caught my wrist. "Tomorrow?"

"Busy."

"Later today then."

I tugged my wrist away. "Nope, still busy."

He opened his lips and the music started.

"What mom?" I yelled, a little too loud as I knocked into his ribs with my elbow as hard as I could. He sputtered and finally moved out of my way.

"Sounds like my mom needs me. Bye."

I pivoted and slammed the door in his face.

Get a clue, mer-moron.

I peered out the window and watched Colin walk across the lawn back toward the Helton's home, the typical bounce missing in his step. A part of me regretted being so mean, but if I wasn't firm, he wouldn't take no for an answer.

"Lovely boy," Mom said as she walked from the kitchen. "Are you two hanging out later?"

"Mom," I forced alarm in my voice to gain her attention. "He's creepy and kind of stalking me. Please, I'm seeing—" I stuttered for a moment. What if Colin had persuaded Mom to tell him all she knew about Fin? She could easily say something accidentally. "If he comes back, just tell him I've moved. Okay?"

"What?" Mom laughed. "Why would I say that? He's a wonderful boy. Just like your father. Who knows? He might be the one."

My jaw hit the floor in sync with her exit. What? After her lecture on keeping my options open? Where my strict yet sensible mom? Geez, mer persuasion was strong.

"Oh, and you have a message on the machine from your coach at Florida Atlantic. They heard about the race, said they're sending flowers."

Flowers?

"We'll be swimming in flowers before we know it. Get it? Swimming." She chuckled as she took a basket of clothes to the laundry room and closed the door.

I went outside and found the slip of white paper Colin had kicked under the begonias.

Dear Ashlyn,

Congrats on your race! We're looking forward to you joining our team!

~ Coach Rick and FAU staff

"Why that little—" I gritted my teeth, curling the note in my palm. I was tempted to chuck it into the bushes, but the evidence was there in black and white. I smiled and ran into the house, note in hand.

"Mom! I have something to show you."

If I couldn't tell her what a douche Colin was, I could sure show her.

15

❧

FIN

Saturday afternoon, April 16th

Dad, Mom, Sissy, and Hans reconvened in the living area of the beach house, giving me and Galadriel question-filled looks. I could care less if Hans and Sissy didn't approve of me, but not Dad. The way he stared me down, as if he knew I'd told Galadriel something I shouldn't, sent a jolt of betrayal directly to my gut. He used to tell me everything and now that I was promised I couldn't do anything right.

Galadriel slammed her hands on the counter, snatching their attention, before I could demand to know what was going on. "I'm bored. I'm going out."

"Not without an escort," Sissy said quickly.

"We leave Natatoria, but Natatoria lives in us…" Galadriel hissed. She held her hand toward me. "Fin?"

To my relief, Sissy moved between us. "No, not Fin. Hans will escort you."

Galadriel pushed past Hans and refused his outstretched hand. She stomped out of the house, but not before a few curt words rolled off her tongue.

"Royalty," Dad mumbled under his breath.

"It's been like this since I grounded her. We had another incident the other day and I'm sick of these love struck puppies showing up here, stalking her, so she must have an escort at all times on land and water." Sissy sighed.

"Incident?" Mom asked.

"Yes. Another boy from the college. We don't know if she's kissed them or not, but with heavy persuasion, we've gotten them all to leave."

"Really? How many has she kissed?" Dad asked

"Jack," Mom jabbed him in the side, "let's not disgrace the poor girl without evidence."

I spotted Hans through the window, struggling to keep up with Galadriel as she strode down the beach ahead of him.

Dad stiffened his shoulders. "Well, it's hard to know, with her hand and all. Maybe she can't be promised..."

Sissy interrupted, "I'm sure she can be, Jack, with or without her ring finger, but it's suspicious. I've suspected she's trying to distract her longing for whoever she's bonded to, but she won't confess to anything and Ferdinand hasn't returned in some time either. She claims she doesn't know why, but without some hard answers, I can't trust her."

Ferdinand? Who was that? And what did she mean distract the longing? Was Galadriel promised, too?

Mom cleared her throat.

Sissy straightened her blouse and smiled grimly at me. "My manners are lacking, Fin. I've forgotten you're separated from your promised one. I'll be more sensitive."

Mom patted my shoulder. "Fin, could you get my bag from the RV. It'll be dark soon and I'd like to change."

"Oh, good idea, Maggie," Sissy said. "First, let me show you to your rooms."

Dad stayed behind as Mom and I followed. Sissy pointed to two adjacent rooms at the end of the hall. One room, no bigger than a sardine can, had a futon and a small dresser. The other I assumed would be my parent's room which was larger with a queen sized bed, a desk, and a chair.

"This was Ferdinand's room, but since he's not here you can store your things here, Fin. I just ask you don't disturb his stuff." She smiled warmly. "And, Maggie, this room is for you and Jack. Sorry it's not larger. I know you're used to more space."

"Oh, no," Mom said. "It's fine."

Mom nudged me, no doubt to encourage me to say thanks and get a move on.

"Thanks." I ducked past them and went outside, mostly to get some air.

I needed to regroup, especially after my conversation with Galadriel. At least with my own room I could close my door, pop in my earbuds to my iPod, and veg out during the day. But at night, my parents weren't going to keep me around. I planned to motor as far away into the Atlantic as I could.

Upon reentering the house with an armful of junk, I found Dad had fallen asleep in a wingback chair, a local paper on his lap, and the women had moved to the table with teacups.

"What do you think it is?" Mom asked quietly.

"We all hold secrets for the King, don't we? Maybe she'll come clean. If not, it's best her secrets die with her mer, don't you think?"

"Hmmm. Maybe."

I walked down the hall, deposited Mom's suitcase on her bed, and dumped my things on the floor of my new room. I kicked back on the futon and strummed out a song on my guitar, aching to call Ash instead. She'd be just about finished with her swim meet by now.

My stomach ached as I played a few sad notes. I'd never heard that kissing another person could distract the longing before. Could this be true? All I'd been told growing up was once you kissed, you'd be bonded for life. Of course, we were warned to wait and kiss the right person, but no one told us the agony of being apart or what it could drive someone to do. Would Ash want to kiss another guy?

I strummed the strings harder. I had to know more.

Sissy's whisper caught my attention over my song. "What if Galadriel ran away for another reason, not because she wanted a human? I've tried to befriend her, but she clams up. I don't know if she's a spy, or in real trouble with her parents."

"I see," I heard Mom say.

"I'm at my wits' end. We can't keep constant watch over her while she's here, and we're having difficulty rescuing the other mers, especially with Ferdinand gone. Missing fingers or not, you and I both know she's not keeping her lips to herself."

"I suppose," Mom said. "The right thing to do is to try and find out who her real mate is, and then everything should work itself out. We shouldn't take her first love from her. Maybe she'll trust me."

"I don't know, Maggie. She keeps hinting about Bone Island, but I'm scared to tell her the truth. If she'll just admit she promised and tell me who he is I'll help her, otherwise, we'll have to convert her, though I hate to do it."

"This is a problem."

The door slammed. Galadriel's annoying voice filled the space. I put down the guitar and turned on my music for real. I started to put my shirts in the dresser when she thumped open my door all the way.

"Oops." She pressed me with a devious smile. "Looks like you got Ferdinand's room."

Though I could hear her, I pretended that I couldn't and continued to unpack. She didn't take the hint and plopped down on my futon. She started to paw through my books.

"Nice choice. I didn't think you could read!" She yelled.

Ironically she held up *The Great Gatsby*. I pulled out my ear buds and frowned. Was she toying with me? The irony she'd admire a book that taught that wanting something was better than actually having it, floored me. I snatched the book from her hands and placed it nicely on the top of my dresser.

"There are a lot of things you don't know about me," I snapped, and moved my bag off the futon. "Why are you in here, anyway? Don't you have something to do?" *Like bother someone else?*

She stretched her long legs out on the futon and lounged back. She twirled her red hair around her finger and watched me. "Let's go somewhere. Do you have keys to the red little jalopy attached to that house on wheels?"

"Do you mind?" I pointed to her feet propped on top of my guitar. She removed them with a coy grin.

"Well, do you?"

"No." I stopped for a second to glare at her before continuing to tuck my shirts in the drawers.

She blew out a gust of air. "If we were in Natatoria, you couldn't refuse me."

I turned and pointed my finger in her face. "Let's get one thing straight, Princess, we aren't in Natatoria anymore, so save your orders. I'm not your slave."

"Crabby." She flicked away my hand with her stump.

"You'd be crabby too if you were looking at the sole reason your sister's in a living hell."

"I'm sure she's fine."

I pitched a brow. "How would you know?"

"Well, you're going to get her, so what's the big deal?"

I didn't feel like arguing. I wanted her out. Maybe if I got personal she'd leave. "How'd you lose your fingers anyway?"

She wiggled the stumps. "A fisherman caught me in his net."

I stopped for a moment, believing her. The corner of her lip turned up. "And I got away, but it cost me my fingers."

"Fish tell tall stories…" I shook my head. "Fine if you won't tell me."

"I did," she grinned mischievously. "A rope… or was it a rusty door? At birth, yeah, that's what happened." She laughed.

"I'm not going to believe anything you say from now on."

"Oh," she pouted out her lips. "Poor merling."

After a few minutes, she started to pluck the strings of the guitar. "Play for me."

"Please leave me alone."

"I just want to go for a drive."

"No."

She sighed, then picked up *How to Win Friends and Influence People*. "Why in Hades would you need this?" She laughed. "You're a merman."

"Because." I lunged for her arm to take back the book.

She held it over her head. I moved closer, tempted to do real damage to her arm if she didn't let go. "I want my book back."

She could learn a thing or two, especially about being a friend. Yes. I was a merman, but I wanted people to like me for me, not because I persuaded them to like me.

Galadriel came face to face with me, the book between our fingers. Her sweet breath tickled my nose. I held my breath as she moved her lips closer.

Freaked at our close vicinity, I let go. "Forget it. You can have it."

She reached beyond me and set it on the dresser, intruding on my personal space again.

"I've already read it," she whispered.

I moved away and bumped the open drawer of the dresser. A collection of smoothed glass stones fell onto the floor behind me.

"Oopsie." She laughed. "That's going to piss off Ferdinand."

"Whatever." I held open the door for her and gestured she leave. "Go."

"You're no fun." She wrinkled her nose, then bounced out of the room.

I closed the door and counted down from ten to keep from punching the wall. The shiny pieces of glass covered the floor.

This was going to be a long month with this nasty spider.

❧

"Ash, I've missed you." I held the phone like it was a lifesaving rope, hoping instead of cinching around my neck, it would bring me closer to her.

"Fin." Her voice sounded happy, no longer skeptical like before. "Me, too."

An instant grin plastered on my face making my cheeks hurt. "How was your day?"

"Crazy, but you first. Are you there? In Florida?"

"Yeah," I said, relieved my ginger girl trusted me again, "we got here about an hour ago. It's... okay."

"Who's there?"

"Oh." I hesitated. Dad had warned not to talk about Galadriel and mentioning the lost princess by name might backfire. Luckily, I hadn't said anything about her yet. "It's Sissy's and Hans' place. They take in runaways. Others come and go."

"What's it like? Tell me everything."

I filled her in on the surfacey stuff, but left out the strained relationship part. She didn't need to know Dad and I were fighting.

"How was the meet?"

"It was really good." She chuckled. "Coach Havor from FAU sent me flowers already."

"Flowers? Already? What, did you break a record or something?"

"You could say that." Her smile oozed through the phone, making me shiver.

"Really!" I could imagine my beautiful swim champion taking

first place. "Wow, that's awesome. You broke the record this time."

"No… well, I didn't break, more like tied."

"So your time was the same?"

"No… I didn't tie my school's record. I tied the NCAA record."

My mouth fell the rest of the way open. I couldn't contain my happiness as it constricted my throat. I knew she could swim well, but wow—I loved she was such a natural.

"Fin." Panic came across the line as she swallowed hard. "I think your blood is still running in my system, or trapped in my muscles. I—I've never been that fast before."

I smirked. "I think it's all you, Ginger."

"Then the promise? Could that have made me swim like a fish?"

"Maybe, but then again I've never met a promised swimmer before." I withheld a laugh unsuccessfully.

"This isn't funny. I'm sure someone somewhere is going to demand a drug test and what if they find fish blood in my system?"

"That sounds sexy."

"I'm serious."

"I'll ask, but I doubt it. Although, that would make sense. What if all Olympic swimmers are promised?" I smiled as an old familiar wish came to mind about swimming in the surf with her a while back. "We should check the athletes for Band-Aid covered fingers."

"This isn't funny. I'm being serious."

"And so am I, but I don't think there's anything to worry about."

She huffed, then sighed. "Do you think there are other land-dwelling mers on land? Like us?" She finally relaxed, and all I wanted was to crush her to me and smother her with kisses.

"I don't think so, maybe. But isn't this what you've always wanted? To win?"

"Yeah… but, I kinda feel like I've cheated, like I didn't do it on my own."

Her words knocked my happiness down a notch. I knew the feeling well—after every time I'd persuaded someone, in fact.

"Do you swim just as fast with legs?"

I snorted. "I don't know. I've never timed myself."

"You're such a brat," she said, the happiness returning in her voice. "I can't describe how exhilarating it was. I thought for sure I'd swim my worst time since I hadn't practiced consistently the past few weeks. But after that race, my parents and my coach were freaked. They want me to try out for the Olympics team in June. It's always been my dream to swim in the Olympics, but now, since we've met, I don't know. It'll delay me from coming to Florida."

I pushed out a long sympathetic sigh because I'd like nothing more than to celebrate next to her—but I knew, with everything, her success brought us further apart. "Maybe I can go with you, wherever that is. I don't want you to have any regrets. We'll take it one step at a time."

She sighed. If it weren't for complete amnesia, I'd lose my fins right this second to be with her forever. She still thought I could make that choice. Now wasn't a good time to tell her the truth.

"Fin?" Galadriel pounded on my door as she tried the knob. "Let's go for a walk."

I cupped the phone, afraid Ash would hear her voice. "I'm busy. I'll be out later."

"Who's that?" Ash asked, brimming with curiosity.

"Um, it's no one. Just the King's annoying daughter."

"I heard that, Fin," Galadriel barked and kicked the door with her foot. "Ouch. You big jerk."

I cringed, hoping Ash's human ears weren't as keen as mine. I'd make my next call far away from the house.

Ash's curiosity peaked. "She's there?"

"Yeah, for a little bit."

"Oh."

"She'll be gone soon, but not soon enough. I'm already sick of her annoying, pretentious, and bossy self," I said, speaking louder than I should.

"You're rude," Galadriel said from down the hall.

I smiled.

"I didn't know she'd be there," Ash said.

"Yeah. She's—uh. It's complicated. She was supposed to convert, but she keeps changing her mind, so...."

"She did? Why?"

"She's afraid she'll be all alone. Something about wanting to find Mr. Darcy or something. She's seriously a nut."

"Oh." Ash grew quiet and I panicked. I'd finally patched things with my sweet girl again just to have Galadriel steal her away. This was exactly why I didn't want to tell Ash about Galadriel in the first place.

"So, what else is going on today?" I asked, hoping to change the subject.

"Besides talking to you as long as I can, nothing, I guess. Just homework. Georgia wants to see a movie later tonight. Did you get the waterproof case yet?"

"I ordered it on the road," I said proudly. "It should be here in a few days."

"That'll be nice so we can at least say goodnight when it's dark on both coasts."

A grin pressed on my lips and I imagined myself floating on my back, looking at the stars as we talked all night—or until my battery died. "Yeah, that will be nice."

A muffled rap through her phone line stole away the vision. "Ash, you've got chores to do today. How much longer? Are you talking to Colin?"

I sat upright on my futon. I could have sworn her mom said Colin's name. "What did she say?"

"NO!" She yelled, blasting my eardrum. "I'm not… I'm talking to Georgia and I'll be out in a second."

"It sounded like your mom said Colin," I corrected.

"No." Ash's voice became hard. "Holyn. She said Holyn."

"Holyn?" I frowned.

"Mom's been overly nosey since my mild breakdown. She has to know everyone I'm talking to, so I—I made up some friends."

"Why can't you tell her you're talking to me?"

"Yeah, well… it's been a little strained here."

"They liked me when I was there, didn't they? Don't they think we're still together?"

She let out a moan. "Yes. They did—do. I'm sorry. I was flustered. I just want her out of my business. Please understand."

Besides being insulted she wouldn't 'fess up she was talking to me, I could have sworn with my merman ears I heard Colin's name. The thought made my skin crawl.

"Is Colin there?"

"Why would you ask me that? No, of course not," she said, sounding insulted.

"I wondered if they'd returned to the house. I'd hate it if we'd left for nothing."

"Well, yeah. I mean, I might have seen someone after you left a few days ago, but not lately. It's pretty quiet now."

"A few days ago? Who'd you see?"

Her voice grew more nervous. "Just men in skirts, like the last time."

I clenched my jaw. I didn't like they'd come back and stuck around. They were too close to Ash and her family, too close for comfort.

Ash's voice picked up in tempo. "Why? Would they be here for another reason? Do they think you're coming home soon? I mean, if no one is there, can't you come back? Please tell me you're coming home."

"No." My chest squeezed at her vulnerability and longing. "I don't think we're ever coming back and actually, I don't know what's happening. My parents aren't telling me anything again."

"Oh, really? Why?"

I made a fist, about to tell another lie. "I think they want to protect me. In case there's…" *a war, retaliation, you name it.* "I don't know."

"So you're not leaving anytime soon to get Tatchi?"

"I don't know." The pause on the line made me nervous. "You still there?"

"Yeah. I'm sorry." I heard her sniffle. "I'm afraid you're going to go and then get trapped in Natatoria, and I'll never see you again, and I won't know how to contact you, or how to help."

Her anxiety ran me over, leaving invisible tire treads on my chest.

"Don't worry, Ash. There's no plan yet. My dad knows I don't want to go until you're here. And maybe, if you think you might like to join us, you could turn mer."

As the suggestion slipped out, I cringed, wishing I could take back what I said. Dad didn't know I wanted to bring Ash along. And now, with our fall out, I could imagine his outrage. But I couldn't leave her on land to wait for my return. He had to understand that at least.

"Oh," she said softly.

The silence ticked on and I bit the inside of my cheek. Mom had warned me not to pressure her. And I hadn't planned to, but somehow I'd thrown that advice aside.

"Whatever you want to do," I said, wrestling in conflict. "There's no pressure. It'll all work out."

"I wish I could give you an answer, Fin. I'm sorry. I still don't know what's the right thing to do."

"We don't need to decide today. We can live as human and merman forever if you want. See? Problem solved."

"That still doesn't fix the issue with you rescuing Tatchi."

"I fought heaven and hell to come back to you then, I'll do it again. They could never keep me from you, understand?"

"Yes." Her voice sounded limp, unconvinced.

"Promise me—if anyone does show up at the house or starts snooping around, you'll tell me, all right? And you'll stay far away from them. Because if they ever suspected we were… just promise."

"Yes, I know," her voice dropped. "You've told me already."

"I'm not trying to be overly protective. I want you to be cautious. They're spineless monsters who would be willing to do anything to get the King's favor."

She remained quiet.

"I'm sorry, Ash. I wanted to stay and I didn't want this to be complicated."

"I know. It's okay. And don't worry about me, I'm fine."

Another knock at my door exploded my rage into a fury. "Go away! I'm busy!"

"Fin, it's Mom," a soft voice said from the other side. "The sun is setting. You need to hang-up and get to the water, before your father—"

I groaned and looked down at my jeans. I'd forgotten to put on my board shorts again. And now, being three hours ahead of Ash's time zone, we had even less time to talk until the case came.

"I'll be there in five minutes."

"No," she said. "It's time."

"I love you, Ash. I'm sorry. I have to go," I said quickly, wishing I could cup her cheeks and lose myself in her kiss instead.

"I know. I love you, too. Have a good night."

As I hung up, a part of me sliced in two. My bare feet hit the wooded floor and I bolted for the front door, locking it behind me. Scales were sprouting on my legs and I knew I wouldn't make it to the water in time.

Tomorrow, I'd be shopping for a new pair of jeans.

16

❦

ASH

Monday morning, April 18th

The alarm ushered me into a world of white as I opened my eyes and peered outside. The groundhog had decided to sleep for longer than six weeks, hiding from an unseasonably cold spring for April.

The thought of Callahan, of all people, popped in my head. An avid snowboarder, he had to be furious waking up to such delectable powder and forced to go to school instead. Personally, I preferred water in liquid form, melted, warmed, and collected in a pool or lake I could dive into. I rolled over with a groan. Everything ached and begged for a hot shower. I must have worked out harder than I'd realized on Saturday.

I padded down the hall and didn't even try the knob. Lucy's pathetic rendition of Kelly Clarkson's *What Doesn't Kill You* filtered through the walls, killing me softly.

I pounded on the door. "I need to go pee!"

"Go downstairs!" she yelled and continued singing.

"Don't take all the hot water!"

She belted the song louder, mumbling through the parts that she'd forgotten the words to.

I trudged downstairs. Mom and Dad bustled in the kitchen. The coffee smelled good for once, though I didn't drink it normally.

"Good morning, sleepy head." Dad tussled my hair. "Excited about the big interview?"

"Not really."

Mom gave me a sideways hug. "You should be getting ready. Why don't you wear the green sweater Gran bought you? It brings out your eyes."

"Yeah, maybe." I looked out the window at the world of white.

The interview wasn't really about me. Coach Madsen had called yesterday all excited because the local news wanted to meet. We were to be filmed while the team worked out in the background behind us. She'd role-played a few questions for me to answer, but if I got frazzled, she volunteered to do most of the talking.

"Oh," Mom said as she tossed me the keys to her car, "come home right after practice today. We're having an early dinner to accommodate a special guest."

I frowned. "Who?"

"Colin," she said in delight as she walked out the door behind Dad.

"What?" I ran to the garage as they climbed into his truck. "No! We can't!"

"He's nice, Ash. I like him." Mom smiled before closing the door.

"I'm with Fin! This is wrong."

She rolled down the window as Dad backed out. "I know, but you're young and there's no reason you can't develop friendships with other boys."

I panicked. If she mentioned Fin, I'd be dead. We'd all be dead. That single mistake was bigger than anyone could imagine.

"Fin doesn't want Colin to know about his family drama, don't you understand? And Colin lied about the flowers."

Mom grimaced. "That was a misunderstanding. Colin explained he was delivering the flowers, not that he'd bought them. Who could be upset with that? He's so sweet and charming."

"But, Mom!"

She waved and rolled up the window. I looked to Dad for help. He only shrugged.

"This is ridiculous!" I yelled as the garage door whirred and rolled shut.

I could still smell the soap in my hair as I drove Lucy to school. The smug look plastered on her face as she bobbed her head to whatever was on her iPod made me sick. Every time she started singing, I slugged her in the arm.

"Ouch!" Lucy pulled out an ear bud. "Stop doing that!"

"Serves you right for hogging all the hot water!"

"I did not."

"I was in there for two seconds, and the water ran cold."

"Gran must have taken a shower, too, or started laundry." She made a face and popped the bud back in.

I stopped on the street opposite the parking lot at her school.

"Get out!" I barked.

"What?" Lucy moaned and folded her arms over her chest. "Drive me to the front."

An evil grin formed on my lips. "I'm late. Get out here."

"A-s-s-sh," she whined, "there's snow."

"Should have thought of that when you hogged all the hot water. I don't have time to wait in line to drop you off. This is your fault and if you don't get out in three seconds, I'm driving off and you'll have to walk further."

"I'm telling Mom!" she said, "and I'm telling her you're talking to Fin all the time!"

What? I gritted my teeth and let up on the brake. The car lurched forward.

"Fine!" she quipped and jumped out anyway. I lingered for an extra second and reveled in her frustration as she tried to maneuver through the snow in her Toms.

❧

At my locker, I grabbed my book and headed for English without much fanfare. No one knew, let alone cared about my accomplishment, which made me extra grateful.

"Ms. Lanski," Coach called.

I swiveled around and blinked, trying to recognize the person in front of me.

"Coach?"

"I wear makeup sometimes, okay? Close your mouth."

I hid my smile. She didn't just apply makeup. Her hair was highlighted, cut, and styled, and she wore a dress.

She gave me a once over. "What are you wearing?"

I looked down at my new black FAU sweatshirt that came shortly after the flowers on Saturday. I figured when I put it on earlier, I might as well advertise, just in case any gawking school poachers didn't know I was taken.

"My new college sweatshirt. Is something wrong with it?"

"You can't wear that. I'm getting calls from all over. You haven't officially signed a contract with FAU, so your options are still open. I've been looking at Stanford, and a few schools in Georgia. You've got the pick of the litter."

"I want to go to FAU."

"You should be thinking about the Olympics," she said and squeezed my shoulder. "After the interview later, I have a coach I want you to meet."

"Sure, but I'm not making any commitments until I talk to my parents," I said as the bell rang. "And get to class."

Her face lit up. "Ash, we're talking the Olympics. Do you understand me? This is an opportunity of a lifetime."

"Yes, I know." A huge grin popped out on my face. My Olympic dream was now within my grasp. Though my love for Fin fought this every step of the way, I wanted to try. I wanted to swim.

17

೨

FIN

Monday afternoon, April 18th

The moment I walked into American Eagle, I knew letting Galadriel tag along was a mistake.

"Oh, Fin-n-n," she crowed, "this is perfect for you-u-u."

She fanned a red and white checked shirt on the hanger like a flag. I rolled my eyes and shook my head. We came here for one purpose: jeans.

Board shorts caught my attention though. I thumbed through a pile on the display while Galadriel disappeared to the back of the store. Maybe a few new pairs and some flip-flops were a better idea, considering the weather in Florida. No one wore jeans here and mine had frayed where I'd sewn in the Velcro strips.

"What about this one?" she yelled across the store, holding up a bright yellow sequined bikini top against her chest.

I glared and shook my head, again. She'd promised to be good, but our definitions apparently weren't the same. I quickly grabbed three pair of shorts and a pair of jeans—no time like the present to adapt to our new surroundings—and headed for the cashier. Then I'd drag Galadriel out of the store for being such a pain in my scales.

"Is this it?" the brown-eyed girl asked while snapping her gum.

"Yeah." I handed her Dad's credit card. Galadriel slid in next to me and put a silver bracelet on the top of the pile.

"This too." She gave me a wink.

"No." I moved the offending item off to the side.

"He's so mean to me." She smirked at the clerk. "Just add it in."

"No," I said again.

The cashier's eyebrows puckered. "Can I see your ID, Jack?" Galadriel snickered. "Yeah, Jack. Let's see some ID." She clicked her nails on the counter. "He had the worst bed head that day when they snapped the shot. I told him to comb it at least."

The back of my neck burned. If Galadriel had stayed at the house like I'd wanted, I would have purchased my items already and been gone without a scene.

I patted my pants. "Oh, I don't have it on me." I tried charming her with the smolder I'd used hundreds of times on weak-minded girls. "It's me. I swear."

Her countenance darkened. "I could lose my job."

I looked up. A camera hung on the ceiling, making things tricky. Galadriel nudged me with her foot. She knew what I needed to do. Would I bend my moral mer ground and use persuasion to get what I wanted?

"This actually isn't Jack. He's dead in the ditch we just left him in," Galadriel whispered as she lifted her index finger to her lips and shushed. "And we'll do the same to you if you don't ring up these items. Or, we could take these and go like we did at that last store, huh, Fin? Oopsie. I said your real name."

The girl blanched.

"Crap." I sang the song of our people and the worry melted off the clerk's face. "Please forget we were here and charge the card with our sale." The girl slid the card through the reader and smiled, following my gentle suggestion. I held up my wallet and flashed an ID anyway, for the cameras watching us.

Galadriel grabbed a pair of earrings. "Can I have these?"

The girl nodded, still under my spell.

"No." I grabbed Galadriel's hand and twisted. "Put them back."

Galadriel's face soured as she yanked her arm away. "Testy."

I snagged the bag and charged through the doors. Behind me, a snap of a metal clicked—the silver bracelet Galadriel stole, no doubt. She'd never be allowed to go anywhere with me again.

"You're no fun, Fin."

I spun around and stared her down. "No fun? You swore you wouldn't make a scene."

"I didn't make a scene."

"Seriously?" I let out a gust of air. "Why do you have to be such a—?" I withheld my insult.

She glared. "Say it. You know you want to."

Within her eyes I saw pain mirrored from my own soul. Did she long for someone, too? Or was she trying desperately to fit into a world that would never accept her, at least not as she was—a mermaid.

"Forget it!" I moved past her and walked to my Jeep.

When she didn't follow, I turned to find her sitting on a bench, head in her hands. Yet another uncontrollable mood swing. If it wasn't one thing, it was another.

"Galadriel, if you don't come, I'm leaving you here."

"Lia? Is that you?" I heard a guy call from across the street. "Lia!"

Galadriel stood up and bolted to my side. "Come on, Fin. Let's go."

She yanked my arm in the opposite direction of the approaching guy. Anger spread across his face as he formed his hand into a fist.

"Who's this guy?" he yelled, firmly walking in our direction.

"My-my brother. He's cool, Matt."

Matt squinted at me, then turned to Galadriel. "Where have you been? I've been worried."

"I—nowhere." She looked down and kicked a rock.

"Who is this, Lia?" I asked, moving aside so she couldn't hide behind me. "We haven't properly been introduced."

She gave me an evil eye. "A friend from the college—"

"How can you say that, Lia?" Matt interrupted. "We're more than just friends." He took her hand. "I'm so glad to find you. You're all I think about, all I care about. And I can't imagine a day away from you." He stooped to one knee. "Lia, will you marry me?"

Galadriel gasped and jumped backward. "Please, Fin—make him stop."

Confused, I studied the skin on his ring finger and found nothing. If he wasn't promised to her, then why was he so obsessed?

Galadriel gripped my hand harder. "Please."

In order to avoid a scene, I conceded and did the worst thing imaginable. I sang to him that his Lia had died, that he needed to move on, that he'd find someone else just as special.

Galadriel's shoulders stooped as the guy broke down in tears and ran from us.

After a moment, she looked up at me, relief plastered on her face. "Thank you."

Anger surged again. I gripped her shoulder and gritted my teeth. According to Sissy, this wasn't the first time this had happened. "Why is he so attached to you?"

"How would I know?" She shrugged me off and slid into the passenger seat.

"Did you kiss him?"

"No…" She checked out her face in the mirror and pushed aside her hair with her deformed hand.

I clamped down my jaw. "You don't think it's odd men are pledging their lives to you?"

"No." She shot me a look of pain and motioned I get inside.

"Did you kiss him or not? Just tell me the truth."

She put on her sunglasses and stared forward. "He… he might have accidentally kissed me."

"Accidentally?" I grabbed her arm and made her face me. "Then why doesn't he have the mark? And why don't you want to be with him?"

She remained tight lipped.

I squeezed a little harder. "Tell me."

She flinched. "You really want to know? Do you?!" She flung off her sunglasses. "He's not my first, okay? Does that make you happy? You can go back and tell everyone—brand me as a tramp."

"You *are* promised," I said in shock, "to who?"

"It's none of your business." She wiggled out of my grip and folded her arms. "I want to go home."

I knew if an unpromised person kissed someone who was promised, they'd bond to them and the other wouldn't feel a thing. Though the bond wasn't quite the same as being promised, the person still felt a strong attachment from the kiss. I was disgusted, not only because she'd kissed Matt, but for her mate she'd disrespected.

I couldn't withhold my sneer. "How cruel."

"You're so much better than me, aren't you? It was an accident, Fin. But you'll soon see. You've only been separated for a few days… pretty soon, all you'll feel is impending doom that you'll never see your delicate flower again." She looked up with wild eyes.

"You're crazy."

"Am I? Is it so horrible of me to want to stop the pain?"

"What do you mean?"

"After Matt kissed me, I no longer felt that awful ache inside… It just went away." She jumped out of the Jeep and traced her hand over my cheek, stopping at my chin. "And, it helps… for a while."

I pushed her off, my stomach flipping in revulsion. "You're disgusting! Get away from me and don't ever put me in that position again. Next time, I won't erase the memory of whoever you kiss. You got it?"

She burst into tears again and ran away from me like I'd done something wrong. I scrubbed my hand through my hair, torn whether or not to let her walk home. Then I smiled. Galadriel no longer had me by the scales. I knew her best-kept secret and with it, I'd no longer be trapped in her web.

But what if Ash was tempted to kiss another guy? I'd hoped she'd never let that happen, but...the thought made me sick. Yes, the longing sucked, but to think of her kissing another. Poseidon! I'd rip his head off.

18

༄

ASH

Monday early evening, April 18th

I bounded into the house, giddy to call Fin and tell him about the ridiculous interview, when the smell of pot roast tickled my nose. I froze.

"Ashlyn, honey," Mom said. "Is that you?"

In the anxiety and rush of everything, I'd forgotten Mom had invited Colin for dinner. Instead of running back outside (like I should have), I tried to tiptoe up the stairs for a quick escape. I'd lock myself in my room if I had to. They couldn't make me eat with him—the enemy. I'd almost made it to freedom when the third step creaked loudly.

"Oh, there you are." Mom dusted her hand off on her most favorite apron—the one with our painted handprints as a Mother's Day gift years ago. "Your new college sweatshirt looks nice on you. That reminds me, I'm going to have to get one of those bumper stickers with *my money and child go to FAU*. How'd the interview go?"

Confused at her cheerfulness, I tucked my hands into the kangaroo pouch of my new FAU sweatshirt in shock. "It went okay."

"Well good. I made your favorite. Drop off your stuff in your room, hang up your towel, and come on down." She lowered her voice to a whisper. "I need a little help with small talk. He's not all that chatty."

I gave a half smile. Of course he's not. The fish-face couldn't possibly know about human culture or even newsworthy facts for conversation.

"I'll be right down," *as in never.* "Let me freshen up."

With my phone in hand, I closed my bedroom door and sat behind it, creating a human door stop. No one would barge in without flattening me in the process. This was Fin time, and neither Colin nor my mother would snatch it from me.

"Fin," I half whispered.

"Ash," he said in relief. "Why so quiet?"

I grinned sappily and leaned my head against the door. His voice magically healed me every time we spoke. "Mom's on a rampage again. But I couldn't wait to call you. I've had the craziest day."

"Rampage? Why?" he asked.

Fish-face is messing with her head for one... "I don't know," I said quickly. "We don't see eye to eye. It'll all be over soon when I move to Florida."

"Yes-s-s," he said with a grin in his voice. "How was the interview?"

I giggled as I told him what happened, complete with details of Georgia's cannon ball that sprayed Coach during the interview. With my other ear, I paid attention to the commotion downstairs. I knew eventually Mom would demand my presence and I'd need to hang up before Fin clued in on what was really going on.

I worried about what would happen if I told Fin his uncle and cousin were here. His family would come to my rescue, then what? What would stop an army of evil fishdoers from capturing Fin's family like they did the last time? I could never see Fin again. The thought sent dread into my soul. Things with Colin were under control and as far as dinner went, little did Mom know a bout of stomach flu was about to hit and I'd have to decline dinner.

Fin rolled in hysterics with me at my retelling and I adored him even more for caring about the smallest details in my life. But what I hadn't mentioned was my eighteenth birthday Friday. I didn't want Fin to feel like he needed to do anything special considering our circumstances, though Georgia wanted to throw a big party. My secret wish was to have a virtual date on the beach and talk with Fin all day. But Georgia insisted on something, so we'd made a date for Thursday night: sushi and a movie since we didn't have school Friday.

"So," I said, hopefully. "Please tell me the case for the phone came today."

"They shipped it to the wrong address," he said, his voice saddening. "So I special ordered another from a store down the street. It should be in tomorrow."

"Oh, really? Awesome. But I have bad news."

"Oh, no. What now?"

"My mom has a friend over for dinner, so I have to cut things short."

"How long do you have?"

"Um—"

As I looked at the clock and listened again. Lucy yelled, "She's on the phone with Fin." My heart stopped.

"Ash? Are you still there?"

I couldn't talk. Only air whooshed out of my mouth.

"Ash?"

Just breathe, Ash.

"Yeah." I swallowed down the rock lodged in my throat. "I have to go now, actually," *and die.*

"I miss you already." Fin sounded disappointed.

"I—I miss you, too. I can't wait 'til you get that case 'cause I can't stand this anymore."

"We'll talk all night tomorrow."

"Good." I forced a smile. "I—I love you so much, Fin."

"I love you, too, my ginger girl. Goodnight and sleep tight."

I held my breath and waited for him to hang up.

In sync, the door slammed into my back. "Ashlyn? Why is this door blocked?"

"Geez, Mom. Hold on, will ya?" I barely made it to my feet before she pushed opened the door the rest of the way.

"What are you doing? We've been waiting for you." Her eyes were frantic, searching for what could possibly have delayed me. "You're not even changed yet. What's taking you so long?" She zeroed in on the phone. I tucked it in my kangaroo pouch.

"Sorry. I needed to make a call. I'm coming."

She held her hand out, palm up and combed her fingers forward. "Give it to me."

"What? Why?"

"Your sister said you made her walk across the parking lot in the snow this morning and she ruined her new Toms, and now you're being rude to our guest. Phone. Please."

That little snitch.

"Did she mention she used all the hot water, too? And that she almost made me late this morning?"

Mom's eyes narrowed. "No… I'll have a talk with her about that. She shouldn't have worn those shoes in the first place, but I still want your phone, at least for the evening."

I pursed my lips. Like she'd ever enforce punishment on her lovely Lucy. I wanted to scream.

"Ashlyn, I don't have time for this."

Reluctantly, I gave her the phone. "Can I have it back later?"

"If things go well tonight, we'll see."

My mouth snapped shut as a snide remark bounced on my tongue.

"I'm sorry," I squeaked out, hoping it would help.

Her face remained stern as she tucked the phone into her apron pocket and exited into the hall. "I know you miss Fin, but that doesn't mean you can sulk around here and ruin the atmosphere for everyone else. Colin is a nice boy and I'd like you to get to know him, so… let's put on a smile, okay?"

I sighed. Little did she know the depths of persuasion Colin had used on her. She'd never be like this with any other boy stalking me. I gulped down my pride and followed, dragging my feet. At the bottom of the stairs, Colin stood with my sister at his side, both of them smug as a catfish. Hot anger pulsed in my veins. Never before had I desired to punch someone as I did now. If it weren't for the fact I'd never see my phone again, I would have.

Mom let out a cleansing breath. "I apologize, Colin. Here's our swim champion." She rubbed my back in glee before ushering everyone into the formal dining room. "Let's all sit down and eat."

Colin's eyes twinkled, his swagger even more pronounced than before. The biggest secret I'd managed to keep from him was out in the open, and for that, I wondered why he didn't just mer mojo everyone, throw me over his shoulder, and cart me off now and forgo the pretenses of dinner.

But he didn't. He just smiled at me, like he enjoyed watching me squirm.

19

～

FIN

Monday before sunset, April 18th

Only an hour remained before sunset and everyone lounged in the living area, still wearing street clothes and snacking on fried fish and chips. Seemed ironic they'd prefer to eat cooked food and wait 'til the last minute to get to sea.

I walked past them with a huge smile on my face. The cellphone store had called right after I hung up with Ash. They had a waterproof case in stock after all. I couldn't wait to get it so I could call Ash tonight and surprise her.

"I'll be back," I said as I palmed the keys off the kitchen island.

Dad looked up from his paper, startled. "What?"

"I have a quick errand to run."

"Son, it's almost sunset," Mom said sternly from the kitchen. "Whatever it is, it can wait."

"I'm going to the cell store on the corner and I'll be back in ten."

"Fin—" Dad started.

But I knew what he was going to say, a big lecture on taking chances. Blah blah blah. I was only going to be gone for a minute. "I'm running out of time. I need to go now."

Dad stood up. "Let's talk outside."

I smirked. Just like Dad to verbally tear me limb from limb out of hearing distance of the rest of the mer. He couldn't risk tainting his perfect fatherly image. But I was ready for this. We'd gone for days without talking, and I was done. He needed to forgive me already.

Once outside, I turned to argue.

Dad held up his hand. "I want to apologize."

"You do?"

Expressionless, he turned toward the water. "I feel bad about how I behaved and I've decided what happened was just as much my fault as yours. Taking the family across country and pushing our limits like that was risky. Any of us could have finned out accidentally. We're lucky you're still mer, and alive! And I've been an ass, so…."

I narrowed my eyes for a moment. Then he hugged me.

"I'm sorry, too, Dad."

He grunted. "Now go get that case—that's what you're getting, right?"

"Yeah," I said and took off running. The store was only two blocks away. Within minutes, I had my phone securely in the case and was back in the Jeep ready to roll. I turned the key, knowing I had plenty of time to spare. But the engine turned over without catching.

Panic set in. The coast was within walking distance, but that meant either streaking across the beach, or wrecking another pair of jeans.

"Please, sweet Poseidon," I begged and turned the ignition again.

The Jeep wouldn't start, taunting me. I smashed my fist into the steering wheel.

"Come on!" I yelled. "Can't I catch a break?"

I turned one last time and the engine sputtered to life with a loud bang. I gassed her good before throwing the shifter into reverse.

"Just take me home, girl."

I cruised down the streets, keeping a steady speed. When the house came into view, I sighed in relief. I knew my reaction to simple car trouble was totally ridiculous, but because Dad and I smoothed things over, it was critical I didn't screw up. I let out a victory whoop once I parked next to the RV in the driveway. A dying breath of smoke coughed out of the tail pipe right when I killed the engine.

"Thank you." I petted the dash.

I'd expected to see the group headed for sea, given we had thirty minutes to spare, when a naked guy limped from the water. After he entered the house, I heard a scream.

Dad ran outside toward me.

"Come on, Son," he said out of breath. "We need your help."

He rummaged through the cabinets inside the RV and grabbed a jar of something.

"Why, who is that?"

"It's Ferdinand," he said over his shoulder as he ran back inside.

I entered the doorway. The naked guy lay sprawled out on the dining table, his legs dangling off the end and resting on a chair. Gashes covered his chest and arms, but thankfully, they'd covered his groin with a towel. Dad dumped the contents of the jar into a mug and fed Ferdinand the liquid.

Ferdinand moaned in Natatorian as he thrashed around. Scales still covered the bulk of his bare legs and he had webbed feet.

Hans held him down to keep him from rolling off. "Shhh, son. Just lay still and drink the tea."

"Get another towel." Sissy flailed her arms for someone to move faster. "I need to stop this bleeding." Mom handed Sissy a towel and she pressed it into his chest and arms.

He moaned louder.

"He's going to die if we don't help this heal." Sissy wiped the sweat off her brow. "And before the sun sets."

Dad took a knife and slit his hand open. He squeezed his blood into the gashes on Ferdinand's torso.

Galadriel appeared at my side, dressed in her bikini top and skirt—ready to go to the water. She watched with a mixture of sadness and relief. Did she not care that this man was most likely tortured at the hands of Natatorians, by the father she hated?

She reached around me and closed the front door. "We don't need the neighbors calling the police." She winked.

Ferdinand thrashed around on the table. Galadriel winced. Dad hoisted Ferdinand up as they slid another towel under his head. Mom continued to feed him more special tea, insisting it worked in the past for me.

"Hmmm." Galadriel watched with intrigue. "Where'd your mom get the tea?"

I held up my hand to show the scars encircling my wrist.

"Oh." She raised her brow. "You know more than my father realizes. Well, I hate to burst your bubble, but if the herbs don't work, then they'll need to use essence. That's the only thing that'll work against the poison."

"What do you mean? What poison?"

Galadriel tisked. "Those cuts on his legs and chest are what's causing the problem. Won't heal otherwise. He was most definitely trying to escape Natatoria."

My heart hammered, not only because of the implications of what she said about Natatoria, but also about the essence. She had to be wrong. We only had one vial left and that was for Ash. I moved closer to see if they could revive him without it—they had to.

"These cuts should be healing." Sissy rubbed the blood between her fingers, inspecting it. "There's something on the wounds. It's gummy almost, and tinted iridescent green."

Dad grimaced. "It can't be—"

"I knew it." Galadriel nudged me in the side. "It's cassava cyanide. Go tell your daddy to use the essence."

My feet wouldn't move. I couldn't accept her lies. He was mer. He'd heal. We all healed, eventually.

"You don't think they're using a different poison, do you?" Mom asked, studying the empty remains in the mug.

"What? No." Sissy brought her hand to her lips. "What would it be? They've outlawed the use of—no!"

Ferdinand's eyes rolled into his head as he convulsed for a brief second, then stopped struggling.

"This is savagery. He's only just a boy," Sissy cried. "Quick, Hans. Do something."

A boy? He looked roughly 22 or 23. Older than me.

"Tell them," Galadriel whispered. "Or do you not believe me? Or—" she smiled evilly.

"It's a message from the King," Hans said grimly. "We either turn ourselves in, or he'll continue to torture and kill the people we care about."

Mom gasped and clutched Dad's arm. "Tatiana?"

"No." Dad's eyebrows pushed together. "Azor loves Tatiana and she's the future Queen. The King wouldn't do anything that drastic, especially against his son. He cares too much about what the mer see. His style is to frame people or make tragedies look like accidents. He'll go after the beta-mers first, like Badger."

Sissy turned to Hans, tears in her eyes. "We're losing him."

I held onto the doorframe for support. The essence was the last we had, the small bit needed for Ash to convert. And now we needed it more than ever. If the situation in Natatoria was this dire, I wasn't going to Natatoria without her. I couldn't. What if we were eternally separated at the enjoyment of a psychotic king?

"Your mermaid or Ferdinand's life," Galadriel whispered in my ear. "Your choice."

"Shut up!" I yelled as I balled up my fist.

Dad appeared by my side and caught me before I had a chance to hit her in the face. "What's this all about?"

I couldn't think. I couldn't breathe.

Galadriel stepped forward. "Give Ferd the essence. It's the only thing that'll heal him against the cassava. And hurry, or we'll all be dragging ourselves down the beach instead of walking."

I wanted to tell everyone that Galadriel was lying, but Mom handed over her necklace anyway. I watched Sissy uncork the vial and pour the contents into Ferdinand's gaping mouth. At first he didn't respond, then he gurgled and swallowed. Within seconds the color returned to his face and the scales disappeared.

Sissy exhaled with a relieved chuckle and hugged onto Ferdinand's neck once he opened his eyes. "Oh, praise Poseidon."

The group collectively sighed—everyone but me. Every horror imaginable flashed through my head, including spending eternity locked up in Azor's cell as the sharks swam by.

Ferdinand's crisis was over and mine had just begun. The endless supply of essence was in Natatoria and if I ever wanted Ash to become a mer, I'd have to go into the warzone for more. My plans collapsed around me.

Dad pulled my arm. "Let's go outside, Son."

I stormed through the open door, one Galadriel had just escaped through, and yanked out a painted rock stuck in the cement along the walkway with inhuman force. Temptation to chuck it at Galadriel gripped me. Instead I lobbed it over her head and watched it land in front of her.

She turned in horror and stuck out her tongue.

"Fin!" Dad grabbed my outstretched arm. "Control yourself."

I yanked it from his grasp. "I'm not going to control myself. Galadriel lied. And now Mom allowed the last of the essence to be used, for what? He would have healed."

"The poison would have killed him."

"What poison?"

"Cassava. I remember hearing of its use a long time ago on nets to prevent mer's from trying to escape Natatoria. Essence back then was also very limited and the only cure."

I scrubbed my hand through my hair, tempted to say numerous evil things I really didn't feel. I wouldn't have wanted Ferdinand to die, but why didn't we hoard more. Emergencies happened all the time.

"We can get more, Son."

"How? Natatoria is a war zone and Tatiana is in the middle of it. If they're using biological weapons designed to kill and possibly shackling everyone in bracelets down there, we'll be trapped. Why didn't Ferdinand bring any back with him?"

"I don't know. I guess we'll find out when he comes to. Hopefully he can tell us what's going on as well."

"Otherwise it would have been for nothing." The words slipped out before I could stop them.

Dad looked at me hard. "So we should have hoped he lived?"

I gulped down my pride and looked away, unable to answer.

"I know you're better than this, Son. You're under duress from the promise so I'm going to let this slide. But Ash's essence saved a life today." Dad squared his shoulders. "So, I advise you to check yourself and let this go."

"Fine," I said. "I'll meet you in the water."

I stormed down the beach to the dock. Galadriel was already in the water, her silver tail reflecting in the setting sun.

She had better keep her distance. At this point I hated everyone and every thing.

"F-i-i-in," Galadriel crowed. "Don't be such a wet blanket."

I gritted my teeth. "Ferdinand better know something, or I'm really going to be pissed."

She burst into laughter, spitting water out of her mouth before diving under. She knew something I didn't, and chances were once I found out, I wouldn't be laughing along with her.

I stripped off my jeans, and dove into the water in my boxers.

20

❧

ASH

Monday before sunset, April 18th

Instead of our typical buffet from the pans on the stove, Mom had the formal dining room table set with china and candles. As we passed the pot roast and mashed potatoes in fancy bowls, I withheld my snort as Colin attempted to use his hands instead of the utensils. Of course, during the blessing, he was overjoyed to hold my hand, but confused about why we were closing our eyes. Afterward, I scooted my chair as far over as possible—straddling the table leg—to put ample distance between us. I didn't want any part of my body touching him, or within his reach.

"So, Colin," Mom said sweetly, "what are your college plans?"

Colin frowned for a moment, before fisting his fork and stabbing a hunk of beef. "I'm not sure yet."

"So, you're just visiting?"

"No," he said. "My dad and I moved here, actually."

So Mr. White Beard was Colin's dad. Interesting. But they sure as heck didn't deserve to live there. I huffed under my breath. Mom noticed and shot me a glare.

"So are you homeschooled, too?" she asked, keeping an eye on me.

"Uh, don't think so," he said as he chomped off a big bite.

I snorted again. Brilliant answer, fish-face. Mom nudged my foot under the table.

Lucy took advantage of the pause and started in on another infamous story about her best friend, Laura Jane. Colin ignored her and watched me with a knowing gleam. My stomach quivered as a trail of grease drizzled down his chin. After a minute, Mom tried to motion to him, then ended up handing him a napkin to wipe his mouth. But by that point, I'd lost my appetite. I resorted to pushing my peas around on my plate.

Everyone, including Dad, seemed a little glazed over. When Fin had come to dinner a few weeks ago, Dad had interrogated him about his future goals and dreams. But today, he was silent.

"So is Jack your dad's brother?" Mom asked.

Colin's eyes lit up. "Yes."

"I have to say, we've missed having the Helton's around since they've left, especially on the pier. People come into the store often asking about Captain Jack's. Fin had said they were looking to sell the business. Are you and your father planning to take over—what's your father's name again?"

I groaned inside for her continual mentioning of Fin's name.

"My dad's name is Alaster," Colin said as he pitched a brow. "We aren't sure yet. My uncle Jack isn't a very savvy business man, I'm afraid. We might need to sell the *Empress* to get out of debt."

My jaw tightened. Sell the boat? What a filthy liar.

"And where did you move from?"

"Lucy, can you pass the peas, please?" I asked to interrupt. "And what were you saying about Laura Jane?"

But Colin had another plan. And just like that, he broke out in song. "It's nothing to worry about, Mrs. Lanski. Let's change the subject."

Hearing his ugly tune made me want to take my steak knife and push it against his conniving merman throat. How dare he come in here and manipulate my family like this. I stomped on his foot.

"Owww," he said, and stopped singing.

"Ashlyn!?" Mom glared.

"I accidentally stepped on Colin's foot." I pushed out my chair and ground my heel in. "Excuse me. Potty break." *And I'd like to barf.*

Mom apologized as I exited the room. Besides enduring Colin's crap, having my phone taken, and losing my appetite, I didn't know what else could go wrong tonight.

After ten minutes, a soft knock on the door rattled my nerves. "I'm in here!"

"Sorry, darlin'. I thought you'd be done by now," Gran said. "I'll go upstairs."

"No." I flushed and quickly opened the door. "I'm finished, Gran. Sorry."

"Didn't mean to rush you. You get old and things don't wait for you like they used to," she said with an endearing smile.

She patted me on the shoulder and went inside.

I returned to the dining room, only because I didn't want Mom to hold my phone hostage longer than she'd planned. But she was staring at me with a frown.

"Who's 'Fish'?" she mumbled. "They keep texting you."

I gulped, wishing I had mer mojo powers to stop her from speaking and force her to give me my phone. I'd reprogrammed my contacts for such a time as this, so she wouldn't know.

But as if an omen followed over my head, things were about to get worse. No one caught what she'd said, though, and I took my seat. Everyone had finished eating.

"I bet it's Fin." Lucy produced an evil smile.

Colin shot me a look. "So you are talking to Fin."

"No," I defended.

Lucy leaned forward. "Oh, yes she is. They're more than just talking, Colin. They're boyfriend and girlfriend."

I glared at Lucy while Colin stared at me, puzzled. Dad remained dumfounded and Mom did the only thing she could do to salvage the meal: get rid of Lucy.

"Lucy, clear the dishes. I think it's time for dessert. Anyone want pie?"

"But..." she said and pouted. "By myself?"

"This is Ashlyn's friend, so clean up. Once you've finished, you can join us in the living room for games. Do you play Gin, Colin?"

"Uh, yeah," Colin said uneasily.

Lucy stormed into the kitchen and crashed around the silverware to show her frustration.

Vindication at last. She was finally getting her just rewards, not for what she should have, but it still worked in my favor.

"Don't mind Lucy." Mom shooed Colin and me into the living area. "Fin's a thing of the past. Right, Sweetheart?"

I took a controlled breath and faced her. "Actually, in all honesty and respect, my relationship status isn't any of Colin's business, Mom."

Mom chuckled and pointed to the couch. "Sit and visit while I dish up pie. Would you like some, Colin?"

"Yes, Mrs. Lanski. Please."

"Oh, you're such a polite man." She smiled before she hurried away.

Colin held out his hand to me. "Lead the way."

"Dad!" I yelled. "Aren't you coming too?"

I needed back-up, fast.

"Yes." He came into the room and sat down in the chair next to me.

"Isn't there anything you want to ask, Dad? Like Colin's goals and dreams? Or if he has any dark secrets?"

Colin coughed, choking on his spit apparently.

"Yeah, I do," Dad said, finally snapping to. "Uh, do you like it here in Tahoe?"

Colin smiled. "Yes. I like Tahoe a lot. It's so much more free than where I come from."

"Oh, that's good," Dad said, "and what does your dad do?"

Colin looked directly at me. "He's a treasure hunter."

"That's interesting. Does he troll the lake?" Dad asked.

"Yes, he does." Colin smirked.

"I bet that takes some specialized equipment."

Yeah, Dad. Go! Ask more questions!

"You should come by and take a look sometime. You'd be amazed." Colin sang again and Dad gazed off into space as if he were sleepwalking. No one was a match to the mer mojo, but I wouldn't concede.

"Well, don't be modest, Dad," I said with a nervous laugh, nudging his arm. "He does have a gun, just so you know. And knows how to start fires and hide evidence, 'cause he is a fireman. And he would like your social security number—to check your record of course." I smiled sweetly at Colin.

His eyes narrowed ever so slightly. "You're so feisty," he said with a smile. "I like that."

"If you're trying to win me over, it's not working. And I don't know what kind of mind tricks you've done to my parents, but I'm not interested in you. It's time for you to leave."

I closed my eyes when the musical notes came out.

Crap.

"Where's Fin?" he asked

"I don't know."

"Why'd your sister say you were talking to him then?"

"My sister likes to lie to get me in trouble," I said robotically.

"So who were you talking to on the phone earlier?"

"Callahan."

He cocked his head to the side. "Who's Callahan?"

I couldn't stop myself from adding in a few extra details. "This super hot guy from school who's nice and wonderful, and I can't stop thinking about him." I leaned in and whispered. "He's my secret boyfriend."

Colin's expression darkened. "Then why did your sister say Fin was your boyfriend?"

"Like I have a clue."

"Interesting." He pushed up the side of his lip into a lopsided grin. "I say you forget about him, and start thinking of me that way."

"I don't want to."

His lips pulled into a straight line. "Why are you being so difficult?"

"Because you're ugly and stink like fish." I couldn't help my smile. Hey, he'd asked and those under the mer persuasion had to tell the truth.

He sat up, dazed and confused, and smelled his armpit. I almost busted up in laughter when the ring tone, *My Jolly Sailor Bold*, chimed on my phone.

Double crap.

My heart sank. It was way past sunset in Florida. Why was he calling? How could he be calling?

"Hello?" I heard my mother ask. "No, this isn't your Ginger Girl."

If Colin found out I lied to him, he'd haul me off to his house, turn me into a fish, then most likely take me to Natatoria. I had no choice. I did the first thing that came to mind and doubled over with heaves, anything to get my mom off the phone. If that didn't work, I'd stick my finger down my throat.

21

✆

FIN

Monday night, April 18th

I lay on my back in the water, admiring the stars as insane thoughts crossed my mind. I wondered how long it would take to swim to the Pacific Ocean, cutting through the Panama Canal. Between Ferdinand using the last of the essence, Galadriel's crazed laughter when I said Ferdinand had better have news from Natatoria, and Ash's mom hanging up on me, I'd finally had enough. No one would control my destiny anymore.

But after hours of waiting for Ash to call, I grew impatient and yelled at the sky. The silence screamed back at me, drowning me softly. Why hadn't Ash called back? Did she even know I was waiting? I needed her, especially after today.

Then the phone rang, but from a number I didn't recognize.

"Hello?" I asked.

"Fin?"

A weight lifted off my chest. I sunk underwater for a second, and sung to her in Natatorian that I loved her.

"I take it you missed me." She giggled. "What did you say?"

"That I loved you more than anything. Poseidon, this has been the longest day of my life. What happened? Why'd your mom answer your phone?"

She groaned, sweetly. "I love you, too, and I am so sorry. I'm grounded again and tonight was the worst of my life. Please come home. Please take me away from here--from this. Please."

My throat tightened and my eyes watered. I couldn't bear to hear her heartache. I wanted more than anything to do just that—to take her away so she'd be happy and with me forever.

"Okay." The words of surrender slipped out on their own.

"What?" she asked, her voice breathless. "How? When?"

I didn't know, but I wouldn't let anything stand between us—not after today. I'd get to her, somehow. But driving the RV after the week we'd just survived unnerved me. And swimming around Central America would most likely bring on a new set of dangers. Could I fly? All the cameras and security—I'd have to do a heck of a lot of persuading.

"I'll figure out something."

Silence lingered on the line, then a sniffle followed.

"Ash? Are you okay?"

"Yes. That—that would be the best birthday present ever."

I smiled, filled with indescribable joy as she quietly sobbed. I hadn't planned anything as spectacular as this for her birthday, more like balloons and eighteen sets of eighteen roses so her family knew for sure I loved her, but this idea was better, perfect.

"When will you leave? Tomorrow?"

I exhaled hard. "Possibly. I need to map a route, but I won't wait long, I promise you that."

Then an idea hit me. I could take out the table and bench seats, and put a portable pool in the living area instead. That way I could drive the most direct route and stay anywhere I wanted. Screw driving from lake to lake.

"I can't believe you're going to be coming back."

"Me neither," I said as the waves rocked me back and forth. I'd never felt more at peace about my decision. "And don't worry about being grounded. I'll persuade your family the moment I get there."

She chuckled lightly. "What phone line are you calling from anyway?"

"Oh," she sniffled, joy infused in her voice. "Mom took my cell, but she didn't say anything about the home line being off limits."

I laughed. "Ingenious. What happened this time?"

"I'd made Lucy walk through the school parking lot in the snow."

"You didn't," I gasped sarcastically. "What a mean sister you are."

"Yeah, well. She deserved it. She made me late."

I wanted to sympathize in the injustice of her grounding, but I couldn't concentrate. I'd finally decided to stand up for myself and my brain was spinning a mile a minute. There was so much to plan. How soon could I be in Tahoe if I drove every second of daylight?

"I can't believe I'm going to see you in a few days."

"I know. Me neither. I can't wait."

Her soft voice curled my fin. She'd be in my arms in less than five days.

"Nothing will have to change. I'll stay at my parents' house."

"Um…" she said with a hard swallow.

"Don't tell me my uncle burned down the house."

"Oh, of course not," she said with a nervous giggle. "It's still there."

"Then what's wrong? Are you worried they'll return?"

"Sort of…" Her voice lowered.

"I'll be careful. There's a lock on the hatch to the lake and deadbolts on the doors, too. And I'll bring my dad's gun with me. If anyone tries to come back, I'll be ready."

"Okay." Her voice was still filled with anxiety.

"Hold on." I plugged in the most direct route on my phone, hoping a definite date would alleviate her worries. "It's 3,000 miles. If I drove nonstop twelve hours a day, I could get there in four days."

"Only four days? Oh, Fin," she crowed.

"I need to smooth things over with my parents first. I need an excuse actually—a good one."

"What if..." Ash's voice suddenly sounded sneaky and completely adorable, "you said that Colin was back? And he was threatening my family."

For a second I imagined this to be true and my blood boiled. "If he were, Poseidon help him. Yeah, I think that'll work."

"Good," she said, sounding satisfied. "Then tell them that."

We decided email would be the best way to communicate in case she couldn't stay on good terms with her mom. She also wanted to know the exact moment I'd arrived in Tahoe. I wanted to surprise her instead. If only I could drive with the bottom half of my body underwater somehow. Regardless, we'd be together again and nothing would stand in our way.

After hours of planning and dreaming together, Ash eventually drifted off to sleep. Her soft breathing kept me company as I listened in, unwilling to hang up. Just knowing she was there—safe—connected me to her.

I was about to close my eyes when I saw my Dad's dorsal fin speeding in my direction.

Crap.

Reluctantly, I hung up the phone.

22

⤳

ASH

Tuesday afternoon, April 19th

With wet hair from swim practice, I jumped into Mom's car anxious to get home and read my email. Had Fin left yet? All day I'd felt naked without my phone. I didn't actually say good-bye last night like I'd wanted, instead I fell asleep and at 4 AM the soft beeping of the cordless signaled the battery had died. In the morning, I tried calling and left a message instead. I hoped he wasn't angry with me for being so rude.

My heart fluttered as I wondered where he was. He'd said he'd more than likely leave later in the day, after he bought food, a mini swimming pool, and a hose. Four days would put him here on my birthday. I couldn't wait.

Guilt and dread swirled in my belly. Though the excuse I'd fed him about Colin was accurate, I feared telling Fin the real truth. I wanted to, so many times, but when I opened my mouth, my voice froze up. But I had to tell him now, otherwise he'd be walking into a trap.

An idea hit me. A decoy. If a barrage of official phone calls, and formal letters from an out-of-state agency appeared, Colin and Alaster would have to take the bait. After all, besides Colin's stupid crush, that's all Azor wanted—the Helton's delivered on a silver platter. If I could lead them away from Tahoe to somewhere coastal, like Maine, I'd be home free.

Then Fin would never have to know how bad things had become, and once he arrived, he could fortify the house and everything would be cool, perfect even. By the time Colin and his dad realized they'd been tricked, we'd be long gone in Florida at college. It could work, if I was smart enough to pull it off.

I parked and skipped down the dock in glee, anxious to start on my mail campaign. Those stupid fish-for-brains mers had no idea who they were dealing with. I bounded up to Mom's office at the store with my swim bag in hand to drop off the keys, when I spotted her—anger had whittled deep grooves into her forehead. I was dead meat.

She lifted a stack of papers off the desk from her new paperweight (my phone) and waved them in my face. "I'm so frustrated with you. Sit."

I sank into the cushions of the loveseat across from her desk. This wasn't going to help operation get-mom-back-on-my-good-side I'd planned to execute today.

"I don't know what to do with you anymore, Ashlyn. I'd hoped after your swim meet on Saturday, your attitude would have turned around. That you'd see that there's so much opportunity knocking at your doorstep. That you have incredible potential and so much ahead in your future."

What possibly could this stack of papers be?

"And I even encouraged a new relationship for you with a boy so much more worthy of your affection—"

I cringed. She had nothing to do with that. If it weren't for Colin's meddling she'd still be crowing in joy over my relationship with Fin, and how he'd bounced me out of my depression.

"—and after last night, I'm so embarrassed with your behavior."

I tried not to smile. I'd successfully puked all over Colin, maiming the upholstery in the process. Mom was furious, but it forced Colin to leave. Cleaning the couch afterward was totally worth it.

"Mom," I said, scared to comment for fear I'd make things worse.

"I've already told you I don't like Colin. He has some weird manipulative hold over you and Dad. Don't you see it? Dad hardly asked any questions last night. When Fin was here—"

"I don't want to hear about Fin." Mom smashed her hand against the desk. "If anyone has a weird manipulative hold…" She groaned. "Do you know what this is?"

I squinted, trying to make out the fine print. "Looks like a bill."

"Yes! It's the phone bill. And you've exceeded your minutes this month to the tune of three hundred and eighty-nine dollars."

"I what? No way. There's a mistake." My mouth fell open. "How?" I could barely talk to Fin as it was. We couldn't have talked over 1,000 minutes this past week.

"This is absolutely ridiculous, Ash. Fin is consuming all your time and thoughts. Your grades are suffering. You're even on your phone during class. And to think your dad and I were actually contemplating buying you a car for your birthday. And then there's college to consider. I—I don't know what to do. We're looking at investing some serious money so you can try out for the Olympics next summer and you're distracted with this boy."

She put her head in her hands. I wanted to say something eloquent, rational even, but Colin's mer mojo had messed with her mind.

"I don't know what to do, Ash. You've been unreasonable and irresponsible, and none of this happened until you met Fin. He is the source of all your rebellion and it has to stop."

My blood boiled at her accusation. "He is not, Mom!" My voice shook. "He's the reason I'm here, why I'm alive. He pulled me from the lake that day I fell in, and I didn't take out the boat because I had a death wish; it was an accident. And I'm glad it happened. It brought the best thing into my life. I love him, Mom and I'm never breaking up with him. So if that makes you worried, then cut me off.

But I will be leaving to go to Florida in June. And I'm going to school on my scholarship with or without your blessing, so deal with it."

I took a deep breath, shocked at myself for telling her the truth, finally.

She blinked at me in disbelief. "After everything your father and I have sacrificed for you, I can't believe you're talking to me like this."

"I'm not trying to be disrespectful. I'm trying to be honest. I'm practically an adult and I don't like Colin. He's the source of all of our problems, don't you see? Please, Mom… I need you to believe me."

"Fine. I get that you don't like Colin, so I won't push you anymore." She looked at me with tears glistening in her eyes. "But you're throwing away your life over a boy and I have to do what's right for you. I'm shutting off your phone and you aren't to talk to Fin anymore. It's over. Do you understand?"

I balled up my hands and threw down my bag on the floor. I couldn't look at her. She couldn't do this to me.

"It'll never be over," I yelled as I ran out of the store and down the beach. This was absolute insanity and Colin had to be stopped.

23

❦

FIN

Tuesday morning, April 19th

"There you are." Dad swam up to me while I drifted in the warm Atlantic current.

I paused, concerned about his stoic demeanor. "What's going on?"

He stared at the phone with curiosity as it floated next to me. "Does it work okay?"

"Yeah." I narrowed my eyes, wondering why the sudden interest in the phone. "So what did Ferdinand say?"

Dad scratched his beard and paused. "I just found out that Ferdinand can't talk. He's apparently a mute."

"He's a what?" Suddenly, Galadriel's acerbic laughter made sense. "How is that possible? I heard him mumbling in Natatorian."

"It's not really words. I guess Sissy found him a few years ago, wandering the Atlantic, and took him in. He's quite odd and does his own thing, but he has helped them find lost mers occasionally. But they've never heard him speak."

"You're kidding me." I rubbed my hands through my wet hair. "That's just great."

"So, I'm leaving with your mom for Loch Ness tonight to talk to Badger's brother-in-law, Dorian. I need to know what's going on and how serious all of this is. We can't put Tatchi's rescue off any longer if things are getting heated in Natatoria."

I swallowed hard and turned from him, conflicted. I wanted to tell him I was going to California and use Ash's excuse—that she was in danger because Colin and Alaster were there—but I didn't want to freak him out, especially not now. "You aren't going in, are you? To get Tatch out?"

"I'd love to sneak her out, but she'd never leave willingly. And this is about justice, too. Azor broke the law and since the Council hasn't enforced a punishment that fits the crime, I will take things into my own hands. I need Badger to round up my men."

"You're talking about a war."

"I was hoping somehow to avoid it, but…."

Challenging the King's son would throw the entire civilization into chaos and Dad didn't know I'd wanted Ash to be with me when that time came. This was all happening too quickly.

"When are you planning to actually go in?" I asked.

Dad grimaced. "If the King isn't letting mers in or out, I need to get a message in to Badger somehow. We'll be in trouble if they seal the gates for good. I also need to take stock in who's captured, get weapons, and formulate a game plan."

My stomach knotted. Though I'd promised Ash I'd leave tomorrow, I wondered why Dad wasn't asking me to go with him. Was now a good time to be running off for California, especially if the rescue would be happening within the next few days?

Dad twitched his tail back and forth impatiently. "So, with your injuries, I don't think you'll be strong enough to flash swim the entire way."

My mouth fell open and I turned away, insulted.

"Mom and I want to get there in a day." He watched me pensively. "And I'd like to bring the cell phone incase we need to contact you. I'm sure we'll find service along the coast."

Like a child, I snatched the floating phone from the water and held it as if he'd arm wrestle me for it. "But, I need my phone."

"There's a phone at the house."

I hesitated, gripping the phone harder. This was Ash's only way to contact me while she was grounded. She didn't know the beach house number.

He creased his brow. "I'll bring it back in a few days." He held out his hand.

We stood off for a moment and then reluctantly, I handed it over. I still had his credit card. I could buy a new phone for the trip and email her the number.

"Hans and Sissy are going up to Iceland to see about things there. Ferdinand is doing better, but who knows if he'll stay. Just keep Galadriel out of trouble."

"Whoa." I backed up in the current. "I'm not babysitting Galadriel."

Dad's shoulders dropped as he shook his head. "I don't understand why you're fighting me. Don't you get how important this is? Galadriel needs to think we've gone to the Bermuda gate to investigate because that's most likely where Ferdinand escaped. I'm not going without your mom, and that only leaves you. I know you two don't get along, but we need your help."

I lowered my head, ashamed at myself. Not only for the fact I wouldn't keep track of Galadriel, but they'd come back from Scotland and I'd be gone. "Fine."

"Good." He gave me a quick hug and pounded me on the back. "I'll see you soon, Son. Just stay by the phone and don't let her get under your scales."

"Yeah. Travel safe."

"I will." Dad nodded and began to swim away.

"Hey," I said quickly. "Could you try to get some essence from Dorian, for Ash?"

He smiled. "I'd already planned to." He gave me the thumbs up.

I smiled, sick inside, feeling like a spineless jellyfish for what I was about to do.

24

ASH

Tuesday afternoon, April 19th

I stomped through the sand, kicking any innocent rock I could find. No amount of deep breathing would slow my racing heart. Though Mom acted out of persuasion, I couldn't believe how irrational she'd become. I closed my eyes and counted to ten. I needed to get Colin and his dad out of town, and fast.

As I continued to walk, my pace slowed. Water shushed lightly against the granite rocks on the beach, stealing my attention. Cold wind dusted over the frigid water and sent a familiar chill over my skin. I'd developed a love/hate relationship with the lake after falling in. She tempted me with her calming and elusive waves, promising if I were to dive in everything would be okay.

"Ash."

I froze at evil-fish-doer-number-one's voice, loathing it more than ever.

"Colin," I turned to greet his smug smile with a tightlipped frown, "stalking me now?"

He pressed his eyebrows together. "No. Just keeping an eye out. You never know what dangers lurk in those waters."

I sneered. *Like you? You little....* I composed myself, unwilling to stoop to his level, and perched a sweet smile on my face. Who needed letters when I could tell him face-to-face?

"I have good news for you."

His eyebrows rose, perked in interest.

I glanced at his Silence is Golden but Duct Tape is Silver T-shirt and couldn't help myself. "You told me to tell you once I heard from Fin. He's in Maine and I think he'd like his shirt back," *freak.*

His eyes grew. "Really?" He tapped his chin, oblivious to my insult. "Where in Maine?"

"Saco Bay. But I don't think they're staying, so you better *chop chop* if you'd like to find them."

I turned my back and strolled in the opposite direction.

"Oh, no, no, no." He appeared at my side. "I'm not letting you get away from me that easily, cutie. We've got a few things to discuss, including our future."

I shoved my finger into his face. "Look, punk. I don't like you. First: you stink like fish bait. Second: you creep me out, okay? And third: you do weird mind mojo to my family. So I want you to leave me alone, or I'm going to file a restraining order on you. *Capicé?*"

"A what?"

"Seriously? You don't know what a restraining order is? It's like you live in a hole."

His nostrils flared. "I've been trying to respect you—but you make it so difficult. My dad says to just do it, but I can't and I won't without your permission."

My forehead crinkled and I walked faster. "He what? You both are sick. People are people, not puppets to play with."

"I have to see." He fastened his hand onto my waist and tugged at the edge of my jeans by my hip.

"What are you doing?" I slapped his hand away and moved backward.

He grimaced before the musical notes poured from his mouth. Suddenly, I realized what "do it" meant and I wasn't about to play along this time. I turned and ran with all my might, losing a shoe in the process.

"Wait!" he called out. "Get back here!"

I pushed my feet harder into the sand, prepared to run the entire way home if I had to.

He caught up easily and latched his hand onto my arm, spinning me around. "How are you able to do that?"

"Ouch," I cried out. "Stop! You're hurting me!"

"You have to obey me." He gritted his teeth. Understanding suddenly flashed in his eyes. "Unless it is true…"

I tried to slip from his grasp and my feet stumbled out from under me. I landed on my butt. "Get away from me."

I tried to get up, but he grabbed my shoulder and flipped me over, face down in the sand. He loosened my pants off my hip once again. I kicked, unable to make contact with him, afraid of what he'd do next.

"Let go of me!" I yelled and tried to scream, but his body weight pressed against my lungs making breathing difficult.

I fought, refusing to succumb to him. I might have been promised to Fin, but Colin could easily still steal my virtue—right here in public, right here on the beach. I clawed my hands forward, shredding my nails against the loamy surface. Was no one around? Could no one see I was about to be raped?

"Hold still," he said with a grunt, pinning me in place.

I continued to struggle, but was no match for his strength. Maybe if he knew I was Fin's girl he'd stop. I turned to look at him, to plead for him to knock it off. Through the curtain of my hair, I witnessed a fist land perfectly into Colin's square jaw. He sailed backward and went down cold a few feet from me. I flipped over and looked up in amazement into chocolate eyes—Callahan.

"What are you doing?" I gasped out.

"Stopping him," he said with a questioning expression before he offered his hand. "Come on, before he wakes up."

I'd never heard a more beautiful suggestion. Beyond, at the picnic tables, Jaime stood with her hand over her mouth. I stumbled forward in a blur and let Callahan escort me to the cab of his truck. Jaime got in on the other side, sitting between us. I held back my tears, my breath coming out ragged.

"Thank you," I finally managed after a long painful stint of silence.

"Who was that guy?" Callahan asked, disgust in his voice.

"I don't really want to talk about it." I looked out at the crystalline water, wishing Fin would pop up out of the waves and save me from this madness.

"Really? You should press charges, Ash. What he did, or was about to do—that wasn't right."

"It's complicated and really it was nothing." I swallowed down the lump forming in my throat. If we told the cops, Colin would just persuade them. I wanted to forget; hide in my house and wait 'til Fin returned. He'd fix everything when he got here.

"It wasn't nothing. I can take you to the precinct now. Both Jaime and I are witnesses."

Jaime nodded quietly.

"I need to get home first," I said, unsure what to do next. Maybe that's what Colin needed, a little heat so his dad would get upset. Then they'd realize I wasn't worth the trouble and investigate Maine instead.

"Has this happened before?" Callahan asked.

"No," I said quietly as he pulled the truck up to my house.

He jumped out and walked around to open my door. His hand, warm and strong, held mine as he helped me outside. The memories hit hard. Last time we were here was after Senior Ball and he'd almost kissed me.

"I'm sorry," I said, wanting to beg for his forgiveness for dumping him without saying a word.

"You're sorry? That asshole attacked you."

"No. About everything else." I swallowed hard, hoping to loosen the lump in my throat.

"Ash, it's fine." He shook his head. "Just promise me you'll be more careful. Tell your dad at least."

"It's not fine. What I did wasn't right, and it wasn't you. I promise. I should have called."

He laughed. "Really? You're going to use the 'it wasn't you, it's me' excuse now?"

I looked down in shame. "I had a really tough time after my accident and I needed time alone."

"Well then follow that instinct and stay away from that loser. You need to take better care of yourself." He put his hand on my shoulder, melting me with his eyes.

"I know…" I soaked in his tenderness, noting a kind and gentle soul.

He patted me on the arm and let his hand linger. "I'm here if you need anything."

Jaime watched us, anxiety and jealousy on her stricken face.

"I'm good, thanks." I forced a smile.

He stared into my eyes a little too deep, as if he longed for something more from me. I ached inside, wanting to return his act of kindness, but we couldn't be friends like that—not anymore. I'd been wrong about Callahan. He did genuinely care and his initial feelings weren't some whim fueled by fleeting lust. I gulped, wondering if we'd be a couple still if I had never taken out the boat.

"Jaime's waiting for you." Her name snapped him from his trance.

He looked away. "Talk to you later."

"Later… and thank you again." I nodded.

"And if you don't do something about that jerk," he said as he rounded his truck, "then I will."

I shook my head. If Colin saw Callahan coming, mer mojo would come into play and Colin would return the sucker punch easily.

I watched the two of them drive away, and instead of going inside, I crumpled onto the porch swing. Under my dirtied jeans, my knees ached, and my hands were a mess of grime and blood.

I glared at Fin's house, afraid of what Colin might do. I prayed he'd leave Tahoe. Over the small ridge, a set of eyes watched me from Fin's porch—Colin's dad. Before he disappeared into the house, I heard his bitter laughter.

25

FIN

Tuesday morning, April 19th

Galadriel sat alone on the sofa with a copy of *Wuthering Heights* in her hand. She gave me a quick once over as I walked through the door. Salt water dripped off my legs onto the rug.

"You're getting water everywhere. Use a towel!" She motioned to hooks by the door. She'd already put on her street clothes for the day—pink tank top and white shorts. "So I assume they left you to babysit me since no one returned?"

"Yup." I toweled off and walked past her, eyeing the house phone. Could I chance a call to Ash now? I counted back three hours from 8 AM. She'd still be sleeping. I took off my shoulder pack and set it on the counter.

"But aren't I dangerous?" Galadriel sauntered over and skimmed her hand across my bare shoulders.

I glared at her. "Maybe if you'd stop fooling around and tell the truth about who you're promised to, then none of us would have to babysit you."

She turned her lip up before retrieving something from her pocket. "You left this."

I squinted as she fanned my one and only picture of Ash in front of me.

"Give me that." I snatched it from her hand.

"She's pretty. And looks an awful lot like—me."

I put the picture safely in my pack and zipped it up. "Let's get one thing straight. Ash is my business, not yours. I'm only here to make sure you don't kiss half of Boca Raton. A little duct tape would solve that in a flash, I'm thinking." I eyed her up and down with a sneer.

She straightened her shoulders and elevated her chin. "That's mean. I'm not kissing half of Boca Raton." She whisked her red hair over her shoulder and returned to the couch.

Yeah, right. I exhaled slowly, keeping my cool. In a few hours, I'd never have to deal with her again.

"Haven't you ever thought maybe Sissy and Hans are holding me hostage?"

I laughed. "Hold you hostage? Uh—as I recall you volunteered for this. I believe they are protecting mankind from your treacherous lips."

She whipped around and gripped the back of the couch with white knuckles. "This makes you feel powerful and better than me, because you can control your desires, doesn't it?"

I raised my brow. "I feel bad for whoever you're promised to."

"You're such a jerk!" She pursed her lips. "I hope Ash has the same control as you."

My nostrils flared and I controlled my temper. She wanted to pick a fight and I wouldn't let her get to me.

When I didn't respond, she slid down on the couch and sat with her back to me. "My bond has nothing to do with this. They're keeping me a mermaid because I know too much. They wouldn't convert me even if I wanted to. They need me for when they go fin-to-fin with my father."

"They've got plenty of dirt on the King and Azor, in spite of your secrets. What they need is for you to want to become human so they don't have to force you or tell us who your mate is." I pushed my hand through my damp hair. "And I don't think you know a thing. You love the attention. But if you want, I'll take up your invitation and convert you in the bathtub right now. That'll solve everybody's problems."

"You wouldn't." She turned. Her eyes grew big.

"Oh, yeah I would."

"What I know involves you."

"Oh, really? That's supposed to stop me?" I rolled my eyes and pawed through the kitchen junk drawer for paper to make a list. The block of kitchen knives caught my eye.

She rose from the couch. "Do you know what proves I'm of royal blood?"

I clenched my jaw. "Go play on the freeway, Glad."

"Look." She moved in front of me and pulled down the edge of her waistband to reveal her hip. "This. The fleur-de-lis."

On her hip was nothing more than a strangely shaped birthmark.

"Are you asking me to remove it, because I can," I reached past her and pulled a paring knife from the cutting block for effect.

She eyed the knife and moved away, pursing her lips. "All mermaids know about the mark. Your sister needs this, or else—" Galadriel sliced her finger over her throat.

I carefully slid my thumb on the blade to check its sharpness. "You're boring me, get to the point."

"When Azor kissed her, the mark should have appeared, like the promise tattoo. It proves her royal transfer."

I leaned my head forward, astonished at her audacity. "Are you suggesting Azor isn't royalty?" I drew a circle in the air with the knife to symbolize a crown.

She gave me a coy smile and shrugged. "It's hard to know. Royal mermen don't have the mark."

I creased my brow. Why was she saying this? Of course Azor was royalty. Silence followed, long and annoying. I waited for the words she refused to speak, for something other than empty ramblings of a crazed mermaid out of water. "And?"

She looked at me arrogantly with her huge blue eyes. "I guess you'll have to check Tatiana's backside when you get down there." She flounced toward the door leading outside. "Aren't you coming?"

"No." I smiled and added duct tape to the list. "I'm busy."

I returned the knife into the block with a thump. Galadriel could go where she wanted as far as I cared—the further away from me the better.

"Fine," she said with a flip of her hair, "let your sister rot in Hades."

I stopped, forming my fist into a ball. "Azor will suffer for what he did to my sister in due time!"

"Is that why you're here and Daddy's on his way to Scotland without you? Looks like you couldn't care less."

I moved around the kitchen island to the door and stood face-to-face with her. "You mind your own business."

"Or what?" she asked snidely.

"Or else—"

Ferdinand walked up behind Galadriel, soaking wet, with a scowl on his face. He towered over Galadriel by ten inches and me by six—much taller than I remembered.

"Nothing." I moved to the counter and retrieved my list. None of this was worth getting punched by a six-foot-ten mute behemoth.

She laughed in victory, then turned, bouncing off his chest. She tried to push him aside, careful not to disturb the tiny cloth covering his manhood..

"Move, you big oaf. Ugh, you're all wet."

With one hand, Ferdinand moved Galadriel inside, and with the other he closed the door. He stood like a statue, blocking her way.

"Move!"

I smiled. Though he acted strange, dressed weird, and couldn't talk, maybe having him around was good after all.

"Fine. Whatever." Galadriel parked herself on the couch.

I stretched out my hand to finally meet him. "Hey, man. I'm Fin."

He acted as if he didn't even see me, and walked past me into my room.

"Hey, where you going?" I called after him.

A weird groan followed.

"Uh, oh." Galadriel smiled deliciously. "You're in trouble now."

My clothing, books, and other things took flight into the air through the doorway heading for the floor.

"Whoa," I yelled, catching my guitar by the neck before it smashed into the wall. "Hey, knock that off!" Papers and clothing continued to soar until there was nothing left.

Galadriel laughed. "Told you so."

He stopped and began carefully arranging his colored rocks in a nice row on the dresser—the same ones I'd knocked off a few days ago.

"That's not cool," I said in exasperation. Ferdinand continued to ignore me. "I know you can hear me. Why'd you do that?"

He glanced at me for a fraction of a second, as if I were an annoying fly, and then walked over my stuff without any acknowledgement.

"Ferdinand. Stop."

He disappeared around the corner as if I'd said nothing.

"Get used to it," Galadriel said playfully. "He does what he wants, when he wants, and ignores the rest. Don't you, ya big lug!"

I scooped up my things and put them in my bag. Yes, I needed to pack, but not like this. "What a mess."

"Stop your griping," she said over the back of the couch. "I'm trying to read over here."

I slung my duffle bag over my shoulder and glared. She smirked in victory while she licked her finger and turned the page.

Ferdinand was in the corner, rearranging the books on the shelf.

"What's he doing?" I dropped my bag on the floor by the door.

Galadriel shrugged. "He likes them in a certain order."

I watched, puzzled for a moment. The length of his back was covered in scars.

"Why doesn't he talk?"

She shrugged again. "Who knows?"

"Where'd he come from?"

"Natatoria, like the rest of us."

I smirked. "Did you kiss him, too?"

She threw her book down and popped off the couch. "Shut-up about that. I'm no mer floozy."

I raised an eyebrow. "That's not what Matt said."

"Oooh!" she yelled, before she slapped me.

I blinked, stunned as the sting lit a fire on my cheek. Reflexively, I raised my hand in the air but stopped. I didn't hit girls.

Ferdinand flew by her side and stood as a barrier between us.

"I'm fine, Ferd. Just—" she wiped her cheek with the back of her deformed hand. "Never mind." She walked past me and went to her room, slamming the door.

Without any emotion, Ferdinand returned to the bookshelf as if nothing happened. I stood speechless, unsure what to do.

After a minute, I put on a shirt, took the RV keys and my parent's credit card off the counter, and headed for the door. Ferdinand continued arranging the bookshelf as if I weren't there.

"Keep an eye on her," I said and shut the door.

࿐

Within a few hours I returned, expecting to find Ferdinand in the same place. No one was around.

"Hello?" I asked without a reply.

Awesome. A quick escape without any questions. I pulled out a pen and paper and headed down the hall. Guilt hit me when I entered my parents' room and caught a glimpse of Mom's favorite possession. Everywhere we'd went, she'd always taken the framed ceramic picture of our handprints and tail prints from when we were merlings.

I traced my sister's hand and my gut clenched. If my parents went to Natatoria without me she'd think I didn't care, that I'd turned my back on her.

I pushed down the worry and regrouped. I wasn't leaving. I was gathering support. Together, Ash and I would be part of the rescue from Azor. The more people on her side the better. Once I convinced Ash of course.

How could my parents blame me? They knew what the dreadful ache was like. Without Ash, I wasn't able to function. And I wasn't leaving forever. I'd be back in a month.

> **Dear Mom and Dad,**
> **When you get this, I should be in California. Sorry I left this way, but Ash is in trouble and I had no choice. Colin and Uncle Alaster have been threatening her family and I'm afraid they'll find out about the promise, and do God knows what. I need to somehow lure them away from her family.**

I stopped writing. Though I wanted to conjure up a really convincing lie, this would send them into a panic and show my stupidity. As if I could show up and threaten my uncle empty-handed. Love was what motivated me. I needed to be with her.

I crinkled the paper and started over.

Dear Mom and Dad,

When you get this, I should be in California. Sorry I left this way. I can't be away from Ash any longer. I hope you understand. We'll meet up in Natatoria when the time comes to rescue Tatiana, or I'll come back to Florida. Either way, I'll only be gone a month. Call me. Here's my new number.

I love you.

Fin.

I folded up the note, stuck it under the frame on the desk. Though I could call and leave a message, this was better. Once they returned, I'd already be safe in California, done braving the wild world of carnivorous humans. But now that I'd decided to leave, I was terrified.

I turned around. Galadriel watched me quizzically.

"Where are you going?"

I looked away. "I'm leaving."

"To where? Tahoe?"

For a second, I contemplated telling her the truth. Though she was pathetic and needy, I did feel sorry for her. She was trapped, unwilling and unable to trust anyone. I hoped she would find her merman, wherever he was. But I brushed my feelings aside. I couldn't afford to care. I needed to distance myself from her toxic ways and get to Ash as soon as possible.

"Doesn't matter where."

"Take me with you."

I stopped for a second to press her with a glare and shook my head. "Like I'd take you anywhere with me."

"Please," she said, her voice broken. "I'll be good."

"You're crazier than I thought."

"I know I've been horrible, but there's a reason. I—I need to escape before they all come back."

I pushed her aside and grabbed my bag. "You can escape once I leave. That is if your guard dog Ferdinand doesn't stop you."

"I can't." Galadriel crumpled to the chair next to me and curled up her arms around her legs. "I can't go by myself. I don't know where to go."

"Then convert like you'd originally planned. Sissy and Hans will give you a new life, and you can start over. You'll be fine."

"But I'll lose the best thing in my life."

Tempted to ask what she meant, I stopped and watched her for a second—a pathetic sniveling mess. I wouldn't miss this drama, not in the slightest. I walked past her to fetch the keys.

"I know you'll miss me, sweetheart, but you'll survive."

The keys weren't on the counter where I'd left them "Where are the keys?"

She stood in the hall. "Please take me."

The heat of her stare burned my anger, bubbling my rage to the surface. "I'm not kidding. Give me the keys. Now."

"Only if you take me."

I took ahold of her shoulder and squeezed. "Maybe you should have thought about this when you left Natatoria. I don't have time for you anymore. Give. Me. The. Keys."

She grabbed my arm. "But you don't understand. There is nothing for me here. I have to go to Tahoe. I can help you. I know stuff that'll save Tatiana's life."

I closed my eyes and forced myself not to react. With all the lies so far, this had to be another. I wouldn't fall again into her web as she dangled my helpless sister over me—nothing but a ploy to keep the attention on the problems she'd created.

"No."

"You don't care?"

I yanked my arm away as she stared helplessly at me, tears in her eyes.

"I don't trust you."

"I know and I'm sorry." She cupped her face in her hands and cried. "I don't know what to do anymore. I've run out of options."

I opened my mouth, but stopped. Did she actually apologize? Her sincerity hit me hard. Galadriel was a cunning liar, yes, but she'd never admitted she was wrong.

She inhaled slowly. "Ever since I was a young mermaid, my younger sisters and I were warned we couldn't promise, even if we were eighteen, until Azor did. I was fine to wait eight years until he was of age, considering the prospects my father had for me were old widowers he wanted to reward with my hand. But then, I met Jax. We'd waited for over two years and though Father was going to allow Azor to promise at seventeen if Tatiana would have him, he wouldn't approve of Jax as my mate. I was furious. So, when we couldn't wait anymore, we kissed. Afterward, I knew we couldn't stay in Natatoria. We had no choice but to run away. But my father found out." She wiped her scarred knuckles over her skin.

"Did he do that you to you?" I pointed to her hand.

"What do you think?" Icy evil poured out from her eyes. "Not only did he chop off my fingers, he had Jax banished to Bone Island to be tethered to a tree and dry to death. But when the longing didn't stop, I knew Jax had escaped. I told my father the bond had broken, and without my fingers he didn't suspect anything. And for over a month I lived in silent agony until I had the perfect opportunity to run away from Natatoria."

My chest squeezed thinking of the cruelty. Her own father cut off her fingers to hide her promise from the mer because of his pride and then attempted to have Jax killed.

"Why didn't the King let you be together? What's wrong with Jax?"

"There's nothing wrong with him. He's perfect and wonderful, but for me to disobey and promise out of order, and in secret; are you kidding? My father strictly forbids anyone choose for love, especially without parental permission. That would loosen his hold and cause a revolt in his precious colony. But he needed to secure Azor's place as King and I screwed that all up, not like I want to become the future Queen or anything. I'd never do that."

"But Azor stole Tatiana's promise without my parent's permission."

"Do you think my father cares? He wants Azor to be the future King and that requires a mate. Besides, Azor always gets what he wants." She threw her hands up in the air. "And he's been salivating over Tatiana for as long as I can remember. I bet my dad took advantage of me running so he could orchestrate everything. He hates your father."

I blinked in shock. She understood far more than I'd ever realized. I nodded my head in silent sorrow for Tatchi and Galadriel: both were sacrificed in this power struggle.

"So then why does your father allow us to live in Tahoe if he hates us so much? Isn't that a special privilege?"

"My father is threatened by Jack. He knows the people like him more. Heck, his own father liked Jack more, so the distance worked in his favor. The King was waiting for your dad to screw up, so he could punish him outright, but my running away gave perfect opportunity. I heard he'd sent a few mers from his private army after Jack to create an accident. Jack is lucky to be alive. I can imagine the lies being spun in Natatoria right now."

I cringed. Dad needed to be warned. They couldn't go into Natatoria without sufficient back up.

"So where's Jax now?"

"I don't know." Galadriel sniffed. "I checked everywhere, and even went to Bone Island, but he wasn't there."

"You know where Bone Island is?"

"Of course I do, I'm royalty. I know a lot of things. And where do you think Hans and Sissy found me? Well, Ferdinand, actually. They've been frequenting the island to rescue the mers for years. I thought for sure Jax would be at the house because our promise was still intact. But, he wasn't, and Sissy refused to talk. The only gate I haven't checked is Tahoe. I'm hoping Jax is trapped in the lake. I've looked everywhere else."

My stomach knotted. If I left her here, they'd eventually convert her. What if Jax was in Tahoe?

"But my dad said he found you in a tub, bleeding to death."

She looked away. "Since I didn't want to convert when Sissy took me in, she insisted I try and acclimate into society. I started school, made some friends, then went to a party. I had one sip of a drink and my head started to spin. The guys surrounded me and they all started to kiss me. I couldn't stop them, then Matt—he rescued me—but he couldn't help kissing me either. In my guilt, I thought Jax knew and killed himself. So, I tried to convert myself, but then Ferd showed up before your dad—I was delirious, but I swear Ferd said his name, 'Jax'. Ferd knows Jax is still alive somehow, but he won't tell me. So, I didn't convert and I'm not a kiss tramp either."

"Sorry." I shifted my weight between my feet. She didn't know we couldn't tolerate liquor? "That wasn't right of me to accuse you."

"I want to check Tahoe. Jax has to be there."

"Fine. You can come," I said, regretting the words once they came out of my mouth.

Galadriel stared at me, stunned. "Really?" She leapt to her feet. "Oh, thank you, Fin. I need to pack."

"Lightly," I yelled behind her as she scrambled down the hall.

"Okay." The loud bang of something solid hitting the wooden floor sent a wave of panic over me. Within minutes she toted a monster pink suitcase on rollers.

"What is that?" I asked.

"My stuff, of course. I'm not leaving it here."

I took one look at her determined smirk and shrugged. Fighting over the bag wasn't worth the energy. We were wasting time.

"How are we going to get there? I've always wanted to fly."

I pinched the bridge of my nose. "There are too many cameras and security. We're driving."

"What?" she whined. "The entire way?"

"If you don't want to drive, then stay here."

"Driving is fine." She forced a smile and produced the keys from within her cleavage.

I took them, noting they were still warm. I slung my duffle bag over my shoulder and held out my hand for her to lead the way. Once we were on the road, I'd call and warn Dad, but since he wasn't prepared to go into Natatoria yet, I hoped he wouldn't go in prematurely without me.

Galadriel chuckled as we paraded down the walkway to the RV, as if she'd influenced my defiance. I sloughed off her enjoyment and remained expressionless. I'd also need to let him know Galadriel was with me. If I helped her find Jax, she'd stop being such a pain in the dorsal fin, and all our problems with her would be solved.

"Oooh, look. A pool," she crowed, as she tried to force her luggage through the small RV door.

Out of nowhere, Ferdinand appeared. He took hold of the suitcase and yanked backward. Galadriel toppled out of the RV onto her butt.

"Ouch," she cried. "Why did you do that?"

He stared at her, still holding the suitcase.

"No, Ferd. Give it back. I'm leaving."

They got in a tug-of-war over the bag. Galadriel's hand slipped off the strap, and Ferdinand tossed it onto the beach behind him. The clasp sprung open and clothing flew out onto the sand.

"You oversized bristleworm!" She stormed over to her things. "You need to stay here. Protect Sissy." She pointed to the house. "Now get inside."

He closed the lid of the suitcase and held it shut with his foot. She banged on his bare toes with her fist.

"Please, Ferdinand. I know it'll be hard, but I need to go find Jax. Please. I don't want to have to hurt you."

He continued to scowl.

"I'm sorry but you leave me no choice."

She stood and pulled something from her shorts pocket. With my merman hearing, I heard a crack. Ferdinand's face softened, then he swayed and fell to the ground with a thump.

"What are you doing?" I came around the RV. Ferdinand lay sprawled out on the walkway, his head split and bleeding.

"No, Fin—"

Something black and oily shimmered in her hands. I inhaled slowly. The pungent scent stung my nose. Then the world around me undulated and swirled, growing dark.

26

❧

ASH

Tuesday evening, April 19th

I limped into the house with a missing shoe and a tender foot. Somewhere between Callahan's suggestion and seeing Alaster on the porch, I'd made a decision. I'd pretend Fin and I were broken up for four short days of his drive, and turn my focus to convince Colin and Alaster to leave Tahoe. Then Fin could persuade my family and everything could return to normal.

Pleased, I headed for the stairs. Mom and Dad emerged from the kitchen and stood side-by-side, both with arms folded over their chests.

"We need to talk." Dad held the dreaded bill.

"Sorry." I lowered my head. "I'll pay you back."

Mom didn't budge for a minute, her lips drawn in a line. "But what about what you threatened earlier?"

"I've had time to think and you're right. My relationship has been distracting me from school and the Olympics. If Fin's right for me, he'll be there afterward. So, to concentrate, I'm swearing off all boys."

Mom inhaled a cleansing breath and her forehead softened. "I'm glad you're finally listening to reason. It's for the best." Her eyes swept over me. "What happened to you?"

I wanted to tell the truth and throw Colin under the bus, but they'd never believe me, not with the mojo hanging on.

"I fell."

"Outside?" she asked, softly. "Oh, honey. You're bleeding. Where's your shoe?"

Before I knew it, she'd ushered me to the bathroom and washed the sand out of my knees. I cried as she gently scrubbed, but not because of the pain.

"It'll be okay, Ash," she said. "I know this is so hard. You're making the right decision."

"I know, Mom."

Though Fin would erase everyone else's memories once he arrived, I wished he could wipe mine after what happened. I could still feel Colin's grimy hands on me and I never wanted to see him again. Why were all the other Natatorian men so nasty? No wonder Tatchi didn't want anything to do with that world. What if choosing to become a mermaid was a mistake? What would my life really be like living under Natatorian law? Was Fin telling the entire truth?

❧

After dinner, I headed to my room to check my email again. Fin still hadn't replied. Was he on the road yet? A soft rapping on my door broke my anxious thoughts.

"Ash?" Mom came into my room. I typed on my keyboard as if I was working on homework.

"Yeah?"

She handed me my phone. "I didn't shut it off. With everything, I think you need it for emergencies. But I'm monitoring your calls and texts, just so you know…."

I looked at my hands and played with the Band-Aid on my finger. "You don't have to worry. I'm not going to call him," *at least not on that phone.* Luckily Fin's cell number was still in the Lake Tahoe area code.

"Well… I know it's hard, but really it's for the best."

For now.

"And, don't worry about Colin. You're right. Now isn't the time for boys."

My head popped up. "Really?"

"Of course." Mom smiled warmly. "After you puked on him last night, I don't think we'll be seeing him anytime soon, anyway."

I tried not to smirk as visions of peas bouncing off his khakis came to mind. Too bad mermen didn't turn into fish when they came into contact with liquid.

"Thanks," I said, genuinely surprised. Maybe the mojo didn't last forever.

I looked out the window. All the lights were on in Fin's house. Colin apparently didn't bite on my leak about the Helton's being in Maine. Maybe they were leaving tomorrow. If not, phase two of Operation Fish and C.H.I.P.'s (Clean House of the Idiot Piranhas) was about to be executed in the form of an ambush of letters and phone calls. Then they'd be stupid not to leave.

Hours passed as I waited in the dark with my bedroom door cracked. A little after midnight my parents finally shut off their light and went to sleep. I tiptoed downstairs and took the cordless off the base. Blood pounded in my ears as the call connected, then rolled directly over to voicemail.

Crap.

"Fin, it's Ash. I don't know where you are, but I'm worried. You promised to email me today, and now I don't know if you've left or not. I really hope I'm worrying for nothing again. I miss you and can't wait to see you. Don't call me back. My parents are on high alert and blame you for this rebellious phase I'm going through. I think mer mojo is the only way to get me out of being grounded. I can't wait 'til you're here and we don't ever have to be apart again. I love you. Goodnight."

As I hung up, a fat tear tricked down my cheek.

27

⤳

FIN

Thursday afternoon, April 21ˢᵗ

My body shifted from side to side, sloshing around in warm liquid. In the background, a girl belted out lyrics to some annoying country song about a red Solo cup.

I moaned, my temples throbbing with each blood-filled beat. I peeled my eyes open. Out the windshield grassy fields waved at me.

"Where am I?" My tongue lolled around in my mouth as if it weren't attached.

"There you are, sleepy head," Galadriel crowed. "Nice of you to finally wake up."

Wake up? I sat upright in the pool, my legs submerged in only a few inches of water. My board shorts hung from my waist like a skirt. I fastened them up at the crotch with weak fingers.

"What did you do to me?"

"Nothing you didn't want done." She shot me a wicked gleam. "Just kidding. I don't take advantage of the unconscious."

What? I ran my tongue over my teeth—film covered them. She'd used octopus ink. That's the only thing that would knock a merman out cold like that.

"You poisoned me?"

"No-o-o. I warned you to stay away and—Ferd. He's just so big; he needed a lot more. But it's okay and now you're fine.

Look. I stuck to our plans."

Our plans?

"Where are we?"

"Um… the middle of Texas somewhere. I'll see a sign soon." Her big smile disconcerted me. "I really like this driving thing, though. You were right. It's so much fun." She honked the horn and waved at a passing trucker.

I held my head still to try to keep my brain from swimming in my skull. She cranked the radio louder and some hick with a heavy twang sang about losing his boots, his truck, and his dog.

"Where'd you learn to drive?" I asked over the racket.

"I found a manual in there." She pointed to the glove box. "At first I wasn't sure where to go, but the people at the gas station were so nice and helpful. They gave me this. I follow along like it says and drive." A map covered the passenger seat complete with pink lines and notes.

"You don't have a license." I rolled out of the pool and crawled on all fours. My body squished into the carpet. "And there's water everywhere."

"Sorry. It's a pain in the anal fin to refill that thing."

Over her shoulder, I watched the RV drift into oncoming traffic.

"Eyes on the road!"

A truck honked. She screamed and swerved, over correcting. I grabbed onto the countertop for dear life as water sloshed all over the inside of the RV.

"I am!" she squealed. "Geez. Stop making me nervous."

My bag rolled over, smacking the opposite wall with an odd thump. A water stain ringed the edge.

"Where's my phone?"

"What phone?"

I limped over and snatched up the bag. Water dripped off the canvas. I tugged the zipper open and found soggy books in between my wet clothes. The new phone sat in the middle of the slushy soup. The cover was fogged up with trapped water.

I cussed in Natatorian. "Galadriel!"

"Now what?"

I held up the dripping contraption.

She shrugged. "Sorry?"

I slumped down on the only chair and emptied the contents of my duffle bag on the table, hoping for one dry shirt, finding nothing. "What day is it?"

"Thursday."

My body jolted, rocketing my head with pain. "Thursday?"

"Yup."

Galadriel sighed and leaned her head back, producing sunglasses from her purse. As she sang along, she applied lip gloss. Somehow she'd morphed into a human girl overnight. Where or how she'd bought all her new trinkets, I was afraid to ask.

My pulse raced as I tried the phone anyway. Nothing worked. Ash had to be sick with worry.

"We have to stop in the next town. I need to make a call and get a new phone."

"Good, 'cause I gotta pee."

My stomach growled at the same time.

Galadriel cruised the RV off at the next exit and pulled into a mini mart parking lot, all with perfect execution. But the payphone was nothing but an empty housing of multicolored wires. Galadriel skipped inside the store and came out a few minutes later with a Big Gulp and a bag of Doritos. According to the map, we were outside of Dallas.

"I thought you had to use the restroom."

"I did," she said with a smile. "I was hungry."

"That stuff will kill you." I rummaged through the cabinets and found an apple and a box of Wheat Thins.

She slurped on the straw and twirled her glasses between her fingers. "The next town is about fifty miles away. That's what the guy inside said. There you can get a new phone."

Crap. I looked off to the vast endless fields. "I need to call Ash now."

"Then persuade someone to use their phone."

I glared. "I can't do that."

"Why? What's the problem?"

Next to the RV, a family in a mini van pulled up. A guy got out and started the pump on the gas, and then went inside the mini mart. Two little girls, maybe ages four and six looked out the windows at us. Galadriel made a face and blew raspberries. They responded and stuck out their tongues. A woman, probably their mother, got out of the passenger side and threw away some trash.

This would be my chance.

I stepped out of the RV with shaking legs and approached her.

"Um, excuse me, miss?" I asked, still keeping my distance.

She looked at me skeptically, eyeing my naked chest and bare feet. "I don't have any money."

"No." I waved my hand. "I don't need any money. I actually was wondering—" I chickened out. "Never mind."

Galadriel appeared and edged me forward. "My friend here needs to use your phone. For a quick call."

The woman furrowed her eyebrows. "I can't help you. I'm sorry."

Galadriel whispered in my ear. "Sing already."

"No." I turned around. "I'm done. Let's go."

Galadriel began to squeal her siren scream.

I yanked her by the arm and shoved her inside the RV as people came outside with their hands over their ears and watched in shock. I crawled into the driver's seat and threw the RV into DRIVE, speeding out of the lot.

"What in Hades do you think you're doing?"

"What am I doing?" she reiterated with a laugh. "One day you're going to fall off your high seahorse and hurt something."

"Don't ever do that again, do you hear me?"

She folded up the map and slid into the passenger seat with her chips. "You're such a baby."

"I bet you didn't even pay for that, did you?" I pointed to her food.

She cocked her head to the side. "Well—what's it to them anyway?"

I growled and merged onto the highway. "If you'd have drained the pool, this wouldn't have happened. I can't believe you octopus inked me. Ugh." I grabbed my head again.

"If you would have listened to me, the octopus ink wouldn't have knocked you out. Actually, everything was going great while you were unconscious." The side of her lip turned up and she pulled out the vial filled with black liquid.

"Put that away!"

She smirked, then jumped up and came back with a pair of sunglasses and the phone. "Here, this will help."

She slid them onto my face and I accepted in desperation. Then she rolled down her window and held the phone outside.

"What are you going to do?" I yelled.

"Get your scales out of a bunch. I'm going to air it out."

It took all my energy to keep the RV on the road and not pull over and kick her out. "If you ever siren scream again, I'm not taking you to Tahoe. Do you hear me?"

"Yes, Daddy." She stuck out her tongue.

I pressed the gas pedal to the floor. The RV barely crept over 72 miles per hour. Time kept me from Ash yet again. She had to be freaking out.

Then a new problem hit me square in the face. I'd be arriving with Galadriel who would say and do just about anything to annoy me. What if Jax wasn't in Tahoe anywhere; then what would I do with her? But more important, how would I explain her—a practical twin—to Ash?

28

ॐ

ASH

Thursday midmorning, April 21st

I walked into class like a zombie. Fin hadn't contacted me in over forty-eight hours and I was losing my mind. Why hadn't he emailed yet, or even called? I'd texted I had my phone back despite Mom's warnings that she'd monitor my calls. I'd called him too, on my cell—several times yesterday and this morning. I had to know. I couldn't wait.

My only comfort was the fact nothing weird hit me like the last time Fin went dark. My undeniable ache for him was strong as ever, which meant he had to be okay. Maybe he was being extra cautious because of my family drama, or the case leaked and wrecked the phone.

As Mr. Branson droned on in History, I zoned out, staring at the cracked paint on the wall. I could feel Callahan's chocolaty eyes on me, questioning me. I did my best to ignore him at lunch after the incident. I'd kept my word to him and so far Colin and I hadn't crossed paths.

"Ms. Lanski." I blinked out of my trance and refocused on Mr. Branson.

"Yes?" My cheeks heated, unsure of what he wanted.

Madelyn, the office TA, stood by his side with a note in her hand.

"You're wanted in the office."

"Oh." I picked up my books and took one look at Callahan before I headed out. He nodded appraisingly, rocking my confidence.

Coach Madsen stood outside the doors in the hall.

"What's up?" I asked.

She ran her hand through her short blonde hair. "You need to take a drug test."

I blinked at her in shock.

"It's no big deal," she said with flushed cheeks. "It's the only thing that will confirm you didn't cheat."

"What?" My mouth hung open. "You're kidding me. They think I'm doing drugs?" *Mer ones maybe.*

"I—I know. It's not me. I've been on the phone all morning with our legal department and Meredith Hamusek's lawyer. At first they wanted the timing equipment tested, but after everything seemed to be working fine, they came after you."

My heart thumped. What if they found mer blood in me?

"I know it's unfair, Lanski, but…" Coach squinted, "if you don't, you'll have to forfeit your time then."

"Seriously? That's ridiculous." I laughed. "What kind of test? A pee one?"

"Hair and blood actually."

The thought of a needle jab sent shivers up my legs. "Why not pee?"

"Those tests are more accurate."

I shook my head. "This is high school, not NCAA."

"You didn't happen to get a blood transfusion in the hospital, did you?"

"Of course not. I lost blood actually." I frowned.

"Okay." She took a deep breath and gently touched my arm. "If you have something to tell me, Ashlyn, I suggest you tell me now. I've defended you all day."

"Yeah, Coach. I'm clean." I pinched my eyebrows together. "But I think I need to talk to my parents first."

"I called your mom and she's agreed already."

I gulped. "She didn't freak?"

"She wasn't thrilled, but after I explained everything, she said you should do it."

"What if I don't?"

"Declining will make you look guilty."

I bit my lip. "Meredith must be pretty mad."

Coach took another deep breath. "Well, she was getting a lot of attention especially since she was favored for the race, and now she's not—so, yes—I'd say she's upset."

Visions of the chem panel returning with reports of foreign antibodies filled my mind. Would they know? Would they haul me away for more tests? Lock me up?

"I don't want to."

Coach raised her brows. "What?"

"I didn't do drugs and I shouldn't have to prove it."

Coach frowned. "Lanski, this is silly. Do the test. It's for everyone's benefit."

"No. I'm standing on principle." I put my hand on my hip.

"Are you afraid of needles?"

I looked away. "Yes, but that's not the point. I shouldn't have to."

She put her hand on my shoulder. "It's a pin prick. There's nothing more to it. They'll test for extra red blood cells and steroids. That's it."

I gulped in worry. I guessed if something weird was in my blood, they'd have already caught it in the hospital. But still—this was a drug test.

"It won't hurt. Come on."

I took a deep breath and stepped through the doors into the nurse's office.

Afterward, I stared at the bandage on my arm as I headed to class. Coach lied. Nurse Nancy collected four vials of blood, each one hurting a lot. But I had to let it all go and hope the lab they were sending my blood to didn't find anything. Fin had sworn our blood didn't mix and I believed him. What if he was wrong?

Fin. Where are you?

My phone vibrated in my pocket with a call. I looked at the caller and almost screamed.

"Fin?" I answered breathless and relieved. "They think I cheated, so I gave blood. I'm afraid they're going to find something. Where are you?"

"Ashlyn," a strange man's voice said. "Ashlyn, it's Fin's Dad, Jack."

I froze mid stride, my knees weakening. "Where's Fin?"

"I was hoping you'd tell me. I got your message and he's not at the house."

My throat tightened. "Why do you have his phone?"

"I borrowed it. He didn't tell you?"

Tell me what? My chest heaved. "Where are you?"

"I can't say. But Fin's not at the house and the RV is gone. Is he driving to California?"

"Yes. Didn't he tell you?"

"No."

The blood drained from my face. Why'd he leave without telling his parents?

"Ashlyn—" Static crackled on the phone. "Ash—whe—call me— touch."

"Mr. Helton. Hello? I can't hear you. Hello?"

"Ashlyn," Principal Wright called down the hall, "hang up and get back to class."

I blinked at her, my phone still against my ear.

"Now!"

I turned and headed to History, but not before calling Fin's dad one last time. The phone rolled over to voicemail.

29

༺

FIN
Thursday afternoon, April 21st

A loud clang from the engine ripped the dreams of my reunion with Ash from my mind—her body wrapped tightly in my arms. Thick black smoke engulfed the vehicle, hiding the road. Then the RV slowed, though I hadn't let off the gas.

"What was that?" Galadriel shrieked.

Blinded, I yanked the wheel to the right. The RV slowed and died on side of the road.

"What'd you do?" Galadriel slugged me in the arm, then jumped out of the vehicle.

"How is this my fault?"

I gripped the steering wheel, unwilling to admit defeat; we had only five miles left to the nearest town. I pulled a lever under the dash and the hood popped open, launching one large smoke signal of doom into the sky. I cursed under my breath and scrubbed my hand through my hair.

Why?

Galadriel ran to the RV side door and threw it open. She tugged on the handle of her suitcase.

"Help me!"

I contorted my face.

She blew her bangs from her eyes and kept yanking. "It's going to explode!"

I laughed as I exited the RV, finally understanding the source of her distress. "Better hurry up then."

Inside the engine compartment, charred remains of a possible oil fire stained the mangled remains. This baby needed some serious work. I wished for my phone to call a tow truck and groaned at the thought of how many days this would put us behind schedule. Beyond the grassy flatlands and sparse trees, a jet climbed high into the sky. Maybe we should fly.

When I finally decided to check what Galadriel was up to, a silver Cutlass sedan pulled along side me.

"Hey man, you going to stay here?" The kid driving wore a black Metallica shirt.

My eyes focused slowly on Galadriel as she smiled at me from the passenger seat.

"Hank, here, has offered to give us a ride, brother." She winked. "Get in."

I stood in shock, unsure what to do. When did she flag down the driver? Should I find a tow truck and deal with a mechanic instead or go with them? Visions of shattered hearts from here to California rocked me.

"Uhhh..."

"Beat ya to Tahoe." Her teeth flashed as she wove her hand within Hank's.

He smiled and I felt sorry for the guy. She could go and I'd finally be rid of her, but my conscience wouldn't let me off the hook. Hank would never be able to fend for himself with this shark. And knowing her, she'd desert him when he was no longer any use and ruin his life.

"Suit yourself, man," Hank said. The tires crunched against the gravel.

"Wait!" I called out, not sure why I cared so much. "I'll go. Let me get my stuff."

I crawled in with my damp duffle bag and rummaged inside for the phone, hoping it would work and remembered Galadriel left it on the dash.

Dang it!

Galadriel toyed with Hank's hair, filling his head with nonsense as he drove. Though he stared at her legs more than the road, I didn't care. As long as we were headed for Tahoe and she kept her lips to herself, I wouldn't complain. How she managed to find someone headed the same direction blew my mind.

"Hank, can Fin borrow your phone real quick?" Galadriel asked sweetly.

"Oh sure," he said, handing it over.

She smiled extra big. "Say hi to Ash for me."

I shot a thankful smile and dialed her house. She'd be out of school already and I hoped she'd answer. Could I chance talking to her mom? Disguise my voice? I almost handed the phone to Galadriel so she could ask for Ash, when a girl answered the phone— my ginger girl.

"Ash," I said, my body filled with relief. "Thank Poseidon."

"Um, no. It's Lucy," she chuckled. "Wow. I'm surprised you're calling here, Fin."

I hiccupped, choosing not to acknowledge her comment. "Hey, Lucy. Is Ash around?"

"Nope. I thought you guys broke up."

My chest constricted. "Not that I know of."

"Well, my sister said she dumped you, but I'm not sure why. I like you a lot better than Colin anyway, so…. Can I leave a message?"

Colin? I wanted to crush Hank's phone in my hand. "Is Colin there?"

"Not right now, no. But yeah, they're dating. Well, maybe. She did throw up all over him the other night."

Bile rose in my throat.

"Which terminal?" Hank asked as he exited the freeway on the 3rd Street exit.

"I don't know. Fin?" Galadriel turned in her seat and smiled at me.

Planes jettisoned off the runway parallel to us.

"Wait. I thought we were driving!"

Hank laughed. "I've got to get to work, man. Lia said you guys only needed a lift to the airport."

Galadriel bit her lip to hide her smile.

I shook my head. "This is ridiculous. We aren't flying."

"What?" Lucy said in my ear. "You're flying here?"

"But we have to. Great-aunt Sissy's funeral." Galadriel started to fake cry. "She was my favorite aunt."

Hank did his best to comfort Galadriel as terror struck me. Colin apparently was manipulating Ash's family. We needed to get to Tahoe today.

"If we don't fly, we'll miss the special day," Galadriel said.

"Fine," I said, unwilling to argue about details while Lucy was listening. We'd have words after he dropped us off. "Take us to the U.S. Airway terminal."

"I'll call back later, Lucy," I said and hung up the phone.

30

⤳

ASH

Thursday afternoon April 21st

After dropping off the keys to Mom, I took a shortcut through Mrs. Culpeper's flowerbed, careful not to crush the pansies. Bruiser, her cockapoo, had to be around somewhere. Without sweet Mrs. Culpeper, he transformed into a white-hot ball of canine terror. But I wasn't taking any chances walking by Fin's house. After what happened on the beach with Colin, I'd walk the entire lake if I had to. Distance was my plan and so far it had worked.

"Ashlyn."

I spun around, clutching my swim bag, ready to bolt. *Why hadn't I packed the knife?* Colin's knowing grin bowled me over; a big yellowish highlighted his jaw.

I held up my fingers in the sign of the cross as if he were a demon. "Stay back, Colin. I'll scream if you come any closer."

"No. Please." He held up his hands. "Hear me out."

"Leave me the hell alone!" I stepped backward, but I couldn't gain any traction without crushing the flowers.

"I'm sorry. I wasn't trying to hurt you, but I had to know—I didn't believe my dad." He lowered down to one knee and bowed his head. "Princess."

Princess? He attacks me yesterday, then calls me princess today? What a wacko. I continued to slide on the slippery rocks edging the flowers, trying to add distance between us, shocked at his display.

He looked up, wide-eyed. "I didn't mean to frighten you. I only wanted to inspect your marking."

"Inspect my marking? Is that what you call it?" I cackled nervously at his strange use of words, unsure if "inspect my marking" was code for some pre-mating ritual. I didn't want to know. Escaping was my goal.

"It's an honor to be in your presence." He bowed his head to the ground.

I pinched my lips together, embarrassed and speechless by his display. "What are you doing?"

Finally after several long seconds he stood. "I'm bowing to you, of course. It'll all make sense when we go home."

Home? As in Natatoria? A Natatorian princess?

I chuckled nervously. "Colin, I'm not a princess."

"Oh, but you are. The mark proves it, and now it makes sense why my song didn't work on you. You're of royal blood."

I repressed a snicker. *It's because I'm promised, sweetheart, and far from royalty. Just ask my mother.* "That mark is called a birthmark and it doesn't mean a thing."

"It means everything and you, my dear beauty, have no clue who you really are."

"Uh, yes I do. I'm Ashlyn Lanski, born and raised in Lake Tahoe, California, captain of the swim team, and I'm really looking forward to leaving for Florida Atlantic University not only to get away from my parents, but also from the likes of you. So, no royal bloodline here."

Colin's face blanched. "You're going to Florida? When?"

I cringed. *Nice job, Ash.* "Uhhh… no time soon. I've still got high school to finish." I took another step backward.

"Well, you can't leave."

I shot a sarcastic smile. "I can, and I will. I decree it, or however royalty make proclamations."

Colin's features hardened. "Princess, you need to return home.

Everyone thinks you've died." His gaze drifted off somewhere dreamy. "I'll finally make my dad proud. I'll be a hero. This'll be the most memorable promising of all time."

"What?"

"Oh, nothing. It'll all make sense when I take you home."

Suddenly everything clicked. They thought I was the lost princess, Galadriel, and Colin expected my hand as a reward for my rescue. How'd they come to the conclusion I was royalty?

"There's been a mistake. I'm not who you think I am, honest. I—I was born hum—here. My mother gave birth to me in this house." I pointed to Gran's place. "There are pictures of my birth, of my childhood, of my entire life. This is my home. Right here. In Tahoe."

Colin pinched his fingers on the bridge of his nose. "How is that possible? Pictures? You remember your childhood?"

"Of course I do. All of it."

"Hmmm… Someone went to great lengths to persuade you and your family. That has to be the only explanation."

He stepped closer to me and my legs wouldn't move.

I gulped. "I have no clue what you're talking about. And I'm late. I need to go."

"You need to come with me." He took ahold of my wrist.

"I won't. No!" I screamed and punched my fist into his rock hard chest.

"Stop fighting me."

If he successfully dragged me to Fin's house, they could convert me and easily take me to Natatoria. Fin wouldn't know where to find me. I'd be gone without a trace.

A barking white ball circled our feet. I braced for Bruiser to attack, but Colin yelped and released his grip on me. I didn't wait; I swiveled, kneed him in the groin, and ran. Colin went down and I didn't look back.

I paced my room and occasionally glanced out the window. I'd barricade my door before I'd let Colin inside to get me. Would he persuade my family and haul me out of the house over his shoulder like a fireman? If only he were a vampire, then I could uninvite him from my house.

Where was Fin? The Heltons' trip took six days. So if Fin left on Tuesday, that would put him here on Sunday. Could I survive three more days? Why'd he leave without his cell phone anyway?

But a princess? Me? I had to laugh again. What a mix-up. Did Colin and Alaster think the Heltons rescued runaway mers? That they'd exiled the lost princess in Tahoe?

After watching for thirty uneventful minutes, I parked my butt in my desk chair and refocused myself. I still had work to do for operation Fish and C.H.I.P.'s. As I printed two letters—one from the Maine DMV requesting Jack Helton pay his fines, and another with info to pick up his impounded RV with a Maine address—I researched fish repellents. DEET seemed to deter fish, according to the more successful anglers that left comments on various fishing forums.

I rummaged through the hall medicine cabinet and found the mosquito repellent. I'd take a bath in the stuff if it worked. I returned to my room and sprayed a thick layer over my body.

Nervous, I glanced at Fin's house again and noted no one was headed over to take me against my will. Today a letter with a court appearance dated for next week in Maine should have arrived. I'd also left a message, stating I, Mrs. Barbie Watkins, was from the insurance company and needed a return call. I didn't have the courage to call today, not after Colin attempted to kidnap me again. I pushed my fingers into my temples and kneaded. Insanity, complete insanity.

"It reeks in here." Lucy pushed open my door with a smug smile.

At least it works on Lucy. I folded up the letters so she wouldn't see what I was doing.

She fidgeted by the door. "Guess who called today."

"Justin Bieber?"

She guffawed. "Nope. Fin."

My face blanched as I dropped the letters on my desk. "He called? What did he say?"

"You lied to Mom and Dad. Why?" A sly grin crept on her face.

Ultimate blackmail. She knew something—if Fin was okay or not—and was turning her info into a weapon. I rushed her and pinned her against the door.

"Tell me what he said." I pressed my forearm against her throat.

A tear crept down her cheek as she coughed. "Ash, you're hurting me."

I swallowed my anger, and stepped backward. I'd never been physical with my sister before. "I—I'm sorry." I looked down, embarrassed. "I'm worried and it's complicated with Mom. Please. What did he say?"

She brushed off the tear and glared. "I'm not telling you anything."

"You don't understand. Mom and Dad are being manipulated by Colin—"

"I understand completely. You want to be with Fin, but Mom doesn't like him. Are you running away?"

I pinched my lips together. "No. But when he gets here, it'll all make sense."

"Well—he's not coming, so there," she said, and walked out of the room.

I stood stunned for a moment. Was she telling the truth? My legs wobbled as I braced for the worst. How could Lucy be so cruel? And now she was going to tell Mom I'd threatened her and my life would be taken away—forever.

I fell to the floor in a sniveling heap. If Fin wasn't on his way, where was he? My life as I knew it was ruined if he wasn't. Forget Mom's wrath. Colin had already threatened to turn me in as his prized princess, and with his mer mojo nothing would stop him.

My life was no longer my own and like Tatchi, I had no way to escape.

31

֍

FIN

Thursday afternoon, April 21st

I walked up to the terminal inside the airport. Galadriel oohed and aahed beside me with her pink suitcase rolling behind her. I eyed the different airline stations and decided to pick U.S. Airways.

"I need two one-way tickets to South Lake Tahoe, please."

The lady, dressed in a blue suit, clicked at the computer embedded into the counter. "For when?"

"Today."

"Today?" Her eyes grew big. "Hmmm… well, we don't fly directly to South Lake Tahoe, but I can get you as close as Reno, Nevada. It's about an hour and a half drive, once you get there."

I'd be with Ash in no time—today in fact. I smiled. "Sounds good."

"I have two available seats on a flight leaving at 4:35 PM arriving in Reno at 8:20 PM. Would that do?"

I grimaced. *Not unless you want fish on the flight.* "Anything sooner?"

"No. Not for today I'm afraid. Tomorrow there's a flight at 8:45 AM arriving at 12:35 PM, but that would be for standby."

"What's standby?"

"If someone cancels you'll take their place, so it's not a guaranteed flight."

I groaned. Such a gamble. We'd lose the few hours left of today's sunlight on a hope we'd get a flight tomorrow. "How long is the drive from here to Tahoe?"

"Oh honey, from Amarillo to California is over a thousand miles. A few days, for sure, unless you drove straight through."

I looked at Galadriel. "Should we do it?"

"Fly? Heck yeah." Her eyes twinkled.

Galadriel didn't care. She only wanted to see what flying was like. But the idea of being that high off the ground in someone else's hands unnerved me. Not only were there cameras watching everyone, planes crashed all the time. People died.

"I'm going to think about it," I said to the lady.

"Don't take too long." She signaled the next person in line.

"What?" Galadriel pushed me aside and slammed her hands down on the counter. "No. We want to book the flight!"

I grabbed Galadriel's shoulder and forced her to step aside so the lady could help the next person who stood impatiently behind us.

"Stop." She yanked against my grip. "How else are we going to get to Tahoe?"

"Rent a car."

"What? She said days, remember? Let's take the flight. You'll see Ash tomorrow, don't you understand?"

"Only if someone cancels."

Galadriel rolled her eyes. "Have you forgotten your most powerful ally?" She perched up her right eyebrow. "Persuasion, lovey. Sing."

I laughed. "I can't sing us a seat if there isn't one available."

Galadriel twirled her hair. "Then, we can be someone else."

I watched the people rushing by, all with important destinations to go. I knew coming here, I'd need to use my song, but to this extent? Without a further thought, I returned to the line.

"Make up your mind, sweetie?" The lady greeted me with a smile when it was our turn.

I closed my eyelids before I sang away my soul. "We need a flight today to Reno, and it needs to arrive before 6:00 PM."

Her eyes floated off on a breeze. "Hmmm… There's a flight leaving in twenty minutes with United. We'll put you in first class. Your names?"

"Um… Jack and Magdalene Helton." I placed Dad's credit card on the counter.

"Good." She typed some more, then printed out boarding passes. "You'll need to hurry or you'll miss it. Your bags?"

Galadriel heaved her pink behemoth onto the scale.

"It's over the weight but I'll let it slide." The woman winked. "And your bag, Mr. Helton?"

I slung the sopping duffle onto the scale. She frowned.

"I had an accident." I smirked.

She shrugged and dropped it onto the conveyor belt behind her. I watched them disappear through a hole in the wall. Were we doing the right thing?

"You two better hurry." She pointed to security.

I frowned at the long line. "Is there another way to our gate?"

"Hmmm..." She signaled to a guy sitting behind the desk. They spoke for a minute.

He called for an escort on his handheld walky-talky. A golf cart arrived and took us to a private security entrance, where I sang to the security guard that they didn't need to see our identification.

We arrived at the gate just as the agent called for first class. A ruckus between two passengers and the ticket agent at the counter drew my attention.

"What do you mean I'm not on this flight? I have boarding passes!" the older man yelled.

Galadriel tugged my hand as the agent scanned our passes. Before we knew it, we were sitting in first class, enjoying drinks and hors d'oeuvres.

"See? That didn't hurt a bit." Galadriel dabbed her lip with her cloth napkin.

I looked out the window as the plane taxied down the runway, a little amazed we didn't have more trouble. For once everything panned out. Within a few hours, I'd be in Lake Tahoe and Ash would be in my arms where she belonged.

I leaned back as the plane jettisoned into the air, tickling my stomach. *I love you, Ash. I'll be there soon.*

༺ༀ༻

I opened my eyes as the plane touched down. Were we here already? Flying proved to be a breeze.

"Guess what, sleepy head," Galadriel said with a soft smile as she tussled my hair. "We're here."

Everyone unlatched their seatbelts and stood in the isles, anxious to leave. I was with them, my pulse pounding. Within two short hours I'd be with Ash once again.

The door to the aircraft opened and people began to file out, until the line slowed and stopped. The attendant motioned to me.

"They want to speak with you."

She pointed toward two men on the gangplank just outside the doors. *Uh oh.* From their stiff stances and starchy attire, they weren't ticket agents. Cops more likely.

Galadriel took my hand. "Just sing," she whispered in my ear as they escorted us into the terminal. I squeezed her hand in return.

"What seems to be the trouble?" I asked once we were separated from the rest of the passengers.

The taller guy spoke first. "Yes, Mr. Helton, we need to check your IDs again, please?"

"What for?"

"You weren't supposed to be on that flight." He held out his hand, palm up.

Galadriel inclined her head against my shoulder, as if to signal I should sing.

With a coy smile, I turned to the agent closest to me. "We aren't the criminals you're looking for. You don't need to check our IDs," I sang.

The guy's eyes glazed over. "Sorry to bother you, Mr. Helton. Enjoy your stay." He turned to his co-worker. "They aren't the ones we're looking for."

I grabbed Galadriel's hand and walked past the cops into the crowded hall.

"They're the ones on the cameras," a woman barked behind us. "Don't let them get away!"

Galadriel took one look at me and we ran through the terminal to the baggage claim. We rolled in hysterics as we rounded the corner and plowed into another set of cops talking on walkie-talkies.

"They went that way," I sang, pointing behind us.

They bounced into one another, then ran in the opposite direction.

We scurried into the baggage area and spotted our bags. I lugged Galadriel's two-ton pink suitcase off the conveyor belt, and she took my soggy duffle bag. Together, we headed for the taxi zone.

We jumped into the backseat of the closest taxi, still laughing.

"Did you see his face once we got away?" Galadriel said with a snort.

"Where to?" the driver asked.

"South Lake Tahoe, and step on it," I said as Galadriel buried her head into my shoulder.

"That'll be $99 for the trip," he said.

"Sure." I handed him my credit card.

I slid my arms around Galadriel's shoulders and she looked up at me with her big blue eyes. "That was the most fun I've had in—forever." Her sweet breath hit me as she moved her lips closer to mine. She looked so beautiful, so enticing. I took one hand and brushed her soft cheek.

"I don't accept Visa, sir," the driver said, snapping me to reality.

"What?" I pushed Galadriel off of me.

She looked at me, stunned, then folded her arms over her chest.

"Cash only, sir."

Galadriel frowned and snapped on her seatbelt. "Just sing."

"No." I glared at her and leaned forward toward the driver. "Can I pay once we get there?"

I was sure Ash had money, or someone in the family could lend me ninety-nine bucks at least.

"No, sir," the driver said, his voice impatient. "And if you don't have the money, then get out."

"Sing," Galadriel said, more forceful this time. "It's almost sunset and we either need to leave, or find water."

"I—" My conscience burned. We'd already ruined someone else's day and kicked them off the flight, and now we'd rip off this guy, too. But the only thing I could think of was Ash.

He sighed and restarted the meter. "Please get out so I can take a paying customer or I'll signal the police."

"You're such a coward," Galadriel said under her breath.

"Am not."

"Well, I'm not waiting. If you don't sing, I will." Memories of her horrible mermaid screech replayed in my mind. "Or maybe kiss him."

"You wouldn't."

"Try me." She pressed me with an evil smile.

"Fine," I sang in defeat. "Please drive us to South Lake Tahoe."

Galadriel snuggled into her seat, pleased. "And step on it."

32

&

ASH

Thursday evening, April 21st

After Lucy's news, I didn't have the strength to move. My only option, since Operation Fish and C.H.I.P.'s wasn't working, was to run away—sooner rather than later. Though my parents would freak, I had to do it. I'd take the rainy day cookie jar money and buy a bus or train ticket. I had run out of options.

But that wouldn't happen until tomorrow. Tonight, Georgia and I were going out for dinner and a movie to celebrate my last day being seventeen. Though I'd originally balked at the idea, the plans were now comforting. At least I'd have one final hurrah with my good friend before I abandoned her unexpectedly.

And like clockwork, the phone rang next to me.

"Hey, Georgia," I said, trying not to sound as if I'd been crying.

"The movie is at seven-thirty. I'll pick you up at six for dinner, okay?"

"Yeah," I said, still lying on the floor in a pathetic heap.

"Have you been crying?"

"No. Just allergies."

"What? I didn't know you had allergies—"

I don't.

"—well take a pill and get dressed. You're going out and you're not cancelling now. Okay?"

"Sounds fabulous." I smiled feebly, hoping some joy would be transferred into my voice.

"Awesome. I'll see ya in an hour. Dress cute."

"Yeah."

Our definitions of cute were vastly different. Jeans and a T-shirt would be my attire, period. She'd scold me, but I didn't care.

༺

Georgia bounced in the driver's seat to the music with an unusually wide grin as she pulled out of the Crazy Sushi parking lot toward the theater. I was still in shock; Mom actually let me go out after everything. She apparently hadn't checked my phone records to see I'd called Fin's number on an OCD rampage the past two days.

"I thought you saw this movie," I said, wondering why she'd be so enthusiastic when she never mentioned the title to me once.

"Movie? Oh, yeah. *Crack of Dawn* is good… so good."

"What's it about?"

"You'll see." She plastered on a huge grin.

I joined in with her as she sang along to the radio. Her usual small talk was noticeably absent, quite possibly the aftereffects of sushi coma. I enjoyed the break. But once we crossed the state line, her face lit up like a firecracker.

She turned into the Montebleu casino parking lot and I cringed. Mom wouldn't be happy if she knew we were coming to this theater. Though we'd be within the safe bounds of those under 21, because of late Grandpa Franks gambling addiction, I wasn't allowed anywhere near a casino, period.

Georgia checked her phone again and giggled.

"Who are you texting?"

"Oh, no one," she said, then peered out the window.

A group of girls in short skirts huddled outside with their phones in their hands. I shook my head at the ridiculous attire for this chilly weather, regardless if they were clubbing or not.

We parked and Georgia flopped her burgeoning bag over her

shoulder.

I chuckled. "What do you have in there, anyway? Did you not get enough sushi?"

"You'll see."

Though she'd regularly smuggled in a few snacks, it looked like she'd thrown in the whole refrigerator. But from the sound of her enthusiasm, the bag was a cover for something else.

She teeter-tottered around the car in her heels and tapped her foot. "Hurry up, already."

I slammed my door and followed, but Georgia didn't wait for me as she practically ran toward the casino.

"We have plenty of time. The movie doesn't start for another…"

The group of girls out front—Shannon, Michele, and Chrissi—rushed Georgia for a group hug. Then the mob pulled me in, too. They cheered, "Surprise!" in unison, bouncing lightly on their heeled feet.

I tried to smile and look happy. "You're coming to the movie too?" *Dressed like that?*

"No, silly. We're going to Déjà Vue!" Shannon pointed behind us to the new nightclub. "It's 18 and over tonight."

Music poured from double doors as glitzy girls and guys stood in a line under the glowing blue sign. I suddenly felt very self-conscious and underdressed.

"But I'm not eighteen yet."

"Not for a few more hours." Georgia patted her bag before she pulled out a slinky black dress. "You'll be looking older and glammed up in no time."

"But… they check IDs."

The entourage laughed and pulled me into the casino. As we crowded into a handicapped stall in the ladies restroom, someone teased my hair while another pulled my shirt over my head and replaced it with a dress that barely covered my butt. Make-up and some extremely high silver shoes completed my ensemble.

"There." Georgia pulled me out of the stall toward the mirror. She now wore a dress as well. "You're finally cute."

A crown adorned the top of my head that read "Birthday Girl." I blinked at my reflection. I'd never worn so much makeup in my life.

"Thank you?" I said, not meaning it to sound like a question.

"Perfect." Georgia handed me a Dixie cup full of clear liquid. "A toast to the fabulous birthday girl. May the music rock and the guys be hot."

They all cheered and slurped down whatever was in the cups.

"Drink." Georgia nudged my arm, sloshing around the thick clear liquid tinged with golden flecks.

"What is it?"

"Something I swiped from Grandma Gee Gee's cabinet," Chrissi said with a giggle.

I sniffed the liquid and recoiled at the pungent cinnamon scent.

"Don't be a poor sport," Georgia whispered and held the cup to my lips.

I allowed a swallow to pass into my mouth and coughed as the liquid burned my throat.

"Okay, time to go." Georgia pushed me toward the door.

"Um… no." I held up my hand. "I'm not eighteen."

"Don't worry," Shannon said with a giggle. "My older brother is the bouncer and he knows it's your birthday. He said he'd let you in a few hours early."

Georgia packed up the last of her things and looped her arm within mine, ushering me outside into the crisp night air. I worked hard not to fall over as the vibrant colors and lights accosted my eyes.

"What's in that stuff?" I mumbled as the whirlwind of perfume, flowing hair, dazzling sparkles, and clicking heels took me through the parking lot.

"Goldschlager," Shannon said with a hum. "It's so yummy."

Since I'd never drank alcohol before, I had no idea how my body would react. I didn't expect it to feel like I'd jumped into a spinning crystal ball. We shuffled past the line to a side door where some guy with hulking tatted arms greeted us. Suddenly we were inside. I wobbled behind the girls, hoping the effects of the alcohol would wear off soon. After tonight, I'd never drink again.

"You okay?" Georgia said, putting her hot hands on my cheeks. Her cinnamon breath rolled my stomach over.

"Yeah." I pushed her off of me. "It's hot in here."

My eyes studied her iridescent hair, floating around her head like she was underwater. The beat of the music pounded into my chest, skipping across my heart. I needed air. I needed cold water. I needed something to quench the fire in my throat.

"Let's dance," she said, whisking me onto the dance floor.

A sea of people swayed hard back and forth like a school of fish. The mob enveloped me and I closed my eyes. My body felt weightless, like I could swim up to the ceiling.

Hands grabbed my hips and swiveled me around. I stared up into a pair of chocolaty eyes.

"Callahan? What are you doing here?" I asked, feeling like my voice was detached from my lips.

"Heard you were having a party." His white teeth glowed bright in the black light. "Happy Birthday."

"But…" I looked up at him as he kept me close to his body. I could smell his clean soapy scent and I wanted to dive my nose into his collar.

"You're so beautiful," he whispered in my ear. "I wish things hadn't ended like they did."

"Aren't you with Jaime now?"

"We're just friends."

He moved his hands further down, holding my hips against his. I molded into him like a rag doll. Something inside me liked it, needed it. His attention dulled the pain I felt from missing Fin.

Fin.

Slow, wet kisses tickled my neck. Callahan's lips moved to my ear, his hot breath elating me as he sucked my earlobe. Goose bumps exploded across my skin. I snorted in laughter as my heart skyrocketed. He chuckled softly in return, then moved along my jaw toward my lips.

"I can't." I pulled away. "Please..."

Our bodies, glued together, continued to bend to the beat as if they had a mind of their own. His sheepish grin faded in and out of clarity, making me woozy. I knew I should sit down, distance myself from his intoxicating smell and electrifying hands, but I couldn't.

"You're so good for me." He brushed my hair from my face. "I'd never let anyone hurt you."

I swooned. Safety. Comfort. To be human and whole, far from mer drama. But he couldn't protect me from Colin. No human could.

"I'm a princess." The words slipped out. I giggled, surprised I'd admitted it.

"Of course you are." He touched the crown on my head. "I'd always treat you as such."

I laughed, wanting to tell him Colin wasn't trying to attack me after all, but thought I was his lost mermaid princess. Oh, and that he decked him a good one. And that my boyfriend was a fish, too, and that I had no clue where he was and was worried we'd never have a normal life together. I wanted to give up—to choose someone safe. Someone with less drama. Someone like Callahan.

"You smell so good," I heard come out of my lips.

"You do, too."

I laughed. He had to be lying. Even I could smell the mosquito repellent over the perfume Georgia doused my body in.

But he started again, kissing my neck lightly. This time I didn't resist. I wanted him—his lips, his hands on me, his body as close as possible. Nothing like this had ever felt so good. This was all so easy. No drama. No decisions. Just Callahan and me.

Fin.

I tried to stop, but the alcohol made my arms limp. He was going to kiss me and I wouldn't be able to stop him this time. The crowd suddenly split Red Sea style and kids tumbled out of the exits like a waterfall. The music stopped as house lights flicked on, blinding everyone.

"Come on, Ash," Callahan said, tugging my hand. "We have to get out of here."

The underlying word I finally heard being breathed over and over from the crowd became crystal clear. Cops.

33

෨

FIN

Thursday evening, April 21st

A high-pitched wail ripped me from my sleep. I slowly opened my eyes. The backseat of the taxi was overflowing with fins and torn clothing.

"What are you?" the driver exclaimed, followed by a string of unintelligible words in another language.

He swerved off the side of the road and skidded the taxi into a fence. Everything played out in slow motion. A hazy blur of barbwire and wooden stakes uprooted and beat the side of the car relentlessly.

"Sing!" Galadriel screamed.

I turned to her, but my lips wouldn't move.

Galadriel shook my arm. "Fin, sing right now!"

My tongue lay flat and heavy in my mouth. Did she poison me again? The driver fled the vehicle like a madman, flailing his arms. Headlights hit my eyes. Tires screeched somewhere in the distance. The twilight revealed we'd chanced fate too long.

Galadriel pulled her body up and hung over the front seat. Her thin tail circled around next to me. She forced the gearshift into drive. The car jerked forward, rolling slowly.

"What are you doing?" I managed to say.

"Getting us out of here!"

She turned the wheel toward the highway. We couldn't merge into traffic, not going five miles an hour.

"You can't possibly think we're going to coast anywhere, do you?"

"Then help me!"

I gave my head a hard shake to release the overwhelming drunkenness assaulting my senses. My tail, thicker than hers, was smashed on the floorboard and wrapped under Galadriel's caudal fin. I rolled over and pulled the lever to lower the driver's seat all the way down. Then I yanked myself forward so my hands could reach the pedals.

"Gas it," she yelled.

I pressed the gas and the car lurched forward, bumping over rocks and potholes. She maneuvered the car to the left. Someone honked, disrupting her confidence. She yanked us onto the bumpy shoulder. I let up on the gas.

"I can't merge over," she squealed.

I wanted to switch places, frustrated all I could see was her terrified face and the night sky out of the passenger window.

"You can do it. Just tell me what to do."

"Okay." She pushed her damp hair off her forehead. "Let me get comfortable."

She flopped her body the rest of the way onto the passenger's seat and moaned. Blood seeped from the side of her dorsal fin. "Crap. That's going to leave a scar."

She leaned further over to the wheel and wove her tail around on the ground. Her fin fanned behind her head. Headlights hit her face as she turned to look behind us. "Okay, on my word, hit it."

"Okay."

"Hit it!"

I pushed down hard on the gas.

She gasped as the car lurched forward. Dirt spun under the tires as we merged onto the road.

"I did it." A smile finally appeared on her face. She studied the road again. "Okay. I think I see the lake."

"Good." I took a deep breath.

"Brake—BRAKE!"

I pushed the brakes hard.

"No, NO! That's too hard. The gas—gas it!"

Cars honked all around us.

"What's going on?"

"Just keep the gas steady!" Galadriel's voice wavered. "Okay—let up. Now give it more. Listen to me, Fin!"

"I am!"

Every instruction took all my concentration as knives pounded into my brain. Why did I knock out like that again?

"Did you drug me?" I asked.

"I—we just—fell asleep—more gas. Not that much! Let up." Her hands shook as she gripped the steering wheel with white knuckles.

My stomach and neck ached from bearing all my weight. I leaned my head against the door.

"Don't fall asleep again!" she yelled in a panic.

"I'm not. This is majorly uncomfortable."

"Well, if you would have sang!"

"I tried. My voice wouldn't work."

Galadriel shook her head. "More gas. Well, I kind of—let up!"

Dirt and rocks embedded themselves into the underside of my arms. I tried not to think about what other disgusting stuff might be on the floor of the taxi. Her ripped up shorts circled her waist. A hint of purple liquid was splattered on the white fabric.

"You octopus inked me!" I yelled. "You wanted me knocked out. Why?"

"It was an accident. I just—Oh, no. OH, NO!" she cried.

A red flicker hit the mirror.

"Where's the lake? Is it close?"

"I don't know. Just—just floor it!"

I pressed the gas as Galadriel swerved the wheel. We jerked left then right and back again. I tucked my head down and tried to stay balanced.

"Just steer us for the lake!" I yelled.

"I don't know where it is—oh wait. I see it!"

"Great! Keep driving towards it."

Tires squealed and sirens blared.

"Can you sing your way out of this one, Fin?"

"Just keep driving."

Galadriel breathed hard, like she'd run a race. "They're gaining on us. And—there are four cars now." A white rectangular block of light from the rear view mirror illuminated the terror behind her eyes.

"Pull over!" I heard blaring behind us as a strobe light lit up the inside of the taxi.

"Just go!" I yelled.

Galadriel whimpered. "There's a motorcycle cop next to me."

"Keep going!"

She turned and waved to someone I couldn't see. "I wish you could sing. Should I roll down the window?"

"He won't hear me. Keep going."

She repeatedly looked to the left hand side of the car. "He's motioning me to pull over."

"Don't."

"Okay."

"How fast are we going?"

"Over a hundred miles per hour. All the cars are out of our way now."

My heart pounded. How long could we do this?

She gasped, freaking me out. "There's the lake, Fin! It's right next to us."

"Can you get us down there?"

"I think I can. It's just—steep."

"Is it drivable?"

"Well, maybe. I—I don't know."

"Is it or isn't it?"

"Yeah. I think I can do it."

I knew singing would be a better way to get out of this mess, but we needed to get into the water and if the lake was right there, I wanted to avoid anymore attention. The police would only let us run for so long before they shot our tires.

Without warning Galadriel screamed, "Here goes nothing!"

She yanked the car to the right and curled up in a ball, hiding her face. Suddenly there wasn't a road under us. We were airborne. I pushed myself backward as the car tipped vertical. Darkness was all I could see through the windshield. I wrapped my arms over my head and tried to protect my face as the car flipped over and my body levitated to the ceiling.

Then we hit, and everything went black.

34

༄

ASH

Thursday evening, April 21st

The fresh air outside of the club felt amazing. I sucked in a bunch of cool sips, trying to slow down my feet and my heart rate.

"Stop pulling me." I yanked my spaghetti arm from my captor.

"We have to keep going," Callahan said. "Where's your car?"

I laughed. Like I could drive. "Georgia drove." My teeth felt like boulders in my mouth. "That's a funny word, Georgia. Who would name their kid after a state. Geor-r-r-gia."

Somehow my feet kept moving. Around me, the dreamy mass of faces and sparkles lessened as we separated ourselves from the swarm of kids.

Shannon appeared at my side and giggled. "Hey, there you are, birthday girl."

I threw my arms around her neck. "Where have you been? I love you, man."

"Who's driving?" Callahan asked.

"Georgia. Where is she?" Chrissi turned to face the club.

"I don't see her," Michele said.

I giggled. "Geor-r-r-gia."

"Shhh." Callahan brushed my hair off my forehead. "I'll drive you home."

"Crap. Maybe they caught her," Shannon said, her voice further away. "Wait. I don't see any cops, do you?"

Callahan gripped me tighter. We were moving again. "Tell Georgia I'm taking Ash home, okay?"

"Yeah," a male voice I didn't recognize said in the distance. "Let's go inside."

Our feet crunched against the gravel and sounded super loud. "What happened?" I asked.

"Don't worry about it. Let's get you home."

I heard a car door open and my body lifted, weightless. Silence surrounded me once he closed me inside the truck. The smell of old leather encased me.

I leaned over, falling horizontal on the seat. The world spun haphazardly and my stomach lurched. I burped. The door opened.

"Oh, no you don't."

My body lifted upright and Callahan snuggled in next to me. His arm appeared on my shoulder as the engine started. "What did you drink?"

I giggled. "Just a sip of Goldshl-l-l-l-ager."

"I think you had more than a sip. We need to get you sober before I take you home."

Nope. Just a sip. "Okay." My head floated around on a tilt-a-whirl. Maybe mermaid princesses didn't handle alcohol very well. I'd have to ask Fin.

He turned onto the frontage road parallel with the lake. The moon bounced off the water, sending sparkles of rainbow light everywhere.

"My boyfriend is a fish," I said.

"Your what?"

"Boyfriend. He came out of the water and rescued me from drowning. Isn't that sweet?"

"I think you've had way more than a sip, my dear."

I closed my eyes and leaned into Callahan's warm shoulder. With him, I didn't care about Colin, or anything. Here I could run away and just be.

"Colin's a fish too. He thinks I'm a princess. They want to kidnap me and take me to Natatoria. Na-ta-to-ria… say it."

Callahan laughed again. "You've got quite an imagination. You should be a writer."

I snorted. "Never. Do you know how many words a book is? Like a bazillion."

We pulled up to the beach area next to my house and I sighed. I didn't want to leave yet.

"How're you feeling?"

Twin Callahan's floated in a circle. "Good. Real good."

I leaned into his chest again. He pulled me tight into his side, then massaged my shoulder, then my arm. His fingers wove into my hair.

"I love your red hair. It's so soft." He kissed my forehead.

I opened my eyes and looked off into the water. A long ripple moved across the surface. Then a head popped up.

"See." I pointed to the lake. "Mer-r-men."

Callahan didn't look. He was more interested in me. His hands molded under my chin as he brought my lips to his. I closed my eyes and let myself go when a dry heave hit me.

"I think I'm going to be sick."

Fast as lightning, he had me outside of the truck. I bent over and let go of my sushi as he held my hair. The fog surrounding my head instantly lifted.

"This is so embarrassing." My cheeks flushed. "Sorry."

"Here, drink this." Callahan handed me a bottle of water.

I took a grateful swig and wondered how I'd ended up at the lake with Callahan to begin with. Did Georgia know I'd left the club? I felt my pocket for my phone. Georgia would be worried.

Over Callahan's shoulder, a silhouette of a man waded in the surf just off shore.

I gasped and walked forward, "Fin?"

"Huh?" Callahan swiveled around.

"Fin?" the merman said, then laughed. Colin.

Another head popped up next to his—Colin's dad, Alaster.

"No," I whispered.

The song came from Alaster's mouth and Callahan robotically moved toward the water.

"No!" I screamed and tugged on his arm. He shrugged me off with ease.

I looked to Alaster in desperation. "What are you doing?"

"If you don't come with us, sweetie, we'll have your friend drown himself." Alaster motioned me forward with his finger.

"No!" Tears poured down my face as Callahan began to walk into the water. "Okay! Okay, whatever you want."

Alaster stopped singing and Callahan stood knee deep in the lake.

"Let's go, Ashlyn," Alaster said. "You agreed."

"But I'm not a mermaid."

He laughed, a deep scary rumble. "Not yet."

I stood solid, my feet at the edge of the lake. "But it's freezing." Haunting flashbacks of the icy water when I fell in hit me.

"If you don't come to us, we'll drown him. Three, two, one—"

"Okay!" I stepped forward. Knives hit my skin. I sucked the air between my teeth as I took a few more steps. Once the water hit my armpits, Colin grabbed me.

Heat from his body helped against the bitter chill. My teeth chattered. "I'm h-h-here. Let h-h-h-him go."

Alaster laughed, then sang again. Callahan turned around and headed for his truck.

"You ready?" Colin whispered in my ear.

"For what?"

He laughed. "Hold your breath."

I sucked in a gasp as he yanked me underwater and sped through the current. After a minute, my lungs ached. Princess or not, suddenly I had a feeling they weren't taking me to Natatoria.

I was the one to be drowned.

35

᠗

FIN

Thursday evening, April 21st

Before opening my eyes, I inhaled. I'd know this clean, snowy water blindfolded—home. My head throbbed and redness tinged the water; I'd survived, barely. I reached out for Galadriel. Only the current touched my fingertips.

"Galadriel?"

The opened passenger door led out into the dark lake without any sign of her or her suitcase. Though the shoreline spanned 72 miles, I knew I'd find her eventually.

I uncurled my fin from the wreckage and swam through the door. The car rested on the lake floor maybe ten-feet below the surface. An array of lights lit the water above me. Anxious to get away before divers showed up, I whipped my tail back and forth to loosen the glass embedded in my scales and surveyed the surroundings. I could have sworn we'd fallen from a cliff, but we'd only jettisoned off the highway a few feet into the bay by Cave Rock, the favorite hang out of the notorious Tahoe Tessie.

My spine cracked as bones relocated and started to heal. Within a few days, no evidence of the crash would show. My head, still groggy, wouldn't clear. Galadriel had poisoned me again in the taxi. But why?

I floated through the soft water toward Emerald Bay. The night was young and Ash would still be awake; I had to look up at her window and see. If I could draw attention to the water, maybe she'd come outside. Knowing her, she'd quite possibly dive in to meet me.

Down below, sixteen hundred feet to be exact, the secret entrance to Natatoria loomed in the dark. Just a few weeks ago Dad had blown

᠗ 210 ᠗

the cave to smithereens. I dove deeper, tempted to check to see if the mers had actually reopened the gate like Badger had said. I had to be careful. According to my brief phone call with Lucy, my annoying cousin Colin was snooping around the lake. After I pummeled his face for trying to take my girl, I'd send him through the gate and arrange another accidental collapse of the tunnel. The less interference from other mers the better.

I swam up to our beach. To my disappointment, the Lanski house was dark. I watched her window. Were they out? Or was she safe, sleeping in her bed? After a few minutes, boredom and responsibility set in. Galadriel couldn't be left unattended, but first I'd take a peak and see what my cousin and uncle had been up to. I cringed thinking of the destruction last time. Good to see the house was still standing.

I swam slowly toward the tunnel leading to the hatch.

36

꩜

ASH

Thursday evening, April 21st

Colin and I surfaced through a hole into a dark cave. I coughed water out of my lungs as he slithered us across a slick surface to another body of water. The change in temperature set my skin on fire.

"It's hot!" I struggled, but Colin had a firm grip on my arm. He clapped two times and the lights magically came on. We were in an indoor pool. A bridge spanned the length above us and a TV hung in the corner. Stairs led up to a closed door. Was this Fin's basement?

My hip kept bumping into the spikes on his sides, tearing at the fabric of my dress. "Ouch."

"Quit struggling."

Alaster popped through the hole and slid into the pool like an oversized slug. "It's about time you started cooperating, Princess."

"I'm not a princess!"

Colin flipped me around and pulled up my dress, revealing my lacy underwear. "Yup, here's the mark just as I remember it."

"Hey!" I slapped his hand and yanked the stretchy fabric down.

Both men laughed.

"She won't be that feisty for long," Alaster said to Colin. "You know what to do. I'll be back by morning with the essence. Pack whatever you want to take with you."

"Sure, Dad," Colin nodded, a proud smile on his face.

"Good job, Son." He clapped Colin on the shoulder before he disappeared down the hole.

My skin quickly adjusted to the tepid pool water and I began to shiver. "I can't stay in here. I'm going to get sick."

Colin rolled his eyes and scanned the deck. I hoped it was for a towel. Instead, he found a rope and tied my wrists before he hoisted me out and sat me on the pool ledge. The chilly air sent a shiver up my spine.

"I need a towel."

"Quit complaining, will you? And why'd you think I was Fin? Are you expecting him?" he asked.

I looked down. "You look like him, that's all."

Colin laughed as I continued to shiver. He finally slid out of the pool and threw a towel over my shoulders.

I wrapped up best I could and watched in wonder at his long tail as it swished back and forth. Two spiked pectoral fins protruding from the sides—the ones that had been poking me earlier—and a larger one jutted from his back. His tail fin wasn't flat like what I imagined a mermaids tail would look like, but shark-like: vertical with a razor sharp on the tip.

"What's wrong with your tail?"

Colin frowned and studied his backside. "Nothing."

"But your fin is sideways."

He howled in laughter. "I'm not a mermaid, Princess. I'm built for power and speed." He dove under and swam in a swift circle to show how functional his tail was.

I smirked and huddled under the towel, finally warm. If I could distract him, I could run up the stairs on my left and escape.

"So," he swam over to me, noting I wasn't impressed, "we can do this the hard way or the easy way."

I cocked my head to the side. "Or you can let me go."

He laughed. All evidence where Callahan had punched him had healed. If I weren't tied, I'd hit him again just to piss him off.

"You're coming with us, so stop begging. When Dad brings the essence, you'll be a mermaid once again."

"Again?" I gulped. "Are you insane?"

"You're the lost princess and my ticket out of mediocrity."

"Right." I struggled against the rope. My wrists rubbed raw under the tight hemp fibers.

"Okay, so… since I can't sing to you, why don't you make this easy and kiss me?" He puckered his lips.

"Kiss you?" I pushed him with my foot. "Heck, no!"

His face hardened as he flipped his tail, mumbling things under his breath. After a few uncomfortable minutes, he turned to me.

"I don't understand why you don't like me. I mean, I'm witty and attractive. When we first met, you were putty in my hands, and then something changed."

"Seriously?" I couldn't help my sarcastic laughter. "Maybe this might be a clue." I held up my bound wrists. "And the fact you've been nothing but a jerk after that."

"Careful, Princess. I don't need your permission to kiss you." He smirked.

"A forced promise is equivalent to rape where I come from."

"I'm not trying to force you, and how do you know about the promising anyway?"

I hid my bound hands under the towel. The Band-Aid on my ring finger barely hung on at this point.

He swam over, creating a large wave of water that drenched me. I tried to move away. He ripped the sopping towel off of me and found the promising tattoo.

"NO!" He pulled hard on my hand and thrust his face in front of mine. "Who is it? Who?"

I gulped down my fear. "Don't hurt me," I said as I turned my cheek.

He gritted his teeth and forced my face to look at him. My heart thumped hard, vibrating my entire body. If I told him, he'd go after Fin. I pushed my lips into a thin line.

Colin's eyes narrowed. "Fin." Below the water, large spikes spread from his side fins, sharp and dangerous looking. "Poseidon, I'm going to kill him."

Colin submerged and darted across the pool. I pulled my feet out of the water and scooted backward. I looked behind me. Here was my chance to escape.

A hand reached up and grabbed my ankle. "Where do you think you're going, Princess?"

I tried to kick myself free. "It won't work, whatever you do. I'm promised and stop calling me princess."

"I'll hunt Fin down and de-fin him to release the bond," he said through clenched teeth. "He can't have you and take everything I deserve. You're mine."

He jettisoned his body out of the water and slid us in one fluid motion across the slick cement to the stairs.

"But he's your cousin."

"Shhh," he said and wrung his hands. "I can't think with you talking."

"But Fin's in Flor—I mean Maine."

"My father isn't going to hear a word of this. As far as he's concerned, we're promised. This mark is mine. And if you say a word, I'll do something drastic. Do you hear me?"

My throat hitched as his face flashed with hateful rage.

Inside I screamed. Why didn't I tell Fin the truth? That Colin and his uncle were here stalking me? This whole time I'd thought they only wanted to know where the Heltons were, but that wasn't the case. They'd been looking for the lost princess, Galadriel. Colin wanted to become promised to her to elevate his position in the mer society—but now that they thought it was me, he'd change me into a mermaid, and claim me for his wife without revocation. I'd be trapped in Natatoria like Tatchi. Fin wouldn't know. I had to convince Colin otherwise.

"Your song didn't work because I'm promised. Don't you see? It has nothing to do with royal blood. But I know where the lost princess is—the one you're looking for."

He stopped for a second, his eyes clouding over in confusion. "What?"

"She's with the Heltons—in Maine."

"But you have the mark."

"It's only a birthmark," I said, pleading. "Please… let me go."

"I can't!" He yelled and leaned up against the wall, thumping his head against the cement bricks. "Don't you understand? That mark says you're royalty and I have to become promised to you, otherwise my dad really will kill me."

Pity filled my heart. This wasn't his plan after all, but something his dad forced him to do. We were trapped together. Maybe I could use this to my advantage for my escape.

I leaned over and took his hand with mine. "Then let's pretend."

He wrinkled his brow. "Pretend?"

"We'll pretend we're promised and then later, you can take me to Fin and I'll set you up with the real princess."

He laughed as something dark crossed his face. "That's all good and convenient for you and Fin, but I don't believe you. You're the princess that's missing and you'll be mine." He grabbed my chin and pulled me forward. "I can still kiss you. Maybe you won't be entirely promised to me at first, but it'll make you want me, and no one in Natatoria will know any different."

I struggled against his grip, braced for his lips to touch mine. Fin never told me what would happen if another merman kissed me. Would our bond break? Would I be promised to them both? Colin said I'd want for him. The thought made my skin crawl.

There was no escape now.

"Touch her and die!"

Colin swiveled backward, mouth agape. "What the heck?"

A mirage of Fin hoisting himself out of the porthole filled the blur in my tear laden eyes.

Colin yelled and charged Fin. "She's mine!"

They collided and tumbled into the pool, creating a giant tidal wave. I struggled to my knees. My eye caught a row of harpoon-like javelins lined against the wall. I crawled to my feet and ran the length of the room to them. I rested the rope against the blade and sawed carefully. Threads began to fray. Once they snapped, I removed the heavy javelin and held it over my head, ready to whack Colin on the head.

I couldn't see a thing in the churning wall of water. Then Fin erupted with his arm around Colin's neck. "You miserable parasite!" Fin's bicep flexed. "Why are you here with Ash? Answer me!"

Colin grunted as his eyes bulged.

"Stop!" I didn't want Colin's death on our consciences.

Fin clenched his jaw, then finally released him in a fit of frustration and threw him to the other side of the pool. "You big coward."

My eyes met Fin's and I couldn't breathe. He was here, finally. I dropped the javelin and lunged for the pool edge, diving in.

Warm hands took ahold of my cheeks, bringing my face to the surface. Our lips crashed together and our hands hungrily gripped one another's faces and bodies. He whisked me to the opposite end from where Colin sulked, and wrapped me up in his glowing warm arms as he whispered sweet apologies for being late, kissing away my tears.

"I'm sorry—I'm so sorry. I'm here. Nothing will harm you again.

Did he hurt you?"

I sobbed and hugged his neck harder as he tried to inspect me.

"Tell me you're all right."

"I'm all right," I choked out. "I'm perfect."

He breathed out a huge sigh and hugged me tighter, kissing my forehead and temple. "I will never let you out of my sight again. Ever."

"Come on," I said impatiently. "We need to go before your uncle returns."

"My uncle is here?" We charged for the porthole, but Alaster sat on the edge.

"Look who's finally home." His hand rested on a thin cord feeding up to the ceiling.

A mesh of heavy ropes fell onto our heads and tiny barbs hooked into my skin.

Fin's eyes rolled back. He sunk down, pulling my body and face under the surface with him. With the little strength I had, I managed to lift my lips above the surface. Through the net, I gasped for air and searched for Alaster. He sat on the pool deck like a big seal, yelling something I couldn't make out. The water swooshed around my ears making listening impossible. Alaster pointed to us, then slapped Colin across the face. I cringed.

Hidden in the rafters above us, nets hung in various places. Silver barbs protruded around the edges and glinted in the light. Booby traps. My hands tingled, unable to lift the net off of our heads. My ears rang as I fought to keep my eyes open.

Colin dove into the water next to me, drowning my face with water. He removed the net and slung my limp body over his shoulder and onto the deck. My eyes fluttered open, paralysis encasing my body. Alaster appeared before me.

He forced my mouth opened. The thick, sweet liquid slid down my throat. I choked and tried to focus on his face. He laughed before he pushed me back into the pool with his hand. I sunk slowly down to the bottom, my arms numb at my side. Something yanked Fin out of the water next to me. I was alone.

Bubbles escaped from my mouth as the two blurry figures hovered on the edge watching me die—Alaster and Colin. What happened to the princess theory? Were they going to turn Fin in instead? The burn to breathe kept building until I couldn't wait anymore. This would be it. My dying breath. Finally, I sucked in a lungful of water.

A searing ache tore at the sides of my neck. Surprisingly, the water gushed in. I shrieked, but only pulled in another hungry thick breath. Again, the water rushed across the raw skin on my neck, bypassing my lungs. Relief filled me. I could breathe underwater. My limbs jolted to life and I touched the flaps of skin protruding from the sides of my neck. Was I becoming a mermaid?

I attempted to kick my feet to swim to the surface when my muscles seized. I cried out and arched my back to stop the biting sting. I twisted and turned. Nothing helped. Then heat began to radiate under my skin, growing warmer by the second. I tried kicking again when something tore down the sides of my legs with a scorching hot burn. I sucked in another gulp of the cool water, hoping to stop the pain.

Hot. My body was in an oven, cooking to death. Hot, so hot. Yes, please. Stop. Anything but this. Instead, the fire stoked under my skin and boiled all around me.

My legs itched uncontrollably. I reached down to scratch the skin. My nail beds sliced open and something sharp protruded out, ripping open my flesh. I screamed, but I couldn't see what I'd done. My eyeballs felt like they were turning inside out, then my ears crackled with a horrific deafening pop. I thrashed in a circle, hoping the rush of water would cool the burn. The bones in my legs crunched and pulled apart with loud pops. I tried to bend my knees; my legs wouldn't respond. Another seizure hit, snapping my legs together like magnets. I yanked to keep them from fusing. Knives carved their way under my flesh anyway, ripping through me with a vengeance. Something yanked hard against my body, stretching me like taffy. I writhed, unable to stop myself from screaming continually as the fire chewed its way over my skin like a piranha.

Fin never warned me about the pain. Though I'd secretly wanted to be a mermaid, this would have been the deal breaker. I couldn't endure this. I didn't care if I'd never see him again, feel his kisses on my lips, fall asleep in his arms.

I wanted to die.

Now.

Please, dear God. Let me die!

But it wouldn't stop. The pain continued on, ripping and tearing me, forming me into something inhuman. I hated Alaster. I wanted to scratch his eyes out with my new claws. If I survived, he'd experience my wrath like no other.

Another seizure tore at my body. Would this happen every sunset? I couldn't do it. I couldn't live with this pain daily.

I keep screaming, crying, begging—I'd give my very soul for peace, but the burning wouldn't stop. When? When would it end?

Fin, please help me!

37

◎

FIN

Thursday evening, April 21ˢᵗ

Someone slapped me across my face. I moved to retaliate, but my arms hung like deadweights chained above my head.

"Wake up, pretty boy." Uncle Alaster's voice sent daggers of rage into my blood stream.

I shook my head. My body was on fire.

"It's no fun if you don't stay awake and watch." His fish breath revolted my stomach.

But my eyes wouldn't stay open. Something dripped on my lips; I ran my tongue along the chapped skin, licking up a few drops of essence.

The sudden infusion cleared my head. "Where's Ash?"

Uncle Alaster's lip pushed up to the side. He looked over at the pool. A small dark figure thrashed around under the water.

"You're full of surprises, Nephew. How could you leave your sweet little honey all alone? No wonder Colin was having such trouble persuading her."

I sat upright. "What did you do?"

"Finished what you started."

A small green fin flipped above the surface of the water—thin and fragile. He'd changed her. She was suffering.

"You son of a bass! When I get out of here—"

"I'd like to see you try—" He dangled a silver key in front of me. "Such poetic justice. My brother provideth, and I taketh away." He leaned forward and whispered. "But in a few hours, you'll be dead—

either by the poison or by exposure. I wish I could stay and watch your princess try her hardest to save you, but I already know what will happen. Don't worry, Fin. After you die, we'll take excellent care of her," he said with a sardonic laugh.

I struggled against the chains and growled. "You're nothing but pure evil."

"Too bad my good-for-nothing brother and his beta-wench didn't come with you. I've had so much fun rigging this place for our happy reunion. Won't your dried carcass be a nice welcome home present?"

I exhaled out of clenched teeth. "You can go to hell."

"Not before you," he laughed. "Come on, Colin. I'm sick of the whining and we can't do anything until the bait dies. Let's give them their last few hours alone."

Colin shot me a mournful look as they disappeared down the porthole. The sound of metal gears rubbing together signaled they'd locked the hatch shut.

"Ash." My lips cracked open and bled. "Ash!"

I took labored breaths in time. I ached for water, my strength diminishing with every second. The incisions on my fin bled from where the barbs cut me, tinged with a weird green glow. Ferdinand had similar wounds when he returned from Natatoria. Uncle Alaster had only given me enough essence to basically bring me around and torture me longer—nothing substantial enough to heal anything.

"Ash, please surface," I said before I closed my eyes. The thought she'd watch me die gripped me. We only had one hope.

"Galadriel," I whispered.

38

∽

ASH

Friday, early morning, April 22nd

The pain finally stopped. I opened my eyes; everything underwater was crystal clear and vibrant. Where my legs used to be, an elegant green fin fluttered in the water, sweet and delicate like butterfly wings. I brought my hand to my mouth. My arms were covered in a fine layer of iridescent scales, soft to the touch. I flitted my tail and zoomed across the pool, faster than I'd ever swam. A squeal escaped my lips. After all the pain, I had a tail. A TAIL! More beautiful than I could imagine.

I tried extending the claws I felt earlier from under my nail beds, but no matter what I tried, nothing would pop out. They'd come in handy, especially when I scratched out Alaster's eyes for what he did to me. *Alaster.*

I breeched the surface of the water to find him. Neither he nor Colin were in the room, but Fin lay lifeless—his fin grey and dull—chained to the wall. He was barely breathing.

"No!" I flipped my tail and flew out of the water, landing next to his body. "Please, no!"

I brushed my hand over his taut face. He sucked in a small breath. I pulled on the chains. They wouldn't budge.

"Water," he croaked out.

I wiggled my hips to get back into the pool and splashed him with my hands.

Frantic, I looked around. They didn't have a hose down here? How'd they fill the pool? Near the soda fountain was a stack of cups.

I swam over and filled two. Most of the water spilled by the time I maneuvered myself back to Fin. I tried to get him to drink and he allowed half to pass his lips. His tail finally twitched.

"Come on. Fight!"

The soggy towel from earlier caught my eye. I strained my arm to grab it, and laid it over his tail. After another labored trip to the pool, I splashed more to drench the towel, but he didn't respond. My arms began to ache.

What did Fin say about being out of the water? How long could we survive? I looked up at the darkened windows along the edge of the ceiling. How long did we have until morning?

A silver ring protruded from the cinderblock and held Fin's chains in place. If I could pull it from the wall, or break away the stone, maybe I could get him free. The javelin could work as a tool.

"Fin, I'm going to break you free. Hang on. Please!"

I held the javelin over my head and chipped away at the stone. Chip, chip, chip. The ring loosened a tiny bit.

I jumped back into the water and splashed him, this time with my tail, before chipping away at the cement again. Chip, chip, chip.

"Hang on."

I splashed again, my energy evaporating. But even with all the effort, the ring barely moved. There was no way I could get him free anytime soon.

"Ugh. God, please!" I pulled on the chain, in desperation; mentally and physically exhausted.

Fin grunted the same time the metal hatch door behind me creaked.

Forgetting I was a mermaid, I tried to run for the javelin on the floor and fell over. Colin popped out of the hatch first.

I shrieked as I circled my fingers around the javelin's shaft. Colin slid over with ease and pushed me into the pool before I could get a firm grip.

When I reemerged, Colin had his arm cocked back with the javelin pointed at Fin.

"No!" With a flip of my tail, my body launched from the pool. I clung to his back, suspended for a moment, my tail swishing around on the ground beneath me, before he shook me free. I fell on the floor in a flippered heap.

"Stop it, Ash, or I'll hit him." He rammed the spear blade into the chain several times. Finally, a link busted open, releasing Fin's wrists. He crumbled onto the floor. I put my hands on Fin's chest.

"Move out of the way!" Colin barked as he elbowed me aside.

He reached under Fin's arms and pulled his limp body into the water with a plop. I clawed forward and dove in after them. Together we sank to the bottom.

"Please." I brushed my lips over his. "Wake up."

Fin's gills moved slowly as he pulled water into his mouth. Colin rested next to us on the pool floor and watched with a twisted frown. I held Fin's face gently and blew water into his mouth from mine. He couldn't leave me. Not now.

"He needs essence," Colin said; the sound was as clear as if we were out of the water.

I turned to Colin and glowered. "You did this!" I tried to slap him. My claws popped out from under my nail beds, surprising me, and I swiped his face.

He turned his cheek, but didn't retaliate. Blood spurted into the water momentarily, before the wounds healed.

"You can hate me all you want later, but we need to get somewhere safe until morning. My Dad is coming back!"

I hung onto Fin as he floated in the water, unconscious. "I don't understand. Why are you helping us now?"

"I didn't agree to this, Ash. To murder. I only wanted to be promised to a princess." He looked away. "I had no idea you and Fin were—it doesn't matter anymore anyway. Let's go."

I breeched the surface and Colin hoisted Fin out of the pool onto the deck.

"Look who escaped!" Alaster appeared at the porthole. He grasped a woman by her red hair—a mermaid. "What are you doing?"

Colin startled, then studied the girl his dad held, confusion clear on his face. "Who's that?"

Alaster pinched his eyes into slits and did a double take as well. The mermaid thrashed under his grip, hissing.

"Put me down, you bottom feeder!" she demanded. "You don't treat royalty this way, you hear me?"

Alaster threw her onto the floor and grabbed a javelin from the wall, pointing it at her.

"Twins?" he breathed in disbelief.

"You'll endure the full extent of the law for kidnapping me," the mermaid seethed. "You'll be taking a one way trip to Bone Island!"

Alaster didn't pay attention. He glowered at me. "This whole time I thought *you* were the lost princess."

The girl looked at me as well, squinting her eyes in curiosity.

Alaster pointed the javelin at Galadriel. "Show me your hip."

She reluctantly turned after he threatened to stab her. We had matching marks.

"How is this possible?" Alaster said, and nudged her with the blunt end of the javelin. "Who are you?"

"Princess Galadriel. Who else would I be?"

"Galadriel?" He studied her, then turned to me in confusion. "Then who are you?"

"Can't you see? She's a princess, too," Colin said offhandedly. "They both have the mark."

Could this really be true after all? I lifted the hem of my tattered dress and ran my hand over the raised iridescent mark above where my scales started. A princess? How did I end up on land then? Were my parents of royal mer blood? Did they leave the colony and escape?

Alaster's brow shot up. "Hmmm…" He eyed the two of us lustfully. "Two princesses."

Fin struggled to breathe as Alaster ran his finger over the tip of the blade, contemplating something. We were running out of time. Fin needed to be in the water, at least.

I held out my hand, ready to push him back in, when—quick as a flash—Alaster bumped me aside and slung Fin's limp body across the floor. He hit the base of the stairs.

"Fin stays out of the water!"

I picked up the fallen javelin and aimed it at Alaster's heart. A vial of the blue liquid hung from his belt. That was what Colin said Fin needed. I charged Alaster determined to stop him and take the blue liquid.

Alaster grabbed my arm and twirled me around, pinning my neck against his chest. He ripped the javelin from my hand. "Feisty little princess." He laughed and gestured to Colin. "Get Galadriel. We're going."

"No, Father. This isn't right. Fin doesn't need to die."

Alaster scowled. "Are you defying me?"

"It's time to let your jealousy over Uncle Jack go. We've got what we want. Fin will be punished for his crimes in Natatoria. I don't want his death on my conscience."

Alaster's chest heaved. "You're not going to be the only one on the royal court, Colin. I will make the decisions around here."

I struggled in Alaster's arm and yanked on the vial chained to his belt. The chain snapped, knocking the vial to the ground. He didn't notice, too busy arguing with Colin. But how was I going to get it to Fin?

Colin protectively moved in front of Galadriel. "Don't do this, Father."

"Do what? Claim my destiny? Give my rotten brother the life of misery he deserves? I was stupid to assume you could handle the power. You're not even royalty yet and you're ordering me around. I'm the one who deserves the praise. I found the princess. Both of them!"

Colin stretched his arm for a javelin on the wall, but Alaster launched the one in his hand first, hitting Colin in the side. Galadriel shrieked and caught him as he flopped onto her, blood pouring from the wound.

"Father?" he said, terror and confusion in his eyes.

"You're as worthless as your mother."

Alaster held me tighter against his body. I gasped as tears spilled over my cheeks. The blood pooled on the deck under Colin.

"You're a monster," Galadriel screamed as she pressed her hand over the wound. "This will not be tolerated!"

"Oh, yeah?" He fastened his arm around my waist and pulled me toward the porthole. "I don't need your approval, Princess. And since I don't need the both of you, I'll take my chances with the compliant one."

Alaster's nostrils flared before he took another javelin off the wall and flung it at Galadriel, hitting her tail. She cried out and fell on top of Colin, blood spilling everywhere.

"No!" I screamed as Alaster dropped me down the hole and pushed my head under the water. He sealed the hatch behind him as I beat on his chest.

"Shut up and come with me." He fisted my hair and pulled me into the belly of the lake.

I shrieked and held onto his hand to stop the pain radiating over my scalp. "I won't go with you! You can't make me!"

He got within inches of my face. "You will go with me and be happy about it. And once we're promised, you'll happily do everything I say or something might happen to that sweet sister of yours. Lucy is it?"

"You wouldn't."

"I would."

I lifted my hand and showed him my tattoo. "But I'm promised to Fin."

He gritted his teeth and then smiled, flashing a gold tooth. "Not for long, love."

He swam off, still holding me by the hair. I watched the opening of the tunnel until it disappeared from sight, unsure where he was taking me.

39

≋

ASH

Friday, early morning, April 22nd

Alaster finally let go of my hair after he pushed me through a hole in the granite on the bottom of Lake Tahoe. I surfaced inside an air-filled corridor. Oddly, bluish-light lit the roughly hewn cave. I couldn't hold in my tears any longer.

"Stop your blubbering already. I need to think!" he yelled.

I sat on a rock in the corner with my arms folded around my new fin and stifled my sobs. The unpredictable monster before me pirated my very breath: one who'd made me endure horrific pain, fatally wounded his son, his nephew, and the Princess Galadriel, all because it benefited him. And if Fin didn't survive, I'd be trapped in Natatoria like Tatchi, promised to Alaster forever, and my human dad couldn't rescue me because I had this—this appendage for legs now. I'd be sentenced to do nothing less than obey him for the rest of my life.

He studied me intently. "Where'd you come from?"

My shoulders slunk in helplessness. "Here, in Tahoe."

"How old are you?"

I turned to hide my smirk at the irony. Most likely midnight had passed making today my birthday. Some present. "I'm eighteen."

"Are you a twin maybe? Or—" He scratched his beard. "How'd you get to Tahoe?"

"I was born here, how else?" I stated firmly, but the details of my birth swirled in my head.

Mom had always joked I was the first homebirth baby mix-up because the ultrasound showed clear as day I was a boy. She'd also bragged how she practically slept through the delivery and awoke in shock to find a 10-pounds, 6-ounce girl in her arms—two pounds heavier than anticipated. Unlike Lucy, who hurt like the dickens at 7-pounds and took thirty hours to grace the world with her presence. Neither my mother nor my sister had a matching mark like Galadriel and I had. Could the birthmark really be a sign of royalty and not a random mark?

Alaster's frustrated growl ripped through my thoughts. "That's not what I meant! Just stop talking!" Alaster treaded water farther from me, mumbling to himself. Then he stopped, stunned and breathless. He began to laugh. "I can't believe it. This is far better than I imagined." He blinked several times; his mouth gaped wide. "So if you're the only promised princess in the King's shoal, and something happened to the royal family, accidentally of course, that would mean I'd be the king. King! Of course, in order to secure my rule, you'd need to give me a son, but that could be managed."

I jolted my head backward. Who cared about the part where he'd become king? I'd die before I ever let him touch me.

"Maybe we should start now." He waggled an eyebrow.

"No!" I twisted to get away.

He came at me quickly, grabbed my wrists, and ground his fat body hard against mine. I screamed and thrashed my tail in the water, but he'd glued me against the wall. He hummed for a moment, obviously enjoying the close touch, then held my hands above my head against the cave wall. I screamed again, clawing and thrashing with all my strength.

His eyes zeroed in on my promising tattoo. "This won't do either."

He yanked my arm outward, and with his free hand, he took a blade from behind his back and sliced through my skin quickly. Painful fire radiated from my fingertips as my bloodied pinkie and ring finger toppled into the water with two soft plops. I screamed in horror and in pain; blood gushed everywhere.

Below us in the deep water, the tattoo shimmered and disappeared out of sight.

"You'll be fine in a minute, so stop your sniveling."

The pain, nothing remotely close to what happened earlier, lessened and the bleeding ceased. Two raw nubs were all that remained. I looked at him and wiped away a tear.

He smirked. "See? I told you. Now we can go."

My face remained tight as I swallowed down the tears and cradled my hand. He'd take me, but he could never have me—not my spirit.

He ran his rough meat-hook hand over my cheek. "Good. I like my girls tough. After all, you'll be queen someday and you'll have to set an example." He arched his brow. "Maybe Fin is dead already."

"What?"

Before I knew it, his hand gripped my chin and his slimy lips were on mine—the taste of seaweed and rotten fish filled my mouth as he slid his tongue inside, practically probing my tonsils. I recoiled and pushed him away, spitting out his slobber. But the deep consuming dread something bad would happen to Fin evaporated off of me, like a heavy blanket had been lifted on a hot summer day. Alaster threw his head back and sucked in a deep breath of air; a smile formed on his lips. "There we go, lovey. You're not so annoying anymore."

I looked at him and felt nothing—just a dull sense of numbness. Was he promised to me now? Colin had mentioned I'd long for whoever kissed me, but he was wrong. I wanted nothing of Alaster, other than his death.

"Now," he moved my wet hair off my forehead, "when we get to Natatoria, you'll follow my lead. You have amnesia. So anything they ask, you don't know. Got it?"

I gritted my teeth; wrapping my fingers around his thick throat and squeezing sounded like a better idea. But he'd hurt Lucy if I didn't cooperate. "Fine."

He moved a little closer and rubbed his tail against me again. "And later, we'll start working on that son. Once you deliver in a few weeks, and I've put together my army, we'll show the proof and overthrow the kingdom."

"Get away from me!" I shrieked and scooted away, still cradling my injured hand.

His eyes clouded in anger as his face went rigid. "Red tide! Isn't that pesky nephew of mine dead yet?"

He looked toward the hole under the water that led out to Lake Tahoe and tugged at my hand.

"Hey, what's going on here?" Two mermen emerged from the other side of the cave, speaking a weird language I could strangely understand. The shorter of the two, the one with dark hair, stopped as our eyes met. His mouth fell open.

"Galadriel?" he whispered.

I blinked, then nodded my head slightly. Maybe if he thought I was the Princess, he'd save me from this monster.

"Yes," I said, but in English. My brain knew how to speak in their language, but the syllables required my tongue to contort in a way I'd never tried before.

The merman startled, then frowned.

"You think this is Galadriel?" Alaster laughed. "Oh, no. She's easy on the eyes, but not as lovely as the Princess is. I could see with the hair how it would confuse you, but I assure you she's not."

"A little young for you, don't you think?" The dark haired merman creased his brow, glaring at Alaster.

The other merman, noticeably taller, had sandy brown hair and clear blue eyes. He didn't focus on any one person or thing—as if he were deaf—and shifted nervously in the water.

"I thought you were in prison, Jax." Alaster's voice grew callous as he put his arm protectively over my shoulder. I tried to shrug it off; he gripped tighter.

"I'm out on bail—aren't I?" Jax nudged his friend with a coy smile. The other merman didn't respond.

"What are you two doing here? This is a private gateway," Alaster said sternly.

"We, uhhh, had a tip about Galadriel." Jax smiled weakly. "But apparently you've found her lookalike, so... we won't be venturing on, I suppose."

Terrified and in shock, I couldn't speak. I trembled, wishing for them to stop Alaster; to save Fin. Numbness still consumed my heart and I wondered if Fin were even alive. I did what I could; I lifted my hand slightly. Jax's gaze flicked at my wound; concern spread on his face.

Alaster noticed. "The human man she lived with beat her. Look at this—" He grabbed my hand and yanked. I yelped in pain. "The jackass cut her fingers when we were trying to escape."

"No—" I tried to say, but Alaster gripped my hand tighter, taking away my breath.

"The girl's still in shock from the change," Alaster interrupted, "speaking gibberish most of the time."

"Oh." Jax ticked his head to the side.

I pleaded with my eyes for help as a tear trickled down my cheek. They couldn't believe him. They needed to probe deeper, to punch him out.

"That's horrible." Jax bowed his head.

"Well, the human has received his justice, so," Alaster lifted his chest, "it's the responsibilities and dangers of guarding a gate, I suppose. I couldn't let her suffer. She's one of the lucky ones, but will require a lot of tender love and care. It's my duty as her new mate. Can I escort you fellas back to Natatoria?"

My stomach pitched a fit and I almost retched. *Help me.*

"You know what, Ferd?" Jax slyly smiled. "I think Alaster is lying.

How about you?"

The rush of fins startled me, as the white water swirled in front of my eyes. I moved out of the way as razor sharp tail fins smashed into the rocky walls. After a minute, Ferd emerged with his arm around Alaster's neck. Jax followed with a punch into Alaster's jaw, knocking him out cold. Alaster's body crumpled like a jellyfish and slipped under the waterline. He came to rest peacefully on the bottom of the cave floor.

"Tough sucker." Jax lifted his tail and ran his finger over one of the spikes. He tasted the liquid. "Totally resistant to my poison."

Ferd looked off to the side, oblivious once again.

I marveled at the relaxed swagger this rag-tag team exuded. "Why did you do that?"

"Honey." Jax took my hand and inspected it. "Did he do this, too? Or was that really from your human?"

The tears poured from my eyes. "Alaster cut my fingers off."

Jax tsked and frowned in sympathy. "I'm sorry. What's your name?"

I bit my lip. Though a criminal, Jax's concern ebbed from his eyes, making me trust him.

"Ashlyn."

"Where's home, Ashlyn?"

"Tahoe."

"Come on, Ferd. Grab the reptile. This all seems a little fishy."

As the three of us swam to Tahoe together, the blood whooshed in my ears. Though they'd rescued me, I didn't know if I'd jumped from the pan into the fire by allowing these criminals to escort me. According to Fin, Galadriel's situation was a secret. Who had given Jax the tip Galadriel was in Tahoe and why did they want to find her first?

"I knew Alaster was a sick and twisted arthropod, but to butcher your hand like hers? I mean, you're a very close knock-off. I thought for a second you were Galadriel, with the red hair and all, but—" He slyly tried to check out my backside. "Did he put a mark on your hip by chance?"

Butcher my hand? Was Alaster secretly trying to pass me off as Galadriel instead?

"No." Thankfulness flooded me. My black dress, though holey, still covered my birthmark, so Jax couldn't be sure and ask more questions. Maybe he'd leave me alone if he suspected I wasn't royalty. But as we swam a little farther, a nervous flutter hit my stomach with a vengeance.

"Shouldn't Alaster be turned in? To your mer police?"

Jax chuckled. "I'm not in the best standing with the police myself, so I'm not sure what we're going to do with him, actually. But I can't leave you here, honey. It's a shark-eat-shark world out there. And though this reptile was anxious to pawn you off as royalty, you're a mermaid now, and unfortunately I'm not privy in how to change you back."

"That's okay. I—I'm good actually. I'll be staying here, so you can go." I jetted into the current away from them. "Thank you," I called out.

If I could get inside the tunnel without them seeing, maybe they'd go away.

Jax caught up with me. "No, Ashlyn. This isn't right. I'm not a hook and release kind of merman."

"I'm okay, seriously."

"I can't leave you."

"I'm not alone. I'm already promised." *I hope.*

"You are? To who?" He flared his tail to slow down. "Is he here?"

My heartbeat accelerated as we neared the tunnel to the hatch. A trail of stinky fish, sweet flowers, Colin's musk, and Fin's clean scent infused my nose. Ferd's anxiety peaked and he dropped Alaster in the current. He rushed for the tunnel first.

"No!" I screamed. "Stop!"

"Wait up, dude," Jax called out and followed closely behind as Ferd swam into the hole.

I followed behind when I heard a scream. My heart dropped. Upon surfacing in the basement, I spotted Galadriel and Jax in one another's arms, but not fighting. She was alive and they were hungrily devouring one another in a passionate kiss.

"You're here!" she kept saying over and over as tears poured from her eyes.

I stopped, my head ping-ponging in confusion. He and Galadriel were promised? I'd completely missed Jax's tattoo. As their lips continued to devour against one another's, I turned away in embarrassment and smiled.

Ferd lingered off to the side, rearranging a stack of beach towels. But beyond, Fin floated in the pool. His eyes were open, watching me. He cracked a smile and feebly lifted his hand. My heart surged.

"Fin!" I dove in to him. "You're okay!"

He grabbed me and drew me close.

"I survived," his voice cracked, "barely. But you, how'd you get away?"

"Jax and Ferd saved me from Alaster." I held him tight and curled my tail around his body. "I'm so sorry. This was all my fault."

"Your fault?" he asked, caressing my face. "I'm the one who should be sorry. I didn't protect you, and now you're a mermaid."

We sunk underwater together. I pressed my body into his thankful the horrific change was finally over. "They say I'm a princess, too. I have some mark on my hip."

"A princess?" He took my face between his hands. "How?"

"This." I pulled up the side of my dress.

"What are you wearing?" He pinned me with a naughty smile.

"Oh." I blushed. "Georgia made me wear it… I'm afraid it's ruined now."

He ran his finger over the mark, tickling the skin where he touched. His face lit up. "Holy carp."

"I know, but that's not the worst of our problems." My tears melted into the water around us. "I didn't tell you Colin and Alaster were here, and now… I screwed up big time."

Fin stroked my cheek with his thumb. "Lucy told me Colin was here when I called. I already knew."

"She did?" I looked down, remembering. Lucy had said he wasn't coming. "She said you weren't coming and I thought the worst. Oh, you must hate me."

"It's okay now" He enveloped me in a hug, pressing my head to his chest. "Ash, I love you and I'm here. We'll never be apart." I heard the smile in his voice.

I wiggled out of his arms, furious. "Why didn't you tell me of the excruciating pain? The torture! And now with everything, how can you say it's okay? Somehow my life has been a lie, your uncle kidnapped me and wanted to make me his," I full body shivered, revolted how close that came into being, "and he tried to kill you and Galadriel. And Colin," I gasped, remembering. "He killed his own son!"

"Colin survived."

"What?"

I pulled away from Fin and surfaced. Colin sat in the corner with a bloody towel wrapped around his legs. His childlike eyes were wide and filled with terror. A large red wound decorated his side.

"He's—human?"

My body involuntarily shook, remembering the pain of the conversion and Alaster's horrible kiss.

"Yes." Fin shifted in the water nervously. "Galadriel didn't have a choice. The barbs had cassava poison on them. I would have died otherwise. After she fed me the essence, Colin had already started to change. He's a little freaked, but once the sun rises, we can get more essence upstairs and change him back."

Pity surged inside me. "He tried to save you."

"Yes, but if I hadn't shown up when I did," Fin's eyes darkened, "he would have laid his filthy lips on you."

Alaster's kiss replayed in my mind and revolted my stomach. I looked away. Fin couldn't know what happened, at least not yet. "He was following his father's orders."

Fin swiveled me to face him. "I'm done talking about them." He pulled me underwater and brought his lips hungrily to mine. A tingle electrified my skin as all my love for him rushed back. I hugged his neck hard in thankfulness. We were still promised. Nothing had changed.

After a minute he studied my face and took my hands. "What are you wearing? How long have you been trapped down here?"

The surprise birthday at the club seemed like lifetimes ago. I brushed my stubby hand against my face.

Fin recoiled in horror. "What did Alaster do to you?!"

"He…." I forced back a sob and tucked my hand behind my dorsal fin.

"Oh, I'm going to slaughter him. Where is he?" Fin popped out of the water and launched himself onto the deck toward the porthole. He yanked on the handle. The hatch didn't open.

"Damn it, Alaster! You bastard!" He banged his fists on the closed hatch.

At the same time, something crashed against the floor above us, shaking the rafters. We all looked up in unison as the room quieted in terror.

40

⌒

FIN

Friday morning, April 22nd

We watched as if the ceiling could cave in at any minute. What had fallen against the floor? Was this another trap? And where was Alaster anyway?

I slid across the suspension bridge to the other end of the basement and hoisted myself up the steps one at a time on my backside. "Please tell me you didn't leave my Uncle in the lake unattended, Jax."

"Dude." Jax held up his hand. "Last I left him, he was out cold and not going anywhere. And your girl didn't say nothing about you and Gladdy being here, so I had no clue what was up. Us finding you was plain luck. Isn't that right, Ferd?"

Ferdinand didn't respond as usual, but Ash shot me an anxious look from the poolside as she hugged her arms. I smiled ruefully.

"Well, someone locked the porthole from the other side, limpet breath, and I don't suppose it was Tahoe Tessie." I popped my shoulder against the basement door. It didn't even budge an inch, barricaded shut. "Son of a biscuit eater! We're locked in."

"Who's Tessie?" Jax frowned.

I scowled. "I can't believe you let Alaster get away so he could lock us in here! Some rescue!"

Galadriel slapped her tail on the water. "You two need to quit arguing! We don't have time for this. Alaster can easily bring back more mindless mermuscles from Natatoria by morning and we need to come up with a plan."

"I say we fight 'em!" Jax rallied. The sound of a javelin unsheathing from the wall ricocheted around the room.

"Doubt we'd last a minute," I mumbled, remembering Colin's tolerance to my merman sting. We'd need something stronger, like octopus ink, to do any damage to Alaster or whoever came to arrest us. I glared at Galadriel, remembering the taxi incident. "You got anymore ink?"

Jax's face lit up. "No way. You holdin' out on us, Gladdy?"

"No." Galadriel was suddenly interested in untangling the wispy netted strips of her swim dress.

"Girl likes to drug her boys." I lifted my right brow and looked at Jax.

Out of the corner of my eye, I caught Galadriel's shocked face.

"Boys?" Jax asked.

If I didn't know Galadriel was a victim of a mob kissing, I would have told him the truth about the flock of love birds showing up at the beach house, considering what a pain in the dorsal fin she'd been. Her silent pleading stopped me.

"Well, me and Ferd. That stuff gives a hangover—let me tell you. Why did you use it in the taxi anyway?"

Judging from her expression, she'd expected me to tell Jax her secret. "I—I didn't think you'd sing and I'd wanted the taxi driver to take a short cut so I could get to Jax sooner. He must have taken us on the long route instead." She smiled at me in thanks. Considering all we'd been through and the fact she'd saved my life, I'd never reveal her secret. I nodded. "So, no. I don't have any more."

Jax scanned the ceiling line. "We could try the window. It looks a little small but once the light comes in, we can lob Gidget through the window."

"Gidget?" I asked.

"Yeah." He pointed at Ash. "Girl midget."

I held my hand out to Galadriel. "Not any shorter than her."

"True. You wanna crawl out, Gladdy?" Jax waggled his eyebrows.

She pursed her lips. "Well, not as a mermaid, I don't."

"Of course not," He curled her up into his arms. She melted. "How else can I look up your skirt?" He laughed And Galadriel punched him in the shoulder.

I did a double take at the two of them. This was what Galadriel called an ideal mate? Her Mr. Darcy? Jax was totally opposite of what I'd expected she wanted. I did have to hand it to him. He had her wrapped around his fin.

"Well I don't want Ash to try because her hand is still healing," I added before I dove into the pool. I draped my arms around her and kissed her forehead. I couldn't believe she was actually here with me. My heart sped up every time I looked at her, knowing I no longer had to worry since she was now a mer like me.

"How are you doing?" I whispered.

She formed a small nervous smile, avoiding the question. "How are we going to get out?"

"I'm not sure yet."

Jax flipped his fin on the deck as if to work off tension. "Sorry about the hand, Ash. Thought the basswipe was a kiss-and-release kinda reptile, not a complete hammerhead." He shrugged apologetically. "Turns out he wanted to pass her off as Gladdy. They do look identical. The resemblance almost blew my fins right off."

"It's because she's royalty," Galadriel said in a commanding voice.

A hush fell over everyone. Ash watched with wide questioning eyes.

"Royalty?" I asked, incredulous. "How is that even possible? Ash was born and raised in Tahoe. I know her parents. The walls of her house are covered in pictures of her growing up."

Galadriel perched her hands on her hips. "Explaining that is the easy part. What I don't get is how you couldn't smell the Sasquatch earlier."

I shot Galadriel a smirk. "Apparently you couldn't either. Or do you like being dragged around by your hair?"

Ash rubbed her scalp while Galadriel gave me a stern look. "I was upstream looking for Jax, invertebrate, but that doesn't excuse the rest of you."

"Smell? Smell what?" Jax asked. "Does Alaster have sulfurous farts?"

She wrinkled her nose and shook her head in exasperation. "You both must have broken olfactory nares. You should have picked up his stench."

Ash nodded her head. "I smell him."

"See?" Galadriel smiled, finally happy.

"He reeks like rotten fish," Ash added.

I sniffed my nose along the water. All I picked up was the sweet honeysuckle of Ash's skin. "I don't smell anything other than Ash." I squeezed her tighter. She remained stiff, but leaned into me.

"Figures. You're sniff-blind. Happens frequently in merman, but that doesn't matter now. We have to get out of here." She tensed her shoulders.

Confusion remained written on Ash's face. "You still haven't explained how I'm royalty."

Galadriel elevated a brow. "The mark on your hip proves you're my full-blooded sister."

"That's what everyone keeps telling me, but how is that possible?" Ash asked.

"Yeah," Jax chimed in. "I know the Queen has a ton of girls, but she's not in the habit of losing her merlings."

Galadriel took in a deep breath and flipped her fin around so it fell gracefully into the water alongside the pool and paused, collecting her thoughts. "By the time I was eight, my mom had given birth to ten girls, infuriating my father, the prince at the time, because without a son, his father wouldn't let him take over the throne. I'd overheard him threatening Mom he'd take another mate if she didn't give him a boy.

"So when the time of delivery came, I hid and watched our nursemaid deliver another girl. Mom was beside herself and so was I. I thought I'd lose my mother to Bone Island, but the nursemaid took the merling away and Mom shut herself alone in her room. No announcement was made of the birth. A few days later the nursemaid returned. And miraculously, Azor was born."

"You're kidding me," I said, flabbergasted. "And the girl?"

"I think you know the answer to that. It isn't a coincidence that Ash looks like me. And let me guess, today's your birthday, right?"

Ash nodded in astonishment.

"So is Azor's," Galadriel said with a perched brow.

"Could this be true?" Ash's bottom lip quivered as she clasped onto Galadriel's outstretched hand. "Me? A mermaid all along?"

Galadriel pulled Ash into a hug and smoothed her hair. "Yes. I watched your birth."

I scowled, angered over the deception. "Then who are Azor's parents?"

Galadriel's chest heaved. "Most likely Ash's human parents and they were persuaded to accept Ash as their own."

I pounded my fist into the water. "So Azor isn't even royalty. After all this. And the King—"

Galadriel turned up the corner of her lip. "His kingdom is built on lies."

"Does the King even know?"

She shrugged. "I doubt it. My nursemaid disappeared shortly after that. But it was a foolish move, because when the truth comes out, and it will eventually, heaven help them all. My mother can't hide the fact Tatiana will not have the mark of royalty."

The Queen was driven by fear over something she had no control over and this proved there wasn't anything she wouldn't do for her family. I instantly worried for Tatchi's safety as I scrubbed my hand through my hair. My conversation with Galadriel from earlier in the beach house suddenly sunk in. Her desire to promise to Jax had to wait all because of a lie. She actually did have secrets—bigger than I could even imagine.

But it now made sense why Ash had the mark.

"Is this why I swim fast?" Ash asked, breaking the tension. "The school took my blood. I wonder what they'll find."

I pulled her into my arms. "You were still human, then."

Ash looked to me with sadness behind her eyes. "I feel so lost now. What are we going to do?"

I exhaled hard. "First we need to get out of here, after that, we'll take it one step at a time."

A stream of morning light trickled through the window and filtered into the water. I felt myself switch without thinking about it. I quickly pulled out my shorts from my shoulder pack. Ash's face contorted as she looked down at herself. Her fin shifted on its own, too. She wiggled her toes. "It is going to hurt again later, when I switch back?"

"No," I said and kissed her temple.

Jax pulled on his mer-skirt, but Ferdinand stood buck-naked by the bar.

"Do you mind, Ferd?" Galadriel asked and turned her head, but motioned to his groin.

Ferdinand smiled slightly and jumped out to get a towel.

"I don't get how he listens to you." I said.

"It's not all the time." Galadriel looked into Jax's eyes. "Must be a wavelength thing."

"That it is," Jax added. "He got my sorry fin off of Bone Island, and then when I went back to Natatoria to find Gladdy and got locked up, Ferd busted me out and led me here. He's a good kid."

Ferd moved back to the bar and placed the red Solo cups in a line compulsively, like he always needed something to put in order during downtime.

"But, when he came to the beach house the last time, he was practically dead? How the heck did you get out?" I asked Jax.

Jax smirked. "Everyone knows Lake Tahoe is a dead end… and Alaster. He's the worst gatekeeper ever. But when Ferd busted me out of jail and I tried to escape through the Bermuda gate, he made me come to Tahoe, and I had no choice but to follow him. But I'm so glad I did." He hugged on Galadriel tighter.

"No choice?" I asked.

"Dude screams like a girl and drags you wherever he thinks you should go, unless you can get away."

But instead of envisioning Ferd throwing a fit, I thought of Azor's palace next to the prison, and my sister living there.

"Tatiana?" I asked anxiously. "Did you see her?"

"I saw her briefly when the King's guards locked me up, but after that." Jax looked down. "Ferd broke me out through the sharks. He's one wild and crazy merman, I tell ya. Maybe the sharks sense he'll tear them up if they get too close."

"So, now what?" Ash asked nervously. "I don't want to be here if Alaster is coming back."

I noted her anxiety.

"Time to lob a girl through the window," Jax said as he hopped onto the deck. "Who's volunteering?"

"Shut your trap and lift me." Galadriel reached up her arms to him. He hoisted her on his shoulders with ease, but she couldn't reach the window ledge. Even on Ferdinand's shoulders, she wasn't tall enough.

Then suddenly, a deep boom rumbled the house, knocking everyone to the floor. I shook my head, unable to hear for a moment as dust and dirt crackled down on our heads. A net fell from the ceiling, missing my leg.

"What was that?" Jax asked.

Another, louder boom made everyone scurry to the pool.

"Mother of Pearl!" Galadriel yelped. "What is that?"

"Alaster," I growled. "When I get out of here, there's no telling what I'm going to do to that sea serpent, especially if he ruins my house, too. Let's get the weapons."

"Sure thing, boss!" Jax leapt out of the pool.

"Wait!" Ash pointed to the nets strung along the ceiling.

"Good idea." I scanned their position. "If we hide around the room and lure the guards under, I can use Alaster's nets to capture them. And for the others, we can use the javelins."

Jax tossed everyone a javelin except Ash because of her hand. I sang to Colin because he was human now, and told him to stay hidden with Ferdinand. Ash cowered behind me as I crouched down by the hatch within reach of the net-release mechanisms. Ferd and Colin hid by the bar, and Jax and Galadriel ducked behind the stack of loungers. I clapped twice to cut the lights. Tension mounted. I scanned the dark room, my eyes roaming from the door to the hatch, waiting for the ambush. Ash clung to my waist, trembling.

"Are you scared?" I whispered.

"Yes."

"It's okay. I'll get us out. Stick close to me."

"Okay." Though she agreed, something in her voice told me she didn't believe me. The lack of faith stabbed me. I had to gain her trust back and prove I could protect her, once and for all.

Upstairs, something slid against the floor. The door opened.

"It's over, Princess!" Alaster barked, followed by laughter.

Gasoline rushed down the stairs like a waterfall. He lit a match and the stair case ignited in flames.

Ash shrieked.

"Into the pool!" I yelled.

We all dove in and phased into our tails so we could splash the staircase. Eventually, the flames went out, but the doorway and beyond was a ring of fire.

"There's no need to panic," I said, not only to myself, but everyone else as the fear gripped my mind. "The bonefish thinks fire is our kryptonite but he doesn't know about firemen."

"Firemen?" Jax asked, his eyes bulging.

"Men who put fires out—with water." Ash touched Jax's arm gently. "My dad's one. They'll come right away, but we'll still need to avoid the smoke."

"Oh," he said relieved, curiosity piqued, "and they know to come?"

"Yes," Ash said, "on land, we're trained to report fires."

Galadriel snuggled up next to Jax. "They're quite brave, or so I've read. We haven't anything to worry about."

Ash's anxiety didn't lessen, though. It was obvious the fire wasn't her only concern.

"You okay?" I tried to comfort her with my arms.

"Colin's out there in the smoke."

"Oh, right." At this point, Colin was the least of my worries.

Ferdinand swam back and forth, and wrung his hands. If he forgot his towel, he'd be streaking until he found another strip of cloth.

I gave the group my most convincing smile. "If all else fails, Jax and I will persuade the humans. We don't have a choice but to wait it out."

Galadriel gave a wink, oblivious to the danger we faced. She reveled anytime I broke down and resorted to persuasion. This time I felt justified. This is why mermen had the power to begin with—to protect the mers' secret identity.

Knowing my house burned above me, when there was nothing I could do about it, infuriated me—all the memories, our furniture, my life as I knew it, destroyed. By Uncle Alaster of all people. There goes my idea of living here until Ash finished high school. What would we do now?

Sirens finally grew closer. Time for the game plan.

"We'll need to leave as soon as we get out of here. Alaster will most likely have an army for our capture. We'll have to persuade someone to drive us or get our hands on a car. If the whole house doesn't burn down, we've got cash hidden. We'll make a run for the Pacific. It's only a three hour trip."

Sadness filled Ash's eyes as she looked away. I squeezed her hand, accidentally touching her knuckle stumps. She cringed. "I'm sorry."

"It's not your fault," she said softly.

"This isn't how I expected everything to play out."

"We should go home," Galadriel interrupted. She held her shoulders high, regal almost. She took Jax's hand.

"Home, as in Florida?" I asked.

She flapped her lips. "Natatoria, of course."

I raised my right eyebrow. "Really?"

"I can no longer sit back and allow my people to be treated like this. Not only the fraud from switching babies, but kidnapping, unassisted conversions, hijacked promisings, and attempted murder, for what? Royal placement? Absurd. I must see my mother, father, Azor and Alaster are punished for their crimes. As eldest daughter, I will take the throne and tell the truth."

"Become the Queen?" I turned to Galadriel in surprise. "Wow. I didn't think you had it in you."

"After everything, I have no choice."

Ash reached out with her good hand to me and squeezed hard.

"I will do my part as well, for Tatchi and my Queen," she whispered in my ear.

I choked back my emotions. I'd never expected Ash to want to change into a mer, let alone fight our fight, and she didn't even know the half of the history behind the King and my dad. I'd never been more proud of her before this moment.

I drew her into a hug. "I guess we'll be going home, then." I wasn't sure if I should be happy, sad, or worried—but to finally get vengeance for everything Alaster and Azor had done put a smile on my face.

"I'll need help with my parents," Ash said softly in my ear, "oh, and Colin. He'll need a family, too."

She tried to remain brave, but I knew this had to be rough on her.

"Sure—or I can look for some essence upstairs."

Galadriel glared and shook her head. "No."

I creased my forehead.

"He's lucky to be alive. We'll leave it at that."

I lifted my hand. "Whatever you say, Queen."

Keeping Colin human was a better idea anyway, quiet and docile. And who knew how he'd react once he had fins again. We didn't need a merman with amnesia tagging along, especially when we stormed the castle. With a little persuasion, the Lanskis would take him in, no problem.

"Is that all?" I asked.

"I think so." Ash forced a smile.

"This is mighty brave of you," I said. "Are you sure you're ready for this?"

"No," she said, fear behind her voice. "But I want to be with you."

"The Lanskis will always be your family." I squeezed her hand.

"I know." She squeezed back.

I popped my head above the water and took in a whiff of smoke by accident. Colin had put the towel up to his nose, but was coughing just the same. Ferdinand leapt to his feet. He grabbed Colin, threw him over his shoulder like a sack of potatoes, and charged up the stairs through the burning doorway.

"No, Ferd!" Jax yelled and jumped up onto the deck.

The smoke poured through the open door like a chimney as we joined Jax on the deck, covering our noses with our hands.

"Now what?" Ash shrieked, clinging to my arm. "Do we run for it?"

Fire rimmed the door jam like a flaming hoop of death. Just watching the flames made me ache for water as badly as when Alaster chained me to the wall and left me to dry.

Masked aliens in yellow appeared. Stuck in mer survival mode, my brain took a second to register they were firemen. They charged down and hoisted Galadriel and Jax over their shoulders. I moved out of the way for them to take Ash first. She fought and cried for me as she disappeared out of sight.

I wanted to follow, but the smoke coated my lungs and the fire licked the walls. I contemplated waiting in the water when my head began to pound and sleepiness took over. I slumped down, content to close my eyes, if only for a second.

41

≋

ASH

Friday morning, April 22nd

"No!" I stretched my fingers for Fin as he disappeared into the billowy blackness below. The masked man carrying me muffled my name. I peered beyond the glass and found blue eyes—my father's.

"Dad," I said as sleepiness took over. "Fin's in there, too. We can't leave him behind."

He nodded and everything went dark.

When I opened my eyes again, a woman in a navy blue paramedic uniform was placing an oxygen mask over my nose and tending to my burns.

"Ashlyn, Thank God you're all right." Dad knelt before me. A tear had made a clean trail through the soot on the side of his cheek. "Who else is in the basement?"

"Fin," I squeaked out.

"Anyone else?"

On my left, Jax and Galadriel sat with paramedics fussing over them. Ferdinand and Colin weren't anywhere. Did they get out? I shook my head.

Dad clenched his jaw. "How did the fire start?"

"We were in the basement, and there was an explosion. We were trapped." I reached up and hugged his neck. "Dad, they have to get Fin out."

"They're inside looking for him right now." He smoothed back my hair and held me close. "I'm so lucky. I almost lost my little girl."

I wiped my cheek with my good hand and hid the other within

the folds of a blanket someone had wrapped around me. Seeing my mutilated hand would freak him out more. I huddled up, though I wasn't cold. Oddly, the early morning breeze didn't chill me like it usually did.

Jax and Galadriel were anxiously watching like me, waiting for someone to pull Fin from the flames. A crash on the right hand side of the house shattered my nerves, and I gaped in horror as part of the walls crumbled inward. Finally, two bundles of black ran through the smoke pouring from the front door—empty handed.

I gasped and tried to stand. "Fin?"

Dad held me tight. "Stay still, honey. Your burns need tending."

Burns? Didn't he see I'd miraculously healed? All the paramedic did was swab dirt off perfectly pink skin. I wiggled to free myself. Fin was still down there.

With my new super-sonic hearing, I picked up bits of conversation between the firemen. They'd gone back inside for the last person and weren't able to find him. Dad put his arm on my shoulder and squeezed.

"But he can't be missing." I pried myself away from Dad's grasp and jumped up, taking off the oxygen mask. "Galadriel! Jax! Do something!"

Jax stood and spoke in Natatorian. "What do I say?"

"Just tell them to keep looking, to find Fin! He's still down there."

At that moment, there was a boom, and the house collapsed and sank in on itself. A huge plume of smoke floated into the early morning sky. I shrieked in horror. "Oh dear God. No!"

Galadriel appeared at my side. She tucked me under her shoulder and stroked my hair. We cried and hugged one another as the flames victoriously devoured the broken remains of Fin's human home. Though the scene looked bad, my heart told me Fin was still alive.

"He's not gone, Galadriel. He can't be."

"I know. It's hard to believe," she said through sobs.

"No," I swiveled and stared into her eyes. "He's alive. I feel him here." I tapped my finger over my heart.

"Really?" Hope washed over her face. "Then how did he get out?"

We looked at the water and spoke in unison. "Alaster."

"I'm on it," Galadriel said as she motioned to Jax.

Jax sang a quick song to tell everyone they were never there as they ran to the water. I started to shrug off the blanket in an attempt to follow when I heard Mom's voice.

"Ashlyn!" she yelled. "Let me through. That's my daughter! William, is Ashlyn there? Is she okay?" Mom muscled her way through the police line and charged over to us. "Are you all right?" Her eyes fell on me in relief. "What happened?"

"Mom." I dipped my head and pulled the blanket up around my shoulders to hide my torn dress. "It's okay. I'm safe. Fin came home last night and... there was an accident."

Her expression morphed from fear to anger. "What do you mean an accident? Ashlyn Frances, you could have died. The house is destroyed. What kind of accident would do this?"

"Karen," Dad said sharply. "Stop! Fin didn't make it out, so…."

Mom blinked, then turned to me. Tears welled in her eyes. "Oh, honey. I'm so sorry."

She enveloped me with her arms and I melted into them. She'd loved me even when I wasn't the boy she'd expected to give birth to, and though our relationship was often disjointed, I wanted her as my real mom more than anything. I sobbed harder. My human life and my family were no longer mine. All of it was a lie and if Fin didn't survive, where would I belong?

"Mom," I breathed in desperation. Fin had to be alive somewhere.

She took my face between her hands. "Where's Colin?"

My brain scrambled for an excuse. Where was he?

"Right here, Mrs. Lanski," he said from behind us.

I turned in shock as he walked up—grimy and gritty. A bloody beach towel circled his waist. He gave me a divided look of understanding and confusion.

"Oh, my dear boy," she exclaimed and hugged him hard around the neck. "What happened? You're bleeding!"

"I'm not. It's only on the towel," Colin said flatly. "Ash, where's my dad?"

"Oh, no! Is he inside as well?" Mom shrieked.

I stared at Colin in astonishment. Did he not remember what happened in the basement?

Colin took Mom's hand. "It's going to be okay, Mrs. Lanski," He sang. "Why don't you go home? And Mr. Lanski, you go ahead and finish up fighting the fire. We can handle things here."

I almost fell over. As a human, he knew how to mer-sing. And like robots, Mom and Dad hugged us both one last time and then followed their persuaded assignments.

"No," I whispered. "How?"

Colin gave a questioning glance. "How what?"

"You're singing."

"Of course I sing. You've heard it lots of times."

"But you converted? How did you convert back?"

"Huh? I didn't convert." Colin wrinkled up his face. "All I remember is being stabbed and then I woke up on the dock." He rubbed the pink scar on his side. "Where is my father by the way?" Hate filled his eyes.

"You converted and had legs in the basement. We were all locked inside and your Dad started the fire, tried to burn us alive… or bury us. Take your pick. You don't remember any of that?"

Colin's eyes narrowed. "I only remember being stabbed."

"Um," I looked away. "Ferdinand must have changed you back.

He's full of surprises."

"Ferdinand?"

"He showed up after you converted. He must have had some essence on him."

"Well, then where's Fin and the Princess?"

Lightning bolts of panic shot into my veins. We were wasting time. "I don't know where Fin is. Galadriel and Jax went in the lake to get him, but she's not back yet—" I was torn. Should I leave and find Fin now? What if he was in Natatoria already? I couldn't leave my parents without an explanation of where I'd gone. "I need to find him."

"Jax? Who's Jax?"

"Ash!" Georgia ran down the small hill with Callahan on her heels. Darkness crossed Callahan's face and his hands formed into fists. His strides lengthened.

Crap.

"You better mind mojo him if you don't want another black eye," I said quickly.

"Why you son of a—," Callahan said through his teeth.

"I mean Ash no harm. I'm her friend. Forget what you saw on the beach," Colin sang.

Callahan blinked and shook his head. He looked off to the side, then his eyes found me, in concern. "Ash, what happened? Are you okay?"

I inhaled deeply in relief. "There was an accident." I looked to Colin for support.

"Yeah," Colin said. "We're lucky to be alive. Ash saved my life."

I chuckled and creased my forehead. "I did no such thing. Don't listen to him."

Georgia took my shoulders in her hands and shook. "Your Mom called our house frantic at 6 this morning looking for you and then

Callahan had your phone for some reason and finally answered it. After the prank at the club, you disappeared. Where did you go last night?"

I opened my mouth as visions of Alaster almost drowning Callahan came back to me. Only air whooshed out. So much had happened.

"Ash came to our house after Callahan dropped her off. Don't you remember Cal?" Colin asked, ticking his head to the side.

Callahan flustered under Georgia's hot stare. He wouldn't remember after Alaster mind mojo'd him.

"Uh, yeah... I dropped her off," he said. "And here's your phone back, Ash."

Georgia hit him in the arm. "Why didn't you tell me that?"

"Sorry." Callahan held up his hands. "The night's a little fuzzy."

Thirty missed calls highlighted the screen, mostly all from Georgia and Mom. There were two from Fin's old number—Fin's Dad—and a message from him. My heart sprung into a gallop. What did Fin's dad want?

Georgia let out a frantic huff then flung her arms around my neck. "This is so crazy. I'm so happy you're alive. I was freaking out."

"I'm okay."

She cried on my shoulder, but all I could think about was Fin. Was he okay? Had Galadriel and Jax found him already? What about Alaster?

"We should be going now." Colin's hand found mine and he squeezed.

"Go?" Callahan's jaw tightened in jealousy. Colin would need to mer mojo that away for me and I couldn't disappear to Natatoria on Georgia without an explanation, like Tatiana had done.

"Yeah." I closed my eyes briefly. "Colin, please tell them I'm going on a trip to... Africa. A mission trip and I won't be home for a while and I'm postponing college and the Olympics."

"What?" Georgia's tone was livid. "No way! What mission trip? Since when—"

At the musical sound of his words, Georgia and Callahan's eyes glazed over. I hated every second of it.

"And tell Callahan to take good care of Jaime. She's a good catch."

Colin creased his brow, but told him anyway. Before I knew it, Georgia and Callahan were hugging me good-bye and wishing me luck. The magic mer-eraser had wiped away two of my friends from me and neither were the wiser. My stomach gave a hot pinch. I wanted to throw up.

"My family—" I breathed out. "I can't leave without explaining."

"Let's do it," he said. "But we have to hurry."

I looked up at Colin as he tipped his head toward the house.

Panic swelled in my heart. "Just go tell them I'll be back later and that I'm okay. I have to find Fin."

I ran for the lake instead.

42

FIN

Friday morning, April 22nd

I awoke to my body whipping in the current as something dragged me by my bound wrists. I fanned out my fins to stop.

"You refuse to die, pretty boy." Alaster chuckled darkly and yanked my body harder. "You're a catfish with your nine lives."

"Where are you taking me?" I muttered through the thick coat of smoky grime in my throat.

"I've changed my mind. You're better to me alive than dead. There's a reward for anyone who brings you in and someone has to pay for Colin's death." He laughed evilly. "You'll make great bait for that tasty lass of yours, if she survived, and for Jack. Finally, my brother will get what he deserves and the King will have to reward me with a princess after all this—your princess I'm hoping."

"Never!" I gritted my teeth and with a quick yank, I pulled myself free from his grasp.

I inhaled the fresh snowy water, gaining strength. We faced off for a moment in the current. Faster than I could dodge, he whipped his tail around and sliced me in the side. My vision clouded as my muscles involuntarily relaxed from his poison.

"You're still susceptible? Incredible!" He sneered as he reached for the rope strung between my wrists. "I bet you Jack never shared that you could build up immunity. My brother, the pacifist."

I swam backward and shook my head. There was a way to gain immunity to the poison? What was he talking about?

But I had the advantage. He didn't know Colin survived. If I couldn't fight Alaster now, maybe that would be my way out of this. Galadriel could switch Colin back and free me from prison with the truth. But was Ash okay? Did they survive the fire? "You'll never win."

"Really?" He sanded his hands together. "It's your word against mine and I think they'll believe me over a criminal."

His tail whacked me again. The pinch from his poisonous barb made me yelp. I drifted sideways in the current unable to stay upright. "Why are you doing this? You're my uncle."

"Why?" Alaster threw his head back and laughed. "Maybe you should ask your dad and his beta-wench. My brother: the golden child, the smarter one, the braver one, the one who could do no wrong. Even the late King Merric wished your dad were his own son. No one ever gave me a chance to shine."

Jealousy and favoritism fueled his vitriol. My energy slipped. I worked to keep my eyes open, but just wanted to sleep. He'd take me into Natatoria and I'd have to await rescue. At least I'd see my sister. I had to hope Galadriel would care for Ash.

"And your little lass… she tasted sweet like honeysuckle," he said in my ear. "I can't wait to make her mine fully. She'll give me another boy."

Rage sizzled down my scales. I arched my back, swiveled my body, and looped the rope around Alaster's neck. "What did you say?"

"Finley," he choked, gripping the rope with his hands. "I can't breathe."

"Did you kiss Ash? Tell me!"

"I thought you were dead. I couldn't help myself. Please—"

I pulled tighter. Alaster thrashed around but his tail couldn't reach me. "You don't deserve to live, Uncle. And if Ash or anyone dies because of you—"

Alaster gagged.

"Fin! Stop!" Galadriel swam up with Jax behind her.

"I have to end it," I said venomously. "He kissed Ash and chopped off her fingers."

"No!" She held up her hands. "Not like this. You'll be no better than him. He needs to deal with his demons on Bone Island where the dead will torment him until he reaches Hades. They deserve the right to usher him from life unto death. Stop! I command you!"

"I don't want to take the chance he'll escape," I said through my teeth, giving Jax an evil eye.

Alaster's body went limp beneath me.

"Not like this." Galadriel caressed my arm. "Let go, Fin. Let's do things the right way, starting now."

I loosened my grip. Alaster floated away from me in the current, his tongue out of his mouth but his gills were moving.

"That's good, Fin," she said. "Jax, restrain Alaster."

Her tiny fingers worked to untie the ropes around my wrists.

"He'll be under Jax's guard the entire time," she said softly, "and he won't let him out of his sight."

Jax puffed out his chest. "Yup."

Ferdinand appeared beside Jax, handing him an extra rope.

"And Ferd, too." She smiled.

"Dude," Jax said. "This slippery fish ain't goin' nowhere. Right, Ferd?"

Ferd looked off to the side as he normally did.

"You have to go, Fin." Galadriel's face grew abruptly serious. "Ash is worried sick about you."

Ash. I turned and pumped my tail hard. The lake would once again have another tidal wave incident, but I didn't care.

All her silent distress in the pool clicked. She worried how I'd react to the kiss.

I needed to see my ginger girl and tell her I knew and that it didn't matter. I loved her and our love could heal anything.

43

ﾟ☙

ASH

Friday morning, April 22nd

My fin sprouted from my hips easily as I dove into the lake. Galadriel and Jax's scents were fresh in the water, but Fin's wasn't anywhere to be found. They would have returned with Fin if they'd found him, so instead of following their trail, I darted over to the tunnel instead. Clean musk that I knew to be Fin's infused the water along with stinky fish smell: Alaster. The bassface went in for Fin after we were rescued by the firemen and they'd recently left the basement together. Was Fin okay? I wanted to rip Alaster's jugular from his throat and chop off his fingers.

My pulse thrummed as I sped along. I knew in my heart Fin was alive, but what did Alaster plan to do with him? What did he tell him? Were they in Natatoria already? Was Alaster taking him before the King? Going to Natatoria alone freaked me out, but I had to find Fin.

I wove past a large school of trout and veered to the left to follow the trail. The scents swirled and faded in the current, abruptly ending.

"Fin!" I called. "Are you here? Fin!"

Scared, the fish darted away, disturbing the water even more.

I returned to the spot where the scents were the strongest and swam in a circle, trying to pick up the trail. Everywhere I swam, the scent ended.

"Fin!" I cried. "Please…"

Knowing most likely they'd end up by the gateway, I swam down into the inky depths and entered the cave, terrified I'd find Alaster instead of Fin. The eerie blue light bounced against the water and created moving shadows along the walls, unnerving me. I froze in terror, remembering all that happened here.

"Fin," I whispered in desperation. "Where are you?"

I sat in the spot where Alaster kissed me and looped my arms around my fin. They'd eventually come this way, so staying here might as well be where I waited. But this place haunted me, the burial ground of my severed fingers. Below me, something in the water sparkled. I swam down and found my pinkie and ring finger stuck between the rocks. I surfaced and held the appendages in my palm. They were pink, as if they were still alive.

Then the pinkie twitched. I shriek and flipped my hand. The fingers snapped onto my raw wounds like magnets.

A slow itch tingled over my skin. I didn't move my hand at first, afraid the fingers would snap off. Involuntarily, they flexed. I touched the fingertips to my thumb. They had feeling. Beyond a tiny hairline scar, the fingers magically reattached themselves. I formed my hand into a fist and squeezed. Good as new.

The water undulated around me. A head of white hair swam up from the cave entrance below the water. Alaster. I screamed. My nightmare was about to relive itself.

Fin popped out of the water. "Ash! It's me."

"Oh, Fin." My body heaved but I couldn't move from the rock.

He spanned the distance between us and took my cheeks between his hands. He kissed me, hot and urgent. I melted into him, hugging him hard. He was alive and okay.

But then I pushed away. He had to know the truth.

"Stop," I said. "You can't. I've… Alaster…"

"Shhh," Fin put his finger to my lips, "I know already."

I blinked in disbelief. "You do? How?"

"He told me." A sliver of darkness slid over his eyes.

Ashamed, I turned my face away from him. "Don't look at me. I'm disgusting."

Fin enfolded me in his arms and pressed his body against mine. "Why would you say that?"

"Because, for you, for the mers, kissing is like…"

He caressed my cheek, inviting me to look at him. "Without the promise, it's just kissing."

"But still." I forced my face downward.

"He's the filthy animal, not you. I love you." He tilted my chin upward with his finger, holding me there. "My uncle broke the law. He violated you. For that you shouldn't be ashamed."

I wanted to believe him, but I couldn't. Nothing changed the fact that it happened.

Fin's eyes narrowed. "My uncle can burn my home, try to kill me, take everything I own, but as long as I'm living, he can't have you—actually, even in my death, he still can't have you."

"But I thought the promise bonded people, regardless of feelings, and they released when one died?"

A coy smile curved his lips. "The promise is just a way of survival for my people. My uncle is a prime example of how the promise isn't a magic wand for love. He's never been happy, even with my late Aunt Grace. You would have never guessed they were bonded. All he cared about was Colin's happiness. Look how quickly that changed. I'm starting to understand the secret. The happiest mer couples are the ones who loved each other first. The promise enhances that relationship; otherwise it could eventually become a nuisance. I loved you before your accident with the boat on the lake."

I sniffled. "So, you still want me?"

Fin rested his forehead against mine. "Of course I want you," he whispered as he wrapped his hands around my jaw. "I'm connected, heart, mind, and soul to you. Please know that."

He ran his hands down my sides and found my hands. Surprise lit his face as he felt over my newly attached fingers. "What?"

I smiled. "They reattached."

"Wow." he blinked in amazement and kissed each one. My scar tingled. "Now, my ginger girl, will you please come with me to Natatoria?"

I didn't respond, my heart ping-ponging around in my ribcage. Though Fin wanted me, I wasn't so sure Natatoria was the place for me anymore. What would my family think? My friends? Everyone?

"Ash, are you okay?"

"No." I looked down, ashamed. "This isn't at all how I wanted it to turn out—when I converted."

He wrapped me up in his arms. "I know and you don't know how sorry I am about that."

"Maybe leaving isn't such a good idea."

Fin pulled away. The corners of his lips turned down. "Why?"

"Well, I mean—school is going to ask questions, my coach, and my friends and family. Colin has told everyone I'm leaving on a mission trip to Africa. They're all going to see through that. It's absurd."

"Colin?"

I swallowed hard. "Ferdinand switched him back into a mer."

"Oh." His eyes tapered as he looked away. "So, are you suggesting we stay here in Tahoe?"

My eyes closed and I took a deep breath. "Or, you could change me back. Just for a while. So I can finish up school."

With a groan he pushed his hand through his hair. "There's something I've been meaning to tell you."

I blinked up at him in concern.

His countenance dropped. "If I change you back into a human, you'll lose your memory."

"What do you mean? You said I could keep my memories."

"Until recently, no one ever explained specifically what happened to one's memories after a conversion."

"What?" I stiffened my shoulders.

"Colin's a prime example. Did you think I made him forget everything after he accidentally converted in the basement?"

"But he remembered later. After he became a merman again, he remembered up until that point."

Fin's face fell in shock. "He what?"

"All he forgot was the time he was human. If you convert me, I'll forget the kiss. I'll only remember up to when Alaster fed me the essence. Then I could finish out high school and we could then talk about when it would be a good time for me to become a mermaid. Plan it better."

"But, Ash…" He moved away from me.

"And you'd be free from the bond so it's not so overwhelming."

"Why are you saying this? Is it because Alaster kissed you?"

"No. Yes. I don't know."

How could he still love me after everything? I didn't want to remember the kiss anymore.

He took me in his arms. "Ash, I don't know where all of this is coming from. But I don't want to take that chance with your memories, not to mention I can't live in a world where I'm not with you. You're my everything and the thought of losing you kills me. I know this is scary and that going to Natatoria won't be easy, but I'll be there. And once we rescue Tatiana and set the kingdom straight, we'll come back and rebuild the house. I want to marry you on our beach in front of God and everyone, under the evergreens. Don't you understand the depths of my love for you?"

I blinked back at him as my lip trembled.

"Please, Ash. Please don't do this to me, to us."

"You'll bring me home to Tahoe?"

"Of course I will. Nothing has to change. I don't want to go to Natatoria without you with me."

His lips came crashing to mine, hard and wanting. I wrapped my hands around his neck and tangled them in his hair. He still desired me, even after everything. Our kiss, hot and delicious, zinged an electric trail down my body to my fin. Joyful tears sprang from my eyes. He loved me and was my life now, and all I wanted was him—forever—on land or water.

44

❧

FIN

Friday morning, April 22nd

As Ash and I swam hand-in-hand to her house, I grew angrier by the second. I'd almost lost my girl again over stupid technicalities of the conversion. Did no one know the truth of what happened to the memories pre and post conversion? Sissy and Hans of all people should, considering they'd converted people all the time. I understood the subject was taboo, but after what I'd experienced, Natatorians needed to talk about it. Everyone needed to know the dangers. When I saw my parents again, they were going to get an earful. Hopefully, Galadriel would change Natatorian customs once she took over, for this and for prearranged promisings.

We emerged, hopped onto the dock, and silently walked the short distance as if it were a gangplank to our death. Ash's newly adhered fingers gripped mine hard as we embarked on the hardest part of our journey. The good-bye. I'd look her father in the eye and tell him I was taking his little girl. I gulped down my nerves. This was completely opposite of my original plan. I'd wanted to ask for Ash's hand without persuasion. But now… we didn't have a choice.

"So, Colin's inside?" I asked to try to distract her.

"Yes."

"And he remembers everything?"

"He seems to, yes."

I sucked in a deep breath, annoyed. I wasn't ready to forgive him for what he'd done. Galadriel wasn't going to be pleased either.

"Oh… I almost completely forgot." From within the folds of the dress that barely covered her body, she produced a waterlogged phone. "Crap."

I chuckled. "You, too?"

She frowned. "Your dad had called earlier and left a message."

"My dad?"

"Yeah." She tapped the phone against her palm. Water dripped out of the sides. "He called after you'd left. I—I thought it was you."

"Oh, right." I exhaled hard. That was lifetimes ago. "What did he say?"

"I didn't have a chance to listen to it before—you know." She shrugged and put the phone back in her pocket. "He must be pretty worried."

I glanced over at the house—all his work up in smoke. There was a lot more to be worried about than just me. "Yeah. I bet he is."

"Why didn't you tell him?"

"He left to go out of town. There wasn't time to explain."

"You can call him in the house, if you want."

"That's a good idea." I gripped her hand tighter. We'd fight one battle at a time.

Ash wrung the extra water from her skirt before we entered the house.

"Ashlyn," Mom said, leaping to her feet. "Where were you— you're all wet? And—what are you wearing?"

"I'm sorry, Mom," Ash walked forward, dripping on the carpet.

I sang for everyone to ignore Ash's attire. Her mom sat back down. Ash ran and grabbed a towel before she joined her mom on the couch. Colin sat on the other side of the sectional, next to Ash's grandma with a smug smile as if he were family. He wore a Lake Tahoe Fire T-shirt and a pair of tan shorts—probably Ash's Dad's.

I glared. "I can take over from here, Cousin."

"Fin," Colin said with a sneer, "nice to see you. I thought you'd bring my princess with you. Where's Galadriel?"

I smirked and shook my head. "Your princess is with Jax, her promised mate. They have your father in custody in the lake. You're welcome to join them. I'm sure Galadriel would love to see you."

"What?" Colin's face fell and I almost laughed at his disappointment. He let out a huff. "Well, that's just great."

Mrs. Lanski's shoulders stiffened. "In the lake? What are you talking about, Fin? What princess? I don't understand, Ash. None of this makes sense." Her volume increased. "You're not finished with school yet. Or swimming. And why are the two of you all wet?"

Ash began to sniffle And my heart broke for her.

I closed my eyes and sang to the family—that I'd take good care of Ash, and her mission in Africa was needed more than they could ever know. I told them not to worry and that we'd be back soon.

Both of the Lanski women's faces softened.

"I'm proud of you, dear." Gran reached over to pat Ash's hand. "To give up your dreams to help others. You be safe, honey."

Ash rolled her eyes and puckered her lip as I walked over and sat next to her.

"This is silly," she whispered. "I don't like this story."

"But it's sort of the truth. You are going on a mission to save Tatchi and the Natatorians."

"Yeah, but not in Africa." She looked off to the side and frowned. "People are going to think my parents are whacked. Who runs off and saves tribes when you're an Olympic hopeful?"

Mrs. Lanski rubbed Ash's knee. "We're so proud of you."

Ash huffed and leaned her head against the back of the couch. "There's nothing to be proud of, Mom."

"If there's something else you'd like me to tell them, I'll tell them whatever you want," I said.

Ash closed her eyes. "Just—just tell them not to worry. That I'm with you and I'll be back soon."

I did again, just to pacify her, but Ash looked pained the entire time.

"Should we wait for your dad?" I asked.

"I don't know." She buried her naked toes into the carpet while her arms stayed firmly tucked across her chest.

The silence grew unbearable.

Colin jumped up and started to pace. "Are we done? I want to see Dad," he said with a growl.

"You're free to go." I pointed to the door.

He leaned against the wall and sighed. "Believe it or not, I do care about this family."

"Whatever." I looked at the clock—just past 10 AM. "Ash, do you think it would be okay if I called now? While we're waiting?"

"Sure. And I need to get one thing from upstairs," Ash said and popped off the couch.

I gave her a quick smile before heading into the kitchen. Emptiness filled her patronizing grin. I wondered if we were doing the right thing. Was I forcing her to go with me? Should I allow her to convert back and stay here?

I picked up the phone and dialed my old cell number. "Dad?"

"Finley Helton!" Dad barked in my ear. "What is going on? Where are you?"

I closed my eyes and held my breath for a moment. This explanation would take patience—for the both of us.

"In California," I said. "It's been quite a journey."

After I explained Ash and Azor's switch at birth, Galadriel's changed demeanor, my uncle's involvement, Colin's conversion and return to the mer, and the status of the house, the phone line went silent.

"Dad? You there?"

"I'm here—just processing," he said, worry oozing from his voice.

"What happened in Scotland?"

"It's bad, Fin. No one will admit who's in my secret army, so the King's putting pressure on everyone. The betas have been locked up, or given bracelets to keep them in Natatoria. And no one is allowed out. There are armed men at every gate. I told Dorian we weren't ready to go in yet, but with Galadriel's willingness to overtake her kingdom and the proof that Azor isn't the King's son—that changes everything. Is it true no one is guarding Tahoe?"

"Jax was able to get through no problem."

"Good. I want you to at least make it into Natatoria okay. Does Galadriel realize it's going to be a bloodbath? Is everyone up for that?"

I thought of Galadriel's small band of warriors. Everyone was fired up, but Ash. This wasn't how I should take her into my city. Could I still protect her if an uprising did get too violent? Could we alone overtake the kingdom? I hadn't considered the culture shock for Ash. Were we rushing things? But I couldn't let this opportunity go. Now was our chance—for Tatiana, for our people—to make big changes in the way mers did things. To provide freedom.

I took a deep breath. "After what happened here today, I think so. It would be nice for once to be on the offensive, not the defensive like last time."

"Alright, Son. I'll trust your judgment," Dad said. "So, you're leaving today?"

"Yeah, as soon as I finish persuading an excuse to Ash's family, we'll   leave."

"Hmmm…" Dad grunted. "Are you sure Ash will be up for this?"

"I can't leave her here—what if something happens?"

He exhaled hard. "If you say so. We'll have to meet in the middle, though. Badger's locked up, so—"

"What?"

"He's a beta-mer, remember? We'll get them all out. And we've got a surprise as well. Sissy and Hans are bringing in the Lost Ones."

"Lost Ones?"

"The mers Sissy and Hans have rescued from Bone Island—the condemned."

My voice stalled in my throat. How many mers had they rescued? And where were they all this time?

"And there's another thing too," Dad said, his voice breaking up. "There's another way to break the bond, without—los—fin—or—die."

"What? What is it?"

"Fin?—" the phone crackled and went dead.

"Dad?" I redialed, but only got the voicemail.

I leaned my hand against the counter to catch my breath. There's another way to break the bond we didn't know about. Tatiana could be saved earlier than expected.

I couldn't believe it. I had to tell Ash.

45

༄

ASH

Friday morning, April 22nd

I sprinted upstairs. With everything we were doing to my family's memories, I needed space. My reflection in the bathroom mirror stopped me. With my stringy hair sticking out from my head in a spastic wild fire and Georgia's stretched-out black dress poorly covering my body, I resembled a piece of lit dynamite. I grabbed a hairbrush and tamed my mane the best I could with a ponytail holder and brushed my teeth.

In my room, I stripped off the dirty dress. A black band from my underwear circled my waist—remnants from when my mertail formed the first time. I stripped that off too, and kicked the heap under my bed.

I wasn't sure what to wear. All my suits were one-piece team-suits and I didn't own anything remotely functional like the fancy glittery tops Galadriel wore. A pink tank-top dress caught my eye. Though it would be ruined by the end of the day from the water, I put it on anyway. Maybe Galadriel could lend me something in Natatoria. The air up my skirt felt a little too free, so I put on a pair of underwear.

I rummaged through my jewelry box and slid the ruby ring on my newly reattached finger. Sunlight caught the stone just right, sending a spray of cinnamon light across the ceiling of my room—my human room. I thought I'd cry or be sad, but everything felt surreal. My new reality hit hard—I'd no longer sleep on a bed, take showers, use electronics, or maybe brush my teeth. Life in the water would drastically alter everything. Was leaving the right thing to do?

"What? No suitcase?" Lucy stood in the middle of the hall, hands on her hips.

My insides jumped. "Oh, hi, Lucy."

"Fin said you're leaving with him. Why aren't you bringing anything?"

I shifted my weight between my feet, unsure what to say. "I'm going to get new clothes when I get there."

"In Africa?"

"Customs is really picky."

She folded her arms. "What about school?"

"I'm dropping out."

She sneered. "Seriously? And swimming, I suppose you're quitting that, too?"

My stomach pinched. I hated that I was giving up my one chance at the Olympics. "I know it doesn't make sense—"

"Is this a joke? Is someone going to jump out and say I'm punked, 'cause I don't believe it."

"It's not a joke." I reached out and tried to touch her shoulder.

Lucy jumped back, revolted, and ran down the stairs. "Don't touch me. This is too weird—"

The musical Natatorian notes started before I reached the bottom of the stairs. Lucy's eyes glazed over. She plopped on the couch next to Mom and Gran. An empty dismalness slid over me as my comatose family zoned out like zombies.

Fin watched me anxiously.

My eyes welled with tears. I bit my lip to stop them. "I was trying to say good-bye."

"I know. They'll be okay."

Really? Okay? Anyone who knew us would label my parents irresponsible for letting me quit school and leave with such a vague destination as Africa with some guy they barely knew. I needed my family to react, to protect me, to care, not to be manipulated so I could sneak away and marry at the young age of eighteen.

I gulped down my hesitation. Back when I had a choice about my change, I appreciated that I could decide if and when it would happen. I'd certainly wanted a less dramatic exit, perhaps even with my parents not being hypnotized. Like what Fin's parents had done—the distancing of myself from human life, so when the time came the switch was easy.

"This isn't at all how I imagined things to go."

He walked to me and stood face to face. "I know it's hard."

"How could you possibly know?" Leaving didn't feel like such a good idea anymore. School would ask questions, my coach, and my friends. Lots of questions. What if someone investigated? What if I became a missing person case in the news? But if I stayed, I wouldn't be with Fin, either. I lose either way.

I looked down and played with my ring, ashamed at my disloyalty.

He took my hand. "Let's talk outside."

I let him drag me to the porch. Before I knew it, he'd dropped down to one knee and cupped my hand in his.

"Ash, I swear on my life that I love you with all that I am and will be yours for the rest of our lives and will die to protect you if you'll have me, but I have to be honest with you. Yes, if it's in my power to bring you back here to live, I will, but that might not happen. When we go to Natatoria, there will most likely be a vicious war in opposition of our rescue of Tatiana. You're probably going to have to confront your real parents. We'll probably fight our way in and out. People we love might die, and if Galadriel isn't successful in taking over the kingdom, we'll have to run. We could be taken as prisoners. We could be separated. One of us could lose their life. There's so much I don't know, but even with all that uncertainty, I want you with me. But I won't make you go if you don't want to.

"I respect the fact that you were forced to drink the essence and by converting back to humanity, you'd forget what Alaster did to you. But what happened, happened, and if you're ever mer again, you'll remember.

"But you can't deny that you aren't mer by staying human. You swim because you are meant to live in the water. You were born a princess and your people need you. You can run away and hide, but you'll always be mer. But my biggest fear is if you choose to stay, you'll want to move on with your human life and I won't be able to support you because I can't be a part of it. And though it kills me, you'll most likely meet someone else. But I won't force you to come with me. You've had too many people do that to you already.

"So, if you find it within your heart that you truly love me and want to spend the rest of your life with me, then let's go to Natatoria together and rescue Tatchi. If not, then tell me so we can start your conversion. But I need to know and I need to know now."

My entire body trembled at his confession. With every word he spoke, I knew in my heart that he was right, but I fought it. I was afraid—of what people at home would think and of the unknown, but mostly of losing him.

But written upon his stunning face was a love so beautiful and vulnerable, I couldn't let him go. Fear couldn't control my destiny any longer.

"I believe you," I whispered as I lowered myself to the ground. "And I'm so sorry for not being completely honest with you." The tears trickled from my eyes. "I was afraid—" Then the truth came to me. "Afraid the promising bond was the only thing holding us together, that if something happened, I'd lose you." I hugged tightly onto Fin. "And I didn't want to trap you either."

His arms squeezed tightly around me. "Never, Ash. I'll always love you."

He lifted my chin and kissed me deeply. His tongue, warm and soft, sent an earthquake to the depths of my soul and a profound peace settled in its place. We were meant for each other. He was designed for me. Together there wasn't any battle we couldn't face as long as we were together. I never wanted to be apart, and most definitely didn't want to take the chance of losing him by switching back.

"And I love you."

"Good," Galadriel said somberly from the lawn below the porch. "Because if you didn't, I'd be losing the one sister I actually liked."

Fin and I stood up together, startled. "Galadriel?" Fin asked. "How long have you been standing there?"

"Long enough." She let out a small chuckle filled with relief. "So, Ash, if you're deciding to come with us, this is for you." Galadriel lifted up a pastel colored garment in her hands. "I had an extra. Sorry it's wet."

The beaded blue wisps of tulle from the skirt blew gently in the wind, catching the light and sparkling in the sun, magnificent and regal.

"It's beautiful," I said breathless as I leaned over the railing and took the garment. We'd be twins.

"Then let's get going." Galadriel laid eyes on Colin who joined us on the porch.

"I'm coming, too," Colin said. "I need to have words with my father."

"What? Don't tell me." Galadriel put her hands on her hips.

Colin gave her a sassy smirk. "I guess I need to thank some guy named Ferdinand."

She rolled her eyes. "Come on, Colin. I could always use another lug in my life."

Colin laughed and joined her by her side. "Is that a good thing?"

She sighed, "I guess."

He followed behind her as they walked the dock. Galadriel dove in first and I looked away when Colin began to strip off my father's borrowed clothing.

"Ash," Dad called out. I spun around. He walked up to the house in his fireman overalls, tired and covered in soot. "The fire is finally out." He stopped and stared. "Is that you, Fin?"

"Yes, Mr. Lanski." Fin gave a small smile.

"You're aliv—okay. I can't believe it. We looked for you and—" Dad let out a relieved exhale.

"I made it out, Mr. Lanski, but..." He looked to me for permission to tell Dad we were leaving and not coming back. I nodded. "I'm going to be taking Ash away with me for a while and it's not going to make sense, but I promise to bring her home. Just know I love her and I'll take good care of her, now and forever. Please, don't worry about her."

Dad's eyes glazed over, his brain becoming mush from the song. Of anyone, he'd be the one I'd hoped wouldn't need mer mojo, but under the circumstances, if he didn't freak, I wouldn't think he loved me.

I looked up into Dad's blue eyes and squeezed his hand. "I love you, Dad."

"I love you, too, Ash." He kissed me on the forehead and hugged me. "I'm so thankful nothing happened to you today."

"Me, too," *but the day isn't over yet.*

He held me for a long time before letting go. We swayed back and forth, and I closed my eyes, pretending away the truth to a simpler time. He'd always be my daddy, no matter who biologically procreated me.

He finally let go and in sadness, I watched him disappear inside and close the door. A piece of me unraveled. Fin wrapped me in his arms as I cried. I appreciated the fact he allowed me time to grieve my human life before we left. But off in the distance, I heard a splash. The others weren't being so patient.

Emotionally exhausted, I didn't want to go through all the good-byes again and change in the house. The boathouse caught my attention.

"I guess I'll change there?"

Fin smiled and took my hand. "Lead the way."

He waited outside the door. Something about wadding up my clothes and leaving them in a rumpled heap felt symbolic of what I was doing to my humanity, to my family. I shrugged the guilt off, knowing I'd made the best decision.

I held up the top. Galadriel definitely had more to fill the cups than I did, but the snaps fit around my ribs securely. So did the skirt. I ran my fingers over the fleur-de-lis on my hip. Being a princess was going to take some getting used to. Air wafted up my legs, reminding me I'd taken off my underwear. I knew I'd have fins shortly enough, but it was awkward not having anything underneath. Then knowing Fin would know too, my cheeks heated.

"Ash? Does it fit okay?" Fin called from the other side of the door.

"Yeah," I said. My voice squeaked. "I'll be out in a sec."

"Please hurry. We have a long way to travel."

I took in a huge breath and opened the door. Fin's eyes grew as his glance gently caressed the length of my body, leaving a tingling sensation deep within my belly.

"Wow," he said, finally closing his jaw.

Though I knew we hadn't time to waste, sexy things came to my mind. But after the initial excitement left his face and the urgency returned, I looked away, slightly disappointed. Apparently our departure couldn't wait.

I bit my lip. "So?"

"Yeah." He gave his head a quick shake. "Let's get moving."

He took my hand and walked to the edge of the dock.

A catcall whistle echoed across the water. Jax, I assumed.

I surveyed the house and the yard one last time. Once we'd disappeared, confusion would linger for my family and friends, but this was the best we could do in the limited time we had. Hopefully, we wouldn't be gone for long and all the horrific things Fin said might happen, didn't.

Maybe once we returned, we could have a cottage built for the new Mr. and Mrs. Helton. Then Tatchi and I could go to the local college, and work for our parents on the dock. We'd be secret mer sisters-in-law in hiding and guard the gate for Galadriel. I could already imagine the wedding now—Lucy, Tatchi, Georgia, and Galadriel, all in evergreen dresses to compliment the everblue of Tahoe. At least I could hope.

Maybe our dreams would come true after all.

Fin's eyes softened as he touched my face. "You accompanying me to my city as my promised mate is the greatest compliment you could ever give me. Do you know that?"

"No," I said with a bashful smile.

We looked into one another's eyes before our lips crashed into one another's once again. I knew I'd never get tired of his kisses.

He hugged me tight. "Happy Birthday, Ash."

I laughed. "I guess it is. And your love is the best present ever."

He held my hand as we walked to the edge of the dock. I curled my toes over the wood and looked down. Last time we where here, he was proposing and had to leave me. Now, we were leaving together. So ironic.

He smiled at me, warm and loving as always, as if the kiss with his uncle never happened.

"Let's go save your kingdom, Princess."

I smiled back. "Yes, let's."

We dove in together and as my green fin sprouted out from my hips, I knew beyond a shadow of a doubt he loved me and we'd never be apart again.

Stay tuned for the next adventure in Everlost, Book #3 of Mer Tales, coming February 2013.

Acknowledgements

I can't believe this is my fifth published book in two years. Wow! I thank God for all His mighty blessings with everything. I also couldn't have done this without the support network of family, friends, fellow authors, and fans—I love you all! Second, I thank my ever-patient husband, Mike. You're my soul mate and give me the precious experience of the mer promise everyday by how you love me and our boys. Your encouragement helps me continue to trudge on. To Savannah and Darci, my second family, for your help day after day with my buddies, and listening to my craziness when I spaz on your couch. I'm so glad my kids love your family as much as I do. To the fab duo of Lisa Langdale and author Lisa Sanchez, for sticking with me. Your love for my characters and their drama is endearing. To author Kristie Cook (and Chrissi), I virtually "accost" you both with a million bazillion more hugs. Thanks for dealing with my whining and my insane deadlines. You're both a treasure in my life. Congrats on 100K. I'm next!

To Mom and Dad, for your example of what true love is and encouraging me every step of my journey. For Jana, Ryan, Jenni, Nate, and Samantha: for the support only family can give, caring about my dreams and cheering me on. For my friends and girls in MOPS, for your friendship while I balance life, motherhood, and writing. To Donna Wright and Lori Moreland, for finding most (smile) of my mistakes and enduring those pet peeve words. To Rhonda Helton (my #1 fan) and Tracy Lanski (my birthday twin) for letting me use your last names. To Jaime and Valia for volunteering to beta and cheering me past the finish line.

To Yara from Once Upon a Twilight, for hosting my book tour and for continually promoting my work. To Jessica from Confessions of a Bookaholic, Jena at Shortie Says, and all the other book bloggers: my books wouldn't see the light of day without your endless enthusiasm and promotion as fabulous wordsmiths, tweetaholics, booklovers, and networkers.

And to you, my dear readers, for your emails, tweets, Facebook posts, and letters. Your enthusiasm for all my books and especially this release has been amazing. I hope you enjoy Evergreen as much as I've enjoyed writing it.

Follow Brenda

brendapandos.blogspot.com

brendapandos.com

Twitter: @BrendaPandos

Facebook: Facebook.com/brendapandos

❦

More from Brenda

The Emerald Talisman
The Sapphire Talisman
The Onyx Talisman

❦

About the Author

Brenda Pandos lives in California with her husband and two boys. She attempts to balance her busy life filled with writing, being a mother and wife, helping at her church and spending time with friends and family.

Working formerly as an I.T. Administrator, she never believed her imagination would be put to good use. After her son was diagnosed with an autism spectrum her life completely changed. Writing fantasy became something she could do at home while tending to the new needs of her children, household, and herself.

You can find out more about her writing, challenges and discoveries on her blog at brendapandos.blogspot.com.

4/16   7   12/15

CPSIA information can be obtained at www.ICGtesting.com
Printed in the USA
LVOW081655031012

301362LV00013B/3/P